I couldn't see his face, I couldn't turn my head around far enough. My left cheek was hard against the wall, my right ear near his mouth. His breath breezed into me when he spoke.

"You don't want to push your luck, kid," he grunted. "Just forget what you saw, understand?"

I sensed his right hand move toward my back and then heard the crack of electricity. There was nothing I could do. The stun gun was pressed into my right kidney and a charge sailed through me. It was like taking a hit from a baseball bat wrapped in barbed wire.

He pulled his right hand back and I buckled, but he wouldn't let me fall. He kept me jacked up against the wall, hard.

"Still feel brave?"

I didn't get to respond. I heard the stun gun charge again. He fired another shot through me. The electricity raced along every inch of my body in a matter of a second. My legs gave out again but he continued to hold me up.

"Hurts, doesn't it?" he said. "Do yourself a favor, remember it. Forget what you saw and remember how this feels."

I turned my head enough so that I could see his eyes. They were small, hateful slits.

It was then I made my move . . .

The Bone Orchard

D. Daniel Judson

BANTAM BOOKS

New York Toronto London
Sydney Auckland

THE BONE ORCHARD

A Bantam Book / April 2002

All rights reserved.

ISBN 0-553-58416-2

Published simultaneously in the United States and Canada

Bantam Books are published by Bantam Books, a division of Random
House, Inc. Its trademark, consisting of the words "Bantam Books" and
the portrayal of a rooster, is Registered in U.S. Patent and Trademark
Office and in other countries. Marca Registrada. Bantam Books, 1540
Broadway, New York, New York 10036.

PRINTED IN THE UNITED STATES OF AMERICA

OPM   10 9 8 7 6 5 4 3 2 1

for my mother and father

The Bone Orchard

One

It was dark when I left my apartment above the Hansom House and went down the two flights of stairs to the street below to wait for Frank Gannon. The stretch of gray clouds hanging low overhead had cores the color of lead, and the few spaces of night between them were starless and empty. I would have been warmer had I remained up in my rooms and watched for Frank from my living room window, but it seemed to me that the early night air was the place to be right then. Frank had called me in the morning and told me that he would come by around five, after I had gotten home from work. It was just five now and I was ready for him, wrapped against the cold in a secondhand overcoat with torn seams, waiting at the curb and wondering a little just what it was he wanted from me now.

I tried to stay clear of Frank as a rule, but Southampton is a small town, particularly in the winter. He had done me a favor when I was in a jam with the chief of police not too far back, but I had paid that off three months ago and was not expecting to hear from him again. He had a phobia about talking on the telephone, so he had hung up this morning before I had the chance to tell him to go to hell. He had simply said, "It's Frank, we need to talk. I'll find you after work." And then he hung up. My first instinct was to pretend I hadn't heard him, but by breakfast I knew there really was no point in that.

The wind was out of the south, an ocean wind, and it stung my face and ears and pried through the weak seams in my coat like long fingers. Just two nights ago it had been Indian summer, days in the seventies, nights in the fifties. In my rooms above, and in the dark bar below, windows remained opened to the mild night air.

The clientele of the Hansom House, mainly local laborers and artists, had sat in their summer clothes at the crowded bar and on the half-dozen overstuffed antique sofas in the main room, listening to live music. One night it was three white boys playing reggae, another it was a jazz quintet made up of kids under twenty.

The Hansom House was an old three-story wreck that had been turned a quarter of a century ago by a local artist into a funky bar and restaurant with apartments above. It was something of a holdout for us year-rounders, and this annual stretch of warm days and nights that came always somewhere between October and Christmas was the hard-earned summer vacation we counted on.

But now, and suddenly, it seemed that winter was here, that maybe it had been here all along. These warm nights had been an illusion or trick. The old elm trees that lined my street were bare, and their branches tapped and hissed in the steady wind. The leaves tumbling across the pavement were dead and brittle and sounded like the quick scuffling feet of the last people to leave town.

I saw headlights turn onto the far end of Elm Street a few hundred feet away and head toward me. I could see that they didn't belong to a silver Cadillac Seville, Frank's car, but instead to an old-style Checker cab that had been long ago repainted red. It was Eddie's cab, and it was slowing down for me.

It pulled over to the curb, its wide tires rubbing against the concrete. Eddie leaned across the seat and jerked the handle of the back door. It swung out, and immediately I smelled clove oil and the pungent odor of cigar.

"You'll freeze to death out here, Mac."

He had been on the East End for almost twenty years, but his Jamaican accent remained for the most part intact. The thick bristles that grew from his face were dull silver, like metal shavings, and by the shape of his face you could tell that he was missing most of his back teeth. What remained were yellowed and seemed to always have an unlit cigar wedged somewhere between them. He didn't smoke as a courtesy to his passengers.

Eddie had a way of sometimes knowing things that

went on around town before anyone else did, and there were times when he sought me out to fill me in on what he knew, when he thought I might do well to know. We didn't in any way socialize, but our paths crossed often enough, and he was there for me in one way or another more times than I could remember.

I leaned forward to tell him that I was waiting for someone, but before I could speak, he said, "Frank Gannon sent me to get you. Come on, get in, it's cold. I'll take you to his office, my friend."

The heated air blowing from the vents under the dashboard felt good. It flowed past me and disappeared fast into the cold night.

Eddie steered us away from the curb and to the end of Elm Street, then turned left and passed the empty train station, then turned left again onto North Main and headed us toward the village. Frank's office was about a mile away, across the alley from the Village Hall, where the police station was. For the past few months I had gone out of my way to avoid either of those places, staying clear of that whole corner of town. It seemed the smart thing to do, and I wasn't happy about being driven toward it now.

The first quarter of a mile Eddie and I rode in silence. I saw that his eyes were fixed on me in the rearview mirror.

"Cold came suddenly," he said.

"Very."

He glanced at the road ahead, then back at me again. "You back working for him again?"

"No. No."

We came to the stoplight on the corner of Newtown Road and Main Street. The village was ahead of us and looked empty; there were maybe a dozen cars lining the length of Main. Frank's office was just beyond our sight. We'd be there in less than a minute.

The clouds over the village were low, brushing the treetops, flying like phantom ships racing into the east. I watched this for a moment, then turned my head and looked into the reflection of Eddie's eyes in the rearview mirror.

I watched his bloodshot eyes. He usually worked sixteen-hour days just to make ends meet. He never charged me a cent for any of the rides he had given me over the years.

"He's a dangerous man," he said. "You know that."

Eddie looked forward after a moment and waited for the light to change. It was obvious from what was around us that within a month Southampton would be little more than a ghost town, and Eddie and I and everyone else like us would be in on that long haul to spring.

His office was dimly lit and sparsely furnished. It ran the length of the top floor of the narrow building. Frank was behind his desk when I came in, reading a file with a look of concentration. He gestured eagerly for me to come in and take a seat on the leather couch by the door. I passed and stood leaning against the brick wall, my hands deep in my overcoat pockets, my eyes on the bare trees outside the storefront window that overlooked Main Street.

A smaller window in the back of that long room over-looked the parking lot behind the Village Hall, where the police patrol cars were parked. Frank could watch the shift change from there and know, if he wanted, which cops were out on any given night. Everyone in town knew this about him. And Frank made a point of letting everyone know.

He glanced up from his reading and looked at me over his half-frame glasses. "Thanks for being on time, Mac-Manus."

The only light on in the room was the desktop read-ing lamp by his right elbow, but I could see him well enough by it. He was fifty-five or so, not very tall but thick through the torso, built like a keg. He wore his black hair slicked back and his dark mustache thick but trimmed just above his upper lip.

"What do you want, Frank?"

He closed the folder, then removed his reading glasses and dropped them on the desktop. He leaned back in his chair, the springs protesting under his weight, and rubbed the bridge of his nose between his index finger and thumb. He seemed genuinely tired, but I really didn't care.

"Augie's coming back to work for me, starting tomor-row night. Did you know about that?"

"Augie's a grown man."

"Grown up more than most people I know. Always has been. See, I don't like to turn friends down when they come to me for help, especially a friend like Augie.

They don't come any better than him. And I know how much he wants to get back to work and put the 'accident' and the past six months behind him. But the truth of it is, he isn't one hundred percent yet. If he wants to work, he's got to work with a partner at first. But of course he'll only partner with one person."

"He'd know I was there to baby-sit him. He'd see through the both of us in a second."

"Not if we told him you were tired of driving around without car insurance and you broke down and came to me for some work."

I wanted to ask Frank how he knew that my insurance had lapsed, but I didn't bother.

"It's simple, Mac. You didn't know he was coming back to work for me, right? So when you came to me tonight it was because you didn't think it was wise driving around without coverage anymore, what with things being the way they are between you and the Chief. You needed money, and I was the only place you could turn. He'll buy it because he has no choice otherwise."

Last May a kid from the high school where Augie's fifteen-year-old daughter, Tina, went died from a heroin overdose. The kid had bought the drugs on school grounds, and when he heard this, Augie waged a one-man war against the pusher. It ended with Augie almost being beaten to death in his own house after taking surveillance photographs of a major player in the local heroin trade. That man was dead now, and the man we believed he had hired to beat Augie, an ugly ex-boxer named Searls, was in prison and blind. I had taken out both his eyes in a fight when he had come after Tina.

Augie had spent three months in the hospital and another four pushing himself toward a full recovery. He had retired from the DEA a few years ago and returned to the East End to live a quiet life. It had been anything but that.

We had met during my brief stint with Frank and had been friends since. Augie was the only man, outside of Eddie, whom I trusted. I wouldn't let anything happen to him, no matter what the cost, to me or anyone else. And Frank knew this, knew this well.

"What's the job?"

"A father wants his son-in-law tailed, thinks the young man has something on the side. Simple documentation. Easy."

"You need two men for that?"

"One to drive, one to take pretty pictures," he said. "The client has very deep pockets, and he wants results. No bullshit, MacManus. I'm telling you exactly how it is, take it or leave it."

"Except, of course, I can't leave it."

Frank sighed and looked down at his hands folded now over his stomach. His fingers were thick, his hands probably twice the mass of mine. "You know, when Augie walked in here with that cane, I wondered, 'Who the hell is this cripple?' To be honest, I don't think he's going to cut it. I think he's setting himself up for a hard fall. But I owe him a shot, if that's what he wants."

The sound of a car door slamming shut echoed up

from just below the front window. Frank looked toward it curiously but didn't get up to check. He just sat there for a moment, alert, listening and waiting for the sound of the street door opening and footsteps moving up his stairs.

I saw the world he lived in then, the world he had created for himself. Maybe for a second I felt for him, but only a second.

"If I do this, Frank, I don't get paid. We have to be clear on this up front. I'm not working for you. That's not why I'm here."

He watched me then, the way a father would a son he didn't understand. He paid well, and I could have used the money badly, everyone knew that. But I didn't ever want to need money badly enough to where I'd take it from a P.I. like Frank Gannon.

"Look, however you want it, MacManus." He was still staring at me, but I got the sense then that maybe a part of him had just given up on me. There was real comfort in that. "There's no reason to make an opera out of it."

I nodded at that. "Good." I removed my right hand from my overcoat pocket and reached for the doorknob. As far as I was concerned, we were done. But I wasn't fooled by the pitch. There was more to this, and I just wanted to see it coming before it hit. "See you around, Frank," I said.

"Take it easy, kid."

It was the next night that we parked on the shoulder of a narrow back road on the edge of town and waited.

There was nothing where we were but the kind of stillness and darkness you'd expect to find so far from the heart of things. There were fields around us, dormant farm fields, and border trees that stood in the distance like hedges of briar against a sky. There was no wind, but it was cold enough without it. The air outside the cab of Augie's pickup truck was arctic air, killing air, and even with the heater running full blast the glass around us was as cold as metal to the touch. I was glad to be inside.

Augie beside me, I was behind the wheel, his camera equipment between us. He was wearing an army field jacket and scarf over a heavy knit sweater, jeans, and Timberland boots. All I had over my jeans and thermal shirt and ten-year-old work boots was my ratty overcoat. I kept my bare hands tucked inside my coat pockets.

Augie and I had barely gotten ourselves settled in for the wait when a car appeared on the dark road behind us. I watched it in the rearview mirror; Augie eyed it from the side mirror mounted outside the passenger door. The car appeared around the sharp turn a hundred feet behind us and approached and passed us fast.

"It's not him," Augie said. I followed the car as it went by. It was a station wagon, not the Fiat that we had been instructed to follow.

We tried to settle in after that. There was the potential for a long wait. Our mark lived less than a mile down this road. The only way for him to get anywhere was to drive by us. His wife was home, so if he was planning to see someone, if there was someone for him to see, he would have to leave and we would follow.

Augie took a deep breath and then let it out. "It's good to be back," he said.

"It's been a long time for you."

"I don't mind telling you, Mac, I was starting to go crazy, pacing around the house all night, standing at my window watching for the dawn 'cause I couldn't sleep, the whole nine yards. I'd open a bottle of Jack and the next thing I knew it was over halfway gone and there was sunlight in my eyes. Poor Tina was ready to kill me. She'd get out of bed in the middle of the night just to tell me to go to sleep. The scary thing is, she'd remind me of her mother so much. When I was half in the bag and she'd come out, I'd swear I was looking at a ghost. After that I'd be too creeped out to sleep, you know."

Tina had stayed with me in my apartment during the three months last summer he was in the hospital. She was fifteen then. Having her there brought me shit, especially from Frank and the Chief. But it was a bad summer for everyone, all around.

"How is she doing?"

Augie shrugged. "Good, as far as I can tell. She's got this boyfriend now. You'll meet him at Thanksgiving. You're still coming, right?"

I nodded. "Is he a decent kid?"

"What's decent these days? He's polite, whatever that means. No piercing, no visible tattoos, no criminal record."

I smiled at that. "It surprises me sometimes just how much of a father you really are when you want to be."

"I'll tell you one thing, Mac, if this kid doesn't already

have a chip on his shoulder about you, he will soon. All Tina does is talk about you, about you and her playing house, about how you saved her life, how you beat the crap out of the two guys who put her badass daddy in the hospital. She's a fan for life, we all know that, but this boy's going to end up with quite a complex before she's through."

"Somebody should explain to her the fragile nature of the male ego."

"She wouldn't listen. I think she's too busy trying to understand her own nature now. Besides, I want the kid distracted, for obvious reasons."

"You know how Tina is. It's going to happen sooner or later, if it hasn't happened already."

"I'm her father, but I'm not blind. I know how she can be. We both do. Hell, you probably know better than anyone. Still, I was spared all this bullshit worry while I was in the hospital. I knew you wouldn't touch her, and I knew soon enough that she'd have a crush on you and that she wouldn't go after anyone else for as long as she felt what she was feeling for you. I'll tell you, that's enough to make me want to check back in and deal with those asshole doctors every day."

"Where is she now, Aug?"

"I didn't want her home alone, so she's supposed to be at her friend Lizzie's house tonight. A sleepover. That's where she's supposed to be."

"If you want, after we knock off, I could take a ride around for you, see if I spot her places she shouldn't be."

"No, Mac, thanks, but no. I'm just a father who isn't so keen on becoming a grandfather yet." He rolled his eyes. "Jesus, just the thought of it twists up my gut."

"I think it's supposed to. But she's a good kid, Aug. She's got a good head on her shoulders, for a teenager."

"It's not her head I'm worried about. See what happens when you've got too much time on your hands. I just kept walking around the house on this fucking cane, looking out my window and wondering if my sixteen-year-old daughter was taking off her jeans for some teenage Romeo with a shitbox Camaro. I'll tell you, I could never get used to being helpless. Never."

Augie took in a breath and let it out slowly. He was looking straight ahead, through the windshield, into all that dark cold out there. "I know you hate this job, I know it cuts against your grain, but this is what I do best, and I need to do it, because without it I'm a guy on a cane heading for a padded room somewhere."

Augie's face was large, heavily boned, his hair buzzed to a crew cut. Even in the dark I could see him clearly. I knew every inch of his face by now. Back when I used to drink we would settle in at his kitchen table in the morning and finish bottles of bourbon while Tina was at school. That was when I heard all about his years in the jungles of Colombia with the DEA, about the guys he had worked with, the people he'd seen die, the death squads and machete squads, the government-sanctioned murder. That was why he had no problem working for Frank, why the whole thing was a walk across the yard on a spring day compared to Colombia. Sometimes, when there was nothing left to talk about, Augie would tell me about Tina's mother and the day that she was killed. Then I would tell him what I knew of my real father, an ex-town cop who sent me when I was a boy to live with a rich family on Gin Lane when my mother died and who disappeared not long after that without a trace.

"Really, Mac, we're in the same boat, you and me, if you think about it," he said. "I can't walk around freely because of my legs. You have to be careful where you walk because of the Chief and his boys. It's different but it's the same. You must get tired of walking that line, day and night. You must walk it in your fucking sleep.

"I know you don't want to hear this, but for you Frank's a good man to keep as a friend for now. He could prove helpful, if the shit starts coming down."

"I don't doubt it," I said.

"If you two really have made peace, you might want to think about keeping it for a while this time. When the Chief does come, he's going to want to do more to you than nail you for operating an uninsured vehicle. He's going to come after you with all his boys and something that'll stick you to the wall. You're going to want more than me on your side then, Mac. It's as simple as that."

I'd heard everything Augie told me, but there was no place in me for those words to take hold. I sat silent and looked at what I could see of his face in the dark.

"You haven't reconciled with Frank, have you? You haven't buried the hatchet with him?"

"Does it matter?"

"I suppose not. If things were reversed, I'd probably make a deal with the devil, too, if I thought you were putting yourself in danger."

"Frank is your friend, Aug. I'm your friend, too."

Augie laughed once and looked away then, grinning.

"I'll shove it up your asses," he said. "Just watch me, Mac. Just watch me."

He turned his head then and fixed his eyes on the mirror mounted outside his door. We didn't say anything for a while after that. The cab of the truck was warm now, a bubble of shelter in the middle of nowhere. Eventually the way Augie was sitting motionless told me that something had caught his attention.

He stared intently at the mirror outside his window, then suddenly turned around and took up watch out the back window. He was looking hard but I don't think he was really seeing anything, not anything that he could point to anyway.

"What?"

"There's someone out there."

I looked from him to the rearview mirror. "Where?"

"I saw someone run from one side of the road to the other, from the grass on the edge of that field there to those trees ten or twenty feet in from the shoulder."

I turned and looked, too, through the back window but could barely see the shape of the bend in the road, let alone anything else. The trees were visible only where they stood against the shifting sky.

"Someone's out there, by that first tree," Augie said. "Give your eyes a minute to adjust. Look by the trunk."

"Who the hell would be out here running around in this cold?"

"I can just see him," Augie whispered. "He's on our side of the tree, like he's hiding from something in the other direction. What the hell is he doing? Wait a minute."

"What?"

"Do you see that?"

"What?"

"He's moving. He's away from the tree. It looks like he's lifting something."

I looked but didn't see anything but stationary shapes in the dark. And then, suddenly, my eyes detected brief motion.

"Wait, now I see it. By that tree. I see something."

Augie was motionless.

"What's going on?" I said.

Augie didn't answer. Something else had caught his attention in the dark behind us.

"Shit."

"What?"

"Headlights."

For some reason I turned and looked into the rearview mirror. I saw the grass that lined the side of the road light up suddenly, and then there it was, rounding the bend and racing past the tree where Augie's man stood concealed. I could tell by the way the car flung around the curve that it was speeding, and I could tell by the way it hung the curve tight that it was a sports car of some kind.

We heard the whining of the motor and the sound of the exhaust tearing down the pipes, but the pitch was lower than I had expected it to be. "It's not the Fiat. It's someone else."

And then it all went to hell.

Without warning the car turned tail first into a spin and veered onto the shoulder, kicking dirt and clumps of grass into the air. Within seconds the nose of the car rounded forward and caught air and rose off the ground, and the spinning turned into a door-over-door tumble down the shoulder. It turned over several times in the matter of a second and seemed as light as a toy. After fifty feet or so the car caught the bank along the road like a boat catching a wave and went up and over it and was gone suddenly from our sight. All that was left of it was debris in the road and a faint cloud of kicked up dust.

"Jesus Christ," Augie said.

He reached for his cell phone while I took hold of the gear shift and turned on the headlights and the flood-lights mounted on the roof above. It was as if daylight had hit the road in front of us. I punched the accelerator and turned sharp onto the narrow road, made a U-turn, and sped us straight into disaster.

The car had gone down a steep bank and landed in a sinkhole pond some fifty feet below the level of the back road. I could barely see from the top of the bank the tail end of it protruding from the dark water. The ambulance and police would be here soon enough, but there was no shaking the thought that someone could still be alive in that car. Augie had made it to the bank, and I looked over at him and could tell by his face that he was thinking the same thing that I was thinking, that something had to be done and had to be done now.

There was really nothing for us to discuss. I looked down at the pond again, fast, and then once more at Augie.

"That water is freezing, Mac. You won't have more than two minutes in it. After that you'll sink like a stone. I don't know what I'd be able to do for you." I patted his shoulder and then went over the bank and down the slope. The degree of decline was severe, the ground frozen solid, and several times I stumbled in the dark and landed hard on my knee or slid and scraped up my bare hands trying to catch myself. At the bottom I tossed off my overcoat and threw it aside and then strode into the pond. A thin film of ice cracked beneath the soles of my work boots, and when I stepped down, the frozen floor of the pond felt solid, like cement. But it was uneven and cratered, and I waded over it as quickly as I could toward the center, where the car had landed. After a few steps the floor sloped suddenly, and all at once I was chest deep in the black water. My soaked shirt clawed at me, and my breath was knocked out of me instantly as if something heavy pressed upon my chest. I rose up on my toes to keep my heart and lungs out of it for as long as I could, but it didn't do me much good.

I realized that Augie was right, I couldn't last long in this. Already I was unable to feel my feet, only the space where they should be between me and the hard pond floor.

It took only a few more steps and then I was up to my chin. Not long after I was forced to swim. I kept my head above the water as best I could, my eyes locked on the bumper that rose just a few inches out into the dark night air. The water around it was churning, bubbles and foam rising from the car breaking the surface. I stroked forward, as fast as I could, but my arms were suddenly heavy, as if the blood that moved through them was becoming lead. Before I was really aware of it my legs were dragging beneath me. My boots were filled with water and I wasn't kicking. My breath was a burst of white that rose past my eyes, brushing my face, fleetingly warm. The bumper was still ahead of me, still visible. I thought that maybe the nose of the car had touched bottom and that the car itself was being kept upright by air trapped in the trunk. If this was so, I could grab onto part of it once I reached it and conserve my strength before tackling what was next.

But before I got within two strokes of the car it started to slide and then sank beneath the churning surface. It went fast, and there was nothing for me to grab hold of anymore.

I flung my weak arms through the water twice, and then once more. I barely moved the distance of a foot, but then I felt my legs bump into something solid. The car was only a yard or so below me. I felt a burst of strength and maneuvered my legs frantically and placed my feet hard on the bumper. The car wobbled. It was upright underwater, its nose resting on the bottom, unstable. Bubbles were still rising from the trunk, and I knew it wouldn't be long before it was filled with water and the car would lean over to one side or another and sink to the bottom.

I moved off the car and tilted my head back and gasped in cold air. My arms had to flail just to keep me up. I took in as much air as I was going to get, then held it and let my arms quit. The weight of my water-filled boots pulled me under and straight down.

Water rushed in my ears and I felt a tremendous stabbing pain deep inside my head. I didn't dare open my eyes and expose them to the freezing water. Besides, in the dark what would I see? I felt my way down the car as I sank, then stopped myself by kicking my tired legs when I found the door. I hung on with one hand and searched frantically for the door handle with the other.

Already my lungs ached. When I found the handle, I yanked it, and the door swung downward and opened quickly. I swam partway into the car and felt the driver's seat, then the passenger's. Both were empty. I reached upward, into the backseat above, and waved my hand through the water. Something brushed past my hand and then was gone. I searched for it and found nothing but empty water. And then, again, it was there, drifting past the back of my hand. I grabbed what felt like an ankle and pulled it as I backed myself out into the open water.

I tugged the body behind me, working it clear of the car interior. I made no effort to be cautious or delicate. I just pulled. My lungs were burning, my throat aching. I had lost all feeling beneath my waist. Still, I pulled and pulled, and once the body was clear of the car and I had it around the waist and against me, I clawed my way to the surface with one arm. It took all I had to keep from breathing till my head cleared and I felt again the brutal cold air around me.

It stung my face and tore my throat as I gasped. I took in water and coughed it out as I held tight to the body, its back pressed against my ribs. Its face was matted with long hair, but through the mesh it made I could see to the bruises beneath, the cuts and blood, the staring, lifeless eyes. I saw no signs of consciousness, felt no movement from the ribs beneath my arm.

I didn't have the strength to keep us both up. Water rushed into my ears and splashed into my mouth as I tried to breathe. I was sinking back into icy cold, and there was nothing I could do about it. I could barely feel the water around me, it was like I was treading air. I tried to find the car with my feet again, and finally did, only to have it tilt over and sink fast beneath me.

I felt myself getting drowsy. I was slipping under, and that was all there was in the world to know. I was seconds from breathing in cold water and drowning, and really maybe that wasn't a bad thing.

But then over my splashing and coughing I heard a rushing sound. I turned my head toward it. Only my nose and eyes were above the water now. I sucked in air through my nose and watched through blurry eyes as Augie's pickup truck backed suddenly into the pond till its front tires were all that remained on land and its rear bumper was well submerged under the black water. The truck stopped and Augie climbed out of the cab and into the tilted back bed and lumbered like a sailor on a rolling deck down into the water till he found the tailgate. He climbed over that to the back bumper and held onto the gate with one hand and leaned out, the water over his waist, and extended his free hand toward me. In it was his cane, and the curved handle hung in space just a foot from my face.

The strain showed on his face. He was in pain. My hand burst from the water and snatched at the trembling handle. I hung onto it as Augie pulled us in toward him.

He lifted the driver into the back of the truck like she was nothing and laid her flat in the bed. Then he grabbed me by the hand and hauled me in. I landed on my knees in the water-filled bed, coughing. Augie immediately checked the girl for a pulse, then began to work to resuscitate her.

She looked to me to be maybe sixteen, no more than that. There was no getting around the fact that she was dead. Her pupils were fixed, large black holes in her head. I pulled myself up the slanted truck bed to the cab and climbed in behind the wheel. My legs ached as if I had just run miles. I shifted into first gear and pressed the accelerator. There was slippage, and then the tires caught and the truck bucked and pulled up onto land. I heard water rushing out of the bed behind me over the sound of the powerful motor. I shifted into park and got out and went around to the back side of the truck. Water was still draining. I opened the tailgate and let it all come rushing out onto the ground.

I looked at Augie. He was kneeling beside the girl and breathing hard into her mouth. I climbed up into the truck bed as quickly as my arms and legs allowed and knelt at the girl's other side and began to press on her sternum with my hands. Augie leaned back and counted off each thrust.

"One. Two. Three. Four . . ."

He was winded already, panting as he spoke. My arms trembled with each downward push I made against the girl, and my breathing wasn't any better than his. I really couldn't think of anyone then more unlucky than this young woman.

As I looked at her I felt betrayed by my own body, by the weakness of it, how the cold could rob me of strength and leave me infirm, unable to perform, useless.

Still, I hung in there, pressing my palm against the girl's chest, one, two, three, four, five, then resting, counting "One, two, three, four, five" while Augie pinched her nose and tilted her head back and breathed into her mouth.

It was after several minutes of this that we heard sirens in the distance. I looked up. There were blue-and-red lights caught in the tops of the bare trees down the road.

This road was in the town of Southampton, and it was the Chief's boys on their way now.

"It's time for you to go, Mac." White puffed from Augie's mouth when he spoke. "They'll find a way to make trouble for you if you stay. Just go, I'll take care of things here. It won't do anyone any good to have you locked up tonight."

The trees that lined the road were full of lights now. The Chief's boys were pulling in, one right after another.

"You'll have to hurry to make it before the cold gets to you," he told me quick. "I'd say, considering what you've already been through here, that you've got maybe ten minutes at the most before things start to turn shitty for you. At the most."

"Don't worry about me."

"My cell phone is in the cab, on the passenger seat. Take it with you. Grab a flare from the glove compartment, in case you get into trouble. C'mon, go, I'll take care of this."

"I'll see you, Aug."

I climbed out of the back and went around to the passenger side door of the truck, leaned into the warm cab, and removed a road flare from the glove compartment and grabbed Augie's cell phone from the seat.

"Call Eddie, have him come and get you. Don't waste time. You don't have long."

I heard voices from the road above then. I told Augie I'd see him soon, then turned and ran blind up the shallow bank and into the open field beyond. I couldn't move fast, my legs were spent and my lungs ached, but I ran as best as I could toward a ditch and once there lay in it so I was out of sight of the pond and the road above it. I could hear the cops, their voices, I could even hear the squelching of their radios. I looked up over the top of the ditch and could see that I really hadn't gotten that far away at all.

I called Eddie on Augie's cell phone. Eddie's wife, Angel, was working the dispatch. She said that he had taken a fare to the airport in Islip and wasn't due back for an hour. I hung up and started thinking that a night with the Chief's boys might not be so bad after all. My soaked jeans were beginning to freeze, hardening into something like cardboard. The material burned where it touched my skin, and creases felt like dull blades trying to cut me. I realized then there was one other person I could call. The number came to me as I dialed. It was a number I had dialed a few times the summer before.

It was late, and the voice that answered was groggy and young-sounding. I wasn't sure what I would have said had one of her parents answered.

"It's Mac, Lizzie. I need to speak with Tina. Is she there?"

There was a brief hesitation, and then I heard the phone get handed off, then muffled talking, and then finally Tina's voice.

"Mac?" she said. "What's going on?"

"I need your help," I told her. "Listen to me carefully."

After I hung up I made my way out of the ditch and

started across the frozen field to the roadside. I bent low so no one could see me. As I went I could watch the Chief's boys making their way down the incline and around the pond to Augie's truck. Paramedics were with them. There were flashlights and a lot of calling, but no one looked out into the field. I stumbled several times, more out of weakness than clumsiness.

I made it to the roadside not long before the car appeared. It had taken me several minutes to cross that field. As the car slowed for me, the passenger door opened, and I climbed inside as fast as I could. I didn't look anywhere but straight ahead, through the windshield. I didn't have to look to know that it was Tina beside me, and by the car I knew it belonged to Lizzie's parents, and that she would be driving.

I told Lizzie to continue on, but slow. The car moved forward, toward the scene of the accident, toward all those lights and the cops running about. I didn't want us to make a suspicious U-turn, I didn't want to get pulled over in the middle of the night with two sixteen-year-old girls. And I wanted to know that Augie was going to be okay.

Tina reached into the backseat and pulled out a blanket and put it around my shoulders. It didn't do much. I was shuddering violently. Tina turned up the heat full blast and one by one aimed each of the vents toward me. But I could barely feel the air that moved past my skin. Tina took my hands and held them together and blew on them and asked me what was going on, but I didn't answer. I didn't even tell her that what she was doing hurt. I just looked out the passenger door window as we approached the point in the road where the car had gone over and told Lizzie to slow it down a little. I looked for Augie and spotted him on the shoulder of the road. He had a wool blanket around his shoulders and was being led toward the ambulance by a paramedic. Augie looked at the car passing slowly, like maybe he recognized it. I quickly told Lizzie to turn on the interior light. His eyes caught mine for a few seconds, and then we nodded. I told Lizzie to switch off the light, and then the back road turned dark and the bare border trees looked arthritic against the winter sky.

"What's going on?" Tina said. I could hear the soft urgency in her voice.

"There was an accident. A car went into a pond. Your father's okay. Don't worry. He's okay."

"You're frozen, Mac. Your fingers are blue. We should take you to the emergency room."

It felt like everything I had left was draining out of me, crawling out like something alive and desperate to get free. I felt one shoulder sinking lower than the other.

"Just get me home, Tina," I said. "Just get me home." The hospital would have more than its share of cops when they brought the girl in. I couldn't be there. My only hope was that Tina would do what I said and not take me there.

"You don't look so good, Mac. You don't look so good at all. Mac? Mac. Mac, you okay?"

All I heard was the sound of the tires spinning over the pavement, but not nearby, far away from me. I don't know how long that lasted, or when exactly I started hearing nothing at all.

Gradually I awoke and became slowly aware of my senses and what they told me. I could tell by the shape of the shadows in the corners that I was in my bedroom, and I could tell by the weight upon me that I was under every blanket that I owned. It was warm under there but uncomfortable. I lay there with my desire to do nothing and followed my senses as they came to me.

I had been awake for a while before I heard the sound of muffled voices coming from somewhere beyond my bedroom door. I could not hear any words, just hushed talk. I didn't think about getting out of bed till I heard the door to my apartment open and then close. The voices stopped, and I half listened to the silence for a while longer till I heard water running in my kitchen. I got out of bed then and put on a sweatshirt and jeans, opened my bedroom door, and stepped out into my dimly lit living room.

I felt like I had been asleep for months. My hands hurt to the bone, and my skin ached, almost burned, as if it had been rubbed harshly. My hair wasn't entirely dry.

Tina was in my kitchen. I saw her briefly as she passed quickly by the open door. I heard the sound of the teakettle being placed on the burner, followed by the burst of a gas flame coming to life. I stayed just outside my bedroom door, so the room would be between us when she came finally out into the living room. Every little bit helped. It felt then a lot like five months ago all over again.

Tina opened and closed cupboard doors, one after another, looking for something. I assumed it was tea. Had she forgotten already where everything was? I heard the last cupboard door close and then she appeared in the kitchen doorway and took a few steps into the living room. She saw me at once and stopped short. She seemed to me to be as much startled as she was diffident. She just stood there across the small room, frozen, her mouth hanging open a bit, staring at me.

I muttered in Spanish, "Who just left?"

I spoke Spanish to her to distract her from the look I was certain all these pains must have placed over the dumb expression on my face. She was studying Spanish and I spoke it to her often. Now I wanted her to think I was sharp, that I wasn't rattled or frightened. Mainly I wanted her to think I didn't need her.

Tina said, "How are you feeling?" She watched my face closely as she waited for me to answer. There was an uncertainty about her that I understood right away. We both knew she wasn't supposed to be here. That was clearly understood. Yet she had helped me, probably even saved my life. I knew for her that maybe this meant things were different now.

As I looked at her I noticed that she didn't really look any different from last summer, except for what she wore and maybe her hair, which was longer now and thicker and maybe even darker; it was hard to tell in the dim light of the room. She had traded in her half shirts and cutoff shorts for a flannel, jeans, and work boots. I was a little relieved to see so little of her now. She had fallen into the habit last summer of forgetting to close the door when she dressed or showered.

I looked away from her and saw a wool pea coat on the chair by the door to my apartment. There was a comfort in knowing that it was there, in knowing that the only thing she needed to grab on her way out was already right there beside the door.

"Who just left, Tina?"

"Lizzie."

"Do you know what time it is?"

"Almost two. How do you feel?"

"Like shit all over."

"I'm making you tea. It should be ready soon."

"Thanks." I opened my mouth to tell her that she should really leave now, but she cut me off fast.

"Mac, what's going on?" she said. "What were you and my father doing out there in that field tonight? Is he in trouble again?"

"He's not in trouble. There was an accident. We stopped to help, that's all."

There were times back when she was staying with me that I would forget that she was a kid, times when I would think that her looks would easily unclose me, when I would forget in the middle of a conversation that

I was twice her age or that the apartment we were in was mine. She was almost my height now, with lanky arms and legs, and gray eyes that shone even in the dimmest light. It was hard to get away from her stare, and when she folded her long arms across her stomach, you knew something was troubling her, you knew something was on her mind, and she had come to talk. There wasn't as far as I knew a question she was afraid to ask. Augie joked that she had probably been an interrogator of some skill in one past life or another. I could see that. But I really think it came from her having to pull every little thing out of her work-obsessed father that she could get.

Her arms now were folded tight across her flat stomach, and her eyes held mine decisively. I just stared back. I could see the worry behind her eyes.

"Is my father working again?"

I nodded. "Yeah." There was no point that I could see in keeping the truth from her.

"For that Frank Gannon guy?"

"Yeah."

"Are you working for him again?"

"No."

"Why were you there? I mean, if you're not working for Frank Gannon, why were you there?"

I shrugged. "Keeping your father company, I guess."

"He pushes himself too far, you know that. He shouldn't be working."

"Cane or no cane, he can take care of himself, Tina. I don't doubt that now."

"I'm not so convinced."

"Give him time."

"I want you to talk him out of working, Mac."

"I couldn't do that even if I wanted to. You know how he is."

She turned her head then, breaking the stare, and looked toward the row of windows at the front of my living room.

"It's not fair," she said, "that I have to sit around and worry about him when he's out doing things he should be smart enough not to do. I'm his daughter, not his wife. It's not fair that he does this to me. I'm not sure I can take it much longer."

"He's only doing surveillance work. It's not dangerous. Frank is concerned about him, too. He won't give your father anything your father can't handle."

"You don't get it, Mac. I'm afraid."

"Of what?"

"I'm afraid that there's going to be trouble, like last time."

"Last time was different, you know that."

She shrugged once. "Maybe it was, but you said it yourself, you go around poking your nose in other people's lives long enough and you get trouble. I don't want my father bringing it home again. I don't want it finding me in my bed one night. The only good night's sleep I get now is when I'm over Lizzie's house. You don't know how many times I wanted to just come over here and sleep on your couch. You don't know how many times I ran through in my mind your reaction to coming home and finding me here. Sometimes you were happy to see me, but most of the time I knew the reaction I'd really get is pretty much the reaction I'm getting from you now.

"I know you want me to go. I know the minute I run out of things to say you're going to tell me to leave. I just remember how safe I felt here, the way I felt knowing you were out here sleeping on the couch or sitting in the kitchen eating or in your chair looking out the window. And I don't really want to let go of that feeling."

I didn't know what to say to that, so I said the only thing I could. "I should probably get some sleep. You should get going."

"Do you really think the Chief's going to pick tonight to make trouble for you? I can stay for just a few hours, leave before it's morning out. No one knows I'm here."

"You and Lizzie didn't drag me up two flights of stairs by yourselves, right? You had help."

"Yeah. The bartender from downstairs helped us. I don't remember his name."

"His name is George. Do you remember what I told you about him last summer? Do you remember what I said to you when you moved in?"

"You said he talks too much."

"Maybe some part of what happened tonight is making its way around town right now. Maybe it isn't. But the chance exists that someone might go running to the Chief with the news, because that's the way it works in this town. You know that better than anybody."

"I'm not fifteen anymore, Mac. I'm not a child."

"It doesn't matter. The Chief doesn't want to make charges stick, he just wants to get my name in the papers. The people in this town will do the rest. All he needs is to make it look like I was busted for statutory rape or some kind of sex crime. Everything else will take care of itself."

"I'd tell the truth. About why I'm here, about last summer. About the lies I told everyone about us being lovers. I'd tell them the truth, that you never touched me, no matter how much I begged. There's nothing they could say."

"It wouldn't matter. They'd just say you're afraid of me, or protecting me, or that you're just afraid of your father finding out. They'd say anything. In the end fighting it would only make things worse. I can't afford to give the Chief anything more than he already has. I need you to leave. I need you to stay away till this whole thing blows over."

She didn't move. She just stood there by the kitchen door with her arms folded and stared at me. I had forgotten how relentless she could be, how much like her father she really was. I had forgotten a lot about her, good and bad.

"He wouldn't let anything happen to you," she said then. "I know for a fact that if the Chief came after you, my father wouldn't sit for it. And neither would that Frank Gannon guy. I've heard him tell my father that if the Chief came after you, it'd be a war."

"No one would win," I said quietly.

"Frank Gannon has something on the Chief, something bad. He said he'd use whatever it is he had to get you out of trouble."

"Frank says a lot."

"Do you want to live like this, like a criminal in hiding? Is that it?"

"I'm just trying to keep the pieces in place, Tina. That's all I want."

"What pieces? What are you talking about?"

"I don't want your father and Frank Gannon and the chief of police cutting each other to pieces because of something I did. I'm doing what I have to do so it doesn't come to that. It's really a small price to pay in my book."

The fine bones in my hands still ached from the cold, and my skin felt as if it had been drawn tight over them to keep them in place, a glove to keep them collected, to keep them from spilling with a sickening noise to the wood floor.

I suddenly craved sleep, a solid unbroken day and night beneath my heavy blankets. I wanted to burrow like some hibernating rodent, on a leave of absence from the whole of the world.

"I can drive you back to Lizzie's, if you want," I said.

Tina shook her head. "It's too cold for you to go out. I'll call Eddie."

She called him from my rotary phone on the table by my couch. I went to my front windows and looked down on Elm Street. No one was around. The trees, everything, was still. The streetlights were on, gleaming off the newer cars parked along the curb. I could feel the cold coming in through the panes of glass. I looked toward the train station, around the corner and halfway down the block, visible through the trees. It was empty but still well lit. There was a single car parked in the small gravel lot alongside the platform. The next train wasn't due till dawn.

After Tina hung up she went into the kitchen. The tea water she had put on was boiling. She poured me a pint glass of green and ginger tea. It was all I had in my cupboards. She brought it out to me, and the heat of the water moved through my hand the instant I gripped the glass.

When I looked up Tina was putting on her wool pea coat. A baggy wool hat was already on her head. After she buttoned up the coat, she pulled mittens from the pockets and held them in her hand. "You should get back to bed."

From outside I heard the sound of Eddie's cab horn. It tooted twice, fast.

"Tell Eddie to come by tomorrow and I'll pay him your fare," I said.

She nodded and turned to the door. I listened to her move down the hallway, then on the stairs till I couldn't hear her any longer. I heard the door to Eddie's cab open and then close. Then it drove off down Elm Street. Not long after that there was nothing to hear at all. I just lay there, relieved that she was gone, too tired to do anything but keep still and listen to nothing.

I feel asleep and dreamed of violence, then awoke to my telephone ringing. I answered it with my eyes closed as a man disconnected from the world, a man with no life to which he was attached. The feeling was gone in seconds, much too soon.

"Yeah."

"You okay?" Augie said.

"What's going on?"

"I'm on my way to your place. You up for a ride?"

"What's going on?"

"I don't know. That's what I want to find out. Meet me outside. I'll be there in two minutes."

"Augie, what's going on?"

"I don't know. Maybe something, maybe nothing. That's what we're going to find out. I'll see you in a minute."

He hung up. I found my tea and drank it down. It was still warm.

We rode back to the pond at the edge of town and parked along the shoulder of the narrow road. The cab of the truck was warm, but the window glass was cold to the touch. The only winter coat I had was gone, taken by the cops, Augie had said, from the scene of the accident. I had only a denim jacket on over my sweatshirt and jeans. Augie kept a change of clothes in his truck, in a mesh duffel bag behind his seat, for emergencies. He took out a spare jacket and gave it to me. It was much too big for me, but my denim jacket filled it out slightly, and anyway it would keep me warm. How I looked was the least of my worries now.

I tried to remember if there were any papers in any of the pockets of my winter coat—bank statements, old mail, pay stubs. I didn't want the Chief's boys to stumble upon anything like that and somehow use it against me. What I had told Tina back at my apartment was only partially true. The Chief would settle for public humiliation, but what he really hungered for was to see me do time for something—that and to keep me for a night in the basement of the police station, just him and his boys and me.

Augie didn't seem that much the worse for wear. He wasn't tired, that much was for certain. He drove alertly, pushing the speed limit all the way. The girl we had tried to save was dead. He told me that right off. But the questions he now wanted answered fed his mind and occupied him in a way he hadn't felt since his beating last May. He was alive, his depression suddenly lifted. He felt useful again, vital. I could see it in everything about him as he drove.

After he parked the truck, Augie climbed out into the cold night air and I followed. The motor was still running, the headlights still on. We stood within their influence and looked from the point where the car went over the bank, a little ahead and to the right of us, to where it had appeared around the curve.

"I'll tell you, Mac, things don't add up here."

"What do you mean?"

"Our friends, the cops, they weren't acting much like cops, you know. They seemed to me more like a clean-up crew than trained and experienced investigators. They towed the car out of the water, loaded it onto a flatbed, and then, boom, it was gone. Not so much as a roll of film or even a single measurement was taken. No one bothered to note the tire marks on the road, nothing. They took my statement fast, then put me in my truck and told me to drive myself to the emergency room. Of course I didn't. I parked up the road and waited and watched the whole thing." He paused. "They were almost acting scared."

I watched his face. His ears were red, and when white fog wasn't bursting from his mouth, it lingered there, churning and then rising slowly past his face.

"When you went over that bank there, did you come across anything on your way down that might slash a car tire to the rim?"

I thought for a quick second, then shook my head and said, "No. Why?"

"I saw the girl's car when they pulled it out of the water. Then later I saw it when they loaded it onto the flatbed. All four tires were cut up, slashed to the rim. On one tire the rim was completely bare, no rubber at all."

"You sure about that?"

"I've got pictures."

"Video?"

"Stills. I crawled in from where I parked and shot a roll. These weren't blowouts, Mac, I can tell you that. I mean, what are the chances of all four tires blowing out all at once? No, these tires were slashed, there's no two ways about it."

"How?"

"Follow me."

Augie led me down the road, toward the curve, toward the cluster of trees where we had seen someone run across the road just before the accident.

When we were near the trees, Augie stopped and said to me, "Would you say this is where the car first lost control?"

I looked around and nodded.

He knelt suddenly, pulling me with him. He took a pocket light from his jacket pocket and shined it on the pavement between us.

I looked closely and saw in the center of the circle of white light several fanglike punctures in the blacktop.

I looked back up at Augie and said, "Cops."

"A spike strip. That's what I thought, too. Come here."

We crossed the road, to the side where Augie's man had hid before bolting across. Augie knelt again and aimed his light on a divot in the dirt bank.

"He nailed it in here and waited till he saw the car come, then dragged it across the road. The spikes tore up all four tires at once. If a car is going fast enough on a winding road like this . . . well, you saw what you saw. Girl dies in a car accident on a back road late at night. That kind of thing happens all the time. No one would think twice about it. And if someone did, no evidence."

"You're talking murder and conspiracy, Aug. You're talking a lot of people, if the Chief's boys are in on it."

"Who else uses spike strips, Mac? Why the shoddy cleanup? You know what money can buy in this town. You know this better than anyone."

He rose and I followed. Together we looked back over the dark, narrow road. The tall grass lining it was dead, bent sharply by the sudden cold. I thought of the pond down the bank and the icy water that almost killed me. I thought of the poor girl, whoever she was. I thought of those home waiting for her.

Augie took a good look around, then said finally, "Something's up. Something's going on. I think it might do us well to find out just what that something is."

"Maybe."

Augie sighed, a puff of white bursting from his mouth, then shrugged. "Let's hope for the best, then. Let's hope it's nothing." He looked at me. "I should get you home," he said. "You look beat."

"I'm okay."

"I'll find out if the car went to the impound lot or a junkyard. Frank has men in Village Hall. I'll have him make a few calls and pull some favors."

"Sounds good."

"Maybe one of my nurses was working at the hospital tonight. I'll see if I can get some information on the girl, ID, address, that kind of thing. Maybe her autopsy'll turn up something interesting."

"If you get a lead on a junkyard, let me know. I

could maybe have a look around tomorrow, between shifts."

We both knew this could be nothing but trouble for me. But I wasn't planning on letting Augie go headfirst into whatever this was alone. I wouldn't have done that before he was put in the hospital, let alone now.

"You're far enough in the shit as it is, Mac," he said. "If this is what we think it is, it'll be hard keeping low like you have been."

"If somebody killed that girl, I'd want to know who did it, cops or no cops. It's my town too, Aug."

We stood together and looked out over the barren farm fields, barely visible in the darkness. After a while, I said, "It's cold, Aug. It's as cold as hell."

We started back down the road toward his truck. Halfway there I heard a sound in the distance behind us, the abrupt sound of a car door shutting and an engine starting. Augie and I stopped and looked back and listened. The car took off, the sound of the motor fading. It was heading away from us, the motor winding up, then pausing as gears changed. Someone was pushing a sports car to its limits along another road somewhere beyond the field behind the cluster of trees. We lingered till the sound of the car was gone, then continued on toward the truck and drove back to the Hansom House.

As we got near it I started to remove the spare field jacket Augie had given me. He told me to keep it for as long as I needed. When we parked at the curb on Elm

Street we shook hands, and I stepped back out into the bitter cold. Augie waved and pulled away as I started up the path toward the door. It wasn't till his truck had turned the corner onto Railroad Plaza and was half down the block and my hand was about to grip the doorknob that I heard the sound of footsteps behind me.

I started to turn but someone slammed into me from behind, the length of his body against mine, and jacked me up against the wall alongside the door, pinning me. I knew right off that whoever the asshole was, he outweighed me significantly, and I could tell by his breath that he was a smoker.

I couldn't see his face, I couldn't turn my head around far enough. My left cheek was hard against the wall, my right ear near his mouth. His breath breezed into me when he spoke.

"You don't want to push your luck, kid," he grunted. "Just forget what you saw, understand? If you don't, I'm going to shit some serious hurt your way."

The only part of me that I could move was my feet. I turned them, swinging my toes to the left, as if trying to point them behind me. I knew the only escape was a reversal. I inched my toes a bit at a time. It was the only way to go. I needed to buy a little time, maybe piss him off so he'd back up to take a swing at me and I could make my move.

"Fuck you, asshole," I said.

"Try a little of this, motherfucker."

I sensed his right hand move toward my back, as if in

a stabbing motion, and then heard the crack of electricity. There was nothing I could do. The stun gun was pressed into my right kidney and a charge sailed through me. It was like taking a hit from a baseball bat wrapped in barbed wire.

He pulled his right hand back and I buckled, but he wouldn't let me fall, he kept me jacked up against the wall, hard.

"Still feel brave, motherfucker?" he said. I didn't get to respond. I heard the stun gun test charge again, and then he leaned close to me and said, "Have a little more, you know you want it."

He fired another shot through me. The electricity raced along every inch of my body in a matter of a second. My legs gave out again but he continued to hold me up.

"Hurts, doesn't it?" he said. "Do yourself a favor, remember it. Forget what you saw and remember how this feels. Next time I set it on high and zap your balls till there's nothing left but smoke."

My legs came back to me more slowly this time. When they did, I turned my feet even more.

"And they told me to look out for you, that you were some kind of badass, some kind of Judo-man. You don't seem so bad to me." He leaned in close to me then, closer than he had been so far. "I wonder if your friend is liking this as much as you are."

My head turned enough then so I could find his eyes. They were small, hateful slits.

"You don't like that, do you? Too bad all you can do about it is stand here and take my shit."

It was then I moved.

The instant the stun gun was off me I spun between him and the wall and crouched slightly, grabbing his balls with my right hand and squeezing with everything I had. I could feel my legs tremble as I drove him backward, my right shoulder in his chest, and hooked his right leg with my left arm for a takedown. He fell at once onto the porch, landing with a crash on the planks. I landed hard on top of him, twisting his balls like a doorknob before letting go and trapping his right arm between my left arm and my rib cage and torquing his elbow till I heard a sickening pop. The stun gun hit the floor of the porch and bounced twice and lay there. I flung it into the bushes. Then I balanced myself over him and landed a half-dozen elbow shots to his head, bouncing it off the planks.

When he wasn't fighting back or screaming or moving any longer, I got up and started toward the Hansom House. George the bartender was standing in the door, his face hung with shock. Beyond him, down a brief hall, was the door to the bar itself. I walked past him, toward the dark bar.

Most of the lights inside were off. George must have been closing up when he heard the commotion. I went fast around the bar and looked around for something, anything, any kind of weapon.

"What's going on?" he said.

"Once I'm gone, call the police. If he tries to leave, don't try to stop him. Just see where he goes, if you can. Lock yourself in here and don't go outside till the cops come."

I didn't have time to go looking in the dark for the stun gun. And anyway that wasn't one of my weapons of choice. I reached for the Galliano bottle, a tall, club-shape bottle of thick, almost unbreakable glass. It was nicknamed "The Bartender's Best Friend." I grabbed it off the top shelf and ran past George and out the door.

My attacker, groggy, was trying to stand, on one leg and a knee. As I passed I swung the bottle with everything I had into the knee of the leg with which he was trying to push off. There was a dull crack, and he screamed out and fell back to the floor. I ran down the path to my LeMans parked across the street, got in, and cranked the ignition. It caught on the third try.

I reached Augie's house in less than five minutes and skidded to a stop at the end of his driveway. I climbed out fast with the Galliano bottle tight in my fist. I saw right away that there were no lights on in or around the house and that the front door was wide open and the storm door had been pushed back on its hinges, broken. There was a dent in its lower panel, like a man had been shoved forcibly into it. I broke into a run up the lawn, bolting toward the house. I ran blindly. All I saw was the open front door and the vague shape of the house around it. I didn't hear anything except for the sound of blood pounding in my ears, the steady lapping of the bay waves against the inlet walls directly behind Augie's house, and the giving way of the frosted grass beneath my feet. I saw myself bursting through the door swinging.

Halfway up the lawn I stumbled over something in the dark and fell hard onto the frozen ground. I had been running full stride and landed badly on my knees and elbows. The ground was just as hard as the ground that surrounded the pond outside of town, and upon impact a jolt went through me that knocked the air from my chest and set my teeth ringing. I looked back to see what it was but could see nothing in the darkness. It seemed there was a heap at my feet, both solid and flimsy, no more than a bag of firewood, though that didn't make any sense. Then it came to me, head-on. It was like hitting the frozen ground for a second time.

I rolled fast onto my back and scurried like a crab away from the body that lay sprawled flat on its back on the lawn. The head lay at a sharp angle from its shoulders, as if the neck were just so much rubber. The mouth gaped open and the limbs hung askew. They all seemed somehow unrelated to each other. It hadn't been dead for long, I could tell this by the fact that the blood I had fallen into and scurried over was still very wet. My first thought was that this was Augie, and my heart couldn't bear that, not one bit.

I moved into a crouch and looked at the body but could barely make out the face and staring eyes in the dark. Blood covered his chest and face. There was a lot of it. Between breaths I muttered, "Jesus," then looked around the yard and up and down the street quickly before moving closer to the body and taking hold of its face and turning it slowly to maybe see it better. "Jesus," I said again.

I leaned over the body, my face just a foot away, and peered close. I put my hand on its shoulder to balance myself and felt cold leather. I shifted my attention to the jacket. It was a leather jacket with a fur lining, not an army-issue field jacket. This wasn't Augie, this wasn't Augie. My heart grabbed at this. My mind and my blood were racing in different directions now. I kept low, in a crouch still, my feet in blood, and picked up the bottle I had dropped when I fell. I counted three breaths, then broke and bolted low across the rest of the lawn.

I flew through the open door and ducked low against a wall, bracing myself against it and listening hard. It was darker inside the house than it was outside. I could barely see my hands. The windows were like shut-off televisions. There was the very pale glow of a digital clock somewhere in the kitchen.

But I knew the house, and I could find my way around it well enough. I stood and started through the living room and down the hallway to the bedrooms and Augie's office. I walked the fine line between the light and the dark and glanced into every room as I passed by their doors. I could only see the shapes of things, when I could see anything at all. But there was nothing, no sign of Augie.

I backtracked down the hall, through the living room and into the dining room. Nothing. Then I moved into the kitchen and saw by the faint bluish light that the back door was open. I started toward it and was just within reach of it when someone came rushing up behind me and I felt metal pressing sharply just behind my ear and I heard a voice order, "Move and you're dead, got it?"

It barely sounded like Augie's. It was full of authority and menace, but it was him, it was his cop voice married with the voice of the man who had just seven months before been ambushed and almost beaten to death in this very same house. His free hand gripped my left arm powerfully, to keep me from turning suddenly around. I didn't move, I didn't breathe, I just stood there in his strong grip, the barrel of his .45 pressed against my skull, and said, "Aug, it's me."

"Jesus, Mac," he said. "Jesus, what are you doing here?" He removed his .45 from my head and dropped his hand from my arm.

I turned to look at him. The light was barely enough to make out the shape of his face. His right arm hung at his side, his gun aimed at the floor. "I thought you might need some help. I had a visitor, too."

He shook his head from side to side a few times. "They didn't waste much time, did they?"

I looked at his forehead and saw a small bump just under his hairline. A faint trickle of blood like a stray thread ran from it to his eyebrow.

"What happened?"

"There were two of them. They jumped me at the front door and tried to push their way in. One hit me with a blackjack. I kicked the other one back into the front yard. He went for his gun. I went for mine. I plugged him. The other one, the one who sapped me, took off when I started shooting. I could have nailed him as he ran, but I wasn't about to shoot an unarmed man in the back, so I let him go."

"You okay?"

"It's just a scrape."

He knew what I was about to say, that he should get it checked out anyway, considering all that he'd been through, but I didn't see the point in wasting our time. Sooner or later the cops would come here and I had to go.

"There's a shit storm coming straight at me, Mac."

"Tell me what you want me to do."

"I'd be able to deal with it a hell of a lot easier if I knew Tina was safe and sound."

I didn't say anything at first. Then I nodded and told him that I'd take care of it.

"I owe you."

"You should call the cops."

"If somebody already hasn't. Either way, you should get going. It's cut and dried self-defense, that's clear, but things are a little fucked now, so maybe they're going to make it rough on me. I think for your sake I shouldn't tell them that you were here tonight."

"I think for your sake, too."

"You look like you've got some blood on you from the guy on my front lawn. It's probably on your boots, too. I'll have to think of a way to explain all these size-nine boot prints all over my house. Then again, fuck it, let them explain it. Just remember, no matter what, you weren't here. We don't change the story for any reason, no matter what happens. Understand?"

I knew he was telling me to stay out of this, to not come forward on his behalf no matter how bad it got. I nodded, studying the side of his face.

"I'll call you as soon as I can. Don't let Tina worry too much."

"You should call your lawyer, Aug. Just to be safe."

"I'll see how it goes first. I'll know pretty much right off what's on their minds by how they treat me."

"There's got to be an easier way to test the winds."

"We'll take what we can get." He patted my right shoulder with his left hand. "You'd better go, Mac. If you don't get out before they get here, then our story's pretty much worthless, isn't it, and you're in deep shit. One of us at a time, okay?"

I felt the need to speak but I had to leave, and it was as simple as that. It seemed now that everything I did to keep out of their path only served to put me right there in the middle of it. There was no avoiding it, no avoiding having to pay for what I had done.

I walked quickly through the cold air to my car, cutting around the body on the grass. I took an old blanket from my backseat and laid it on the front seat to keep from leaving a bloodstain. I untied my boots and took them off and laid them on the other half of the blanket on the passenger seat, then cranked the ignition, shifted into gear, and made a U-turn, heading back down Little Neck Road, toward Montauk Highway.

Augie's house was on a peninsula that jutted briefly out into the Shinnecock Bay. There was only one way in and out of his neighborhood. When I was near the end of Little Neck Road I heard the first siren in the distance. It was closing fast. I killed my lights and swung my Le-Mans into the nearest driveway. A patrol car swerved around the corner and sped past me. Less than a minute later another followed. There was a third siren lagging behind. It was the ambulance. I waited till it made the corner before I shifted in reverse and backed fast out of the driveway.

When I paused on the street to shift into drive I took a quick look at the house in whose driveway I had parked and saw someone watching me from between the curtains of the front bay window. I could see no face, just the shape of a head framed by dim back light. I started my car forward and flipped on my headlights. The head remained there, turning to follow me as I rode through the stop sign and turned right onto Montauk.

In town I stopped at a pay phone on Job's Lane and called Lizzie's house yet again. It was past four in the morning, but she sounded awake when she answered her extension. I told her I needed to speak to Tina, and she put her on.

"Meet me out front in two minutes," I said.

"What's going on?"

"Just meet me."

I hung up and got back into my car and drove to where Lizzie lived. Tina was waiting by the curb when I pulled up. She was wearing her pea coat and wool hat, her hands deep in her jeans pockets. I had her sit in the back to keep her from the blood and drove her to the Hansom House. I parked in the spot I had vacated not a half hour ago and killed the motor and lights. I took a good look around but saw no one. The house was still, the street empty.

Inside I turned on the living room light—it was a weak bulb—and Tina saw all the blood on me and started asking me what had happened. I told her as I took a duffel bag from my closet and removed Augie's field jacket and stuffed it inside that someone had tried to break into their house and that Augie had shot a man.

She stood there in the middle of the room and stared at me without moving. Her hands hung past the middle of her thighs. I assured her that Augie was okay, that I was just with him and that he seemed fine. Then I told her there were some precautions that I had to take for both Augie's sake and mine and that she couldn't ask any more questions.

I took off my shirt and socks and stuffed them into the bag, then went into the bathroom and scrubbed the blood from my hands, digging out with the tip of a scissors blade the residue that had gotten caught under my nails. I dried my hands on a ratty hand towel I kept under the sink and threw that into the duffel bag. From there I went into the bedroom and removed my jeans and stuffed them in.

Tina was standing just outside my door, watching me. I don't think she realized what she was doing. She was still in shock. But there was nothing I could do about that now. I put on a clean pair of jeans, a wool sweater and socks, then pulled a pair of old sneakers out from under my bed and put them on. I moved past Tina and through the living room to the kitchen, got a spray bottle full of window cleaner and some paper towels from under the sink, then grabbed my denim jacket and put it on.

I looked at Tina. She was still standing outside my bedroom doorway, but she had turned and was facing me. I was at one end of the living room and she was at the other, just like before.

"You stay here," I told her. "Don't answer the door or phone. If I need to call, I'll let it ring twice, then hang up and call back. Got it?"

"What if it's my father?"

"I'll be back before he calls, don't worry."

"Where are you going?"

"I'm going to get rid of all this. I'll be back as soon as I can."

I drove west on Sunrise because there'd be fewer cops

on that road this time of night. Along the way I cleaned the steering wheel with the window cleaner and put the dirty paper towels into the bag. I stopped at the side of the highway and grabbed two rocks twice the size of my fist and put them in the duffel bag. Then I stuffed in my boots and finally the blanket and tied the bag closed. I continued west, till I came to a bridge over the Shinnecock Canal, then pulled over to the side of the road and took a screwdriver from my glove compartment and poked a half-dozen air holes through the heavy cotton of the bag and flung it into the night air. I heard it land in the rushing water and then got back into my LeMans.

I thought of what I could have done differently to keep from ending up where I was. But I didn't see anything that would have kept me out of all this. I was where I was supposed to be, which was as disconcerting as it was comforting. If there was a debt to pay here, I wanted to pay it and get it over with and move on.

I was telling myself that the night was over, that things had come to a natural pause and would resume again on their own sometime tomorrow, when those involved had time to consider what had occurred and plan their next move. But when I entered my apartment I found Tina standing in the living room beside my couch with the phone to her ear and a look of wild fear in her eyes, and I knew then there would be no such pause at all, that this night would bleed gradually into the morning and all I could do was stand there and watch it.

"What's going on?"

She extended her long arm, as if to push the receiver off on me. I could hear the sound of a male voice coming through the earpiece, tinny, talking fast. I stepped toward her and reached out for the phone, and just as I was bringing it to my ear, she muttered, "They've arrested my father."

We looked at each other for a moment, and then I said into the phone, "Augie, what's going on?"

The line cracked twice, and there was a heavy hissing in the background. It was obviously a pay phone line, but the voice came through clear enough.

"I thought you had more sense than this, Mac-Manus." It wasn't Augie on the other end, it was Frank Gannon. "Just don't tell me it's true love. I've got a weak stomach."

I ignored that and said, "Why's Augie been arrested?"

"No, not over the phone. Be at my office in the morning, around nine. I'll fill you in then."

"But is he okay?" I glanced at Tina.

"All I know is he's under arrest. I'll find out more in the morning."

"I have to be at work by eight."

"Seven-thirty, then. I'll send Eddie."

"Don't bother. I'll get there."

"You're going to have to do something with that little plaything of yours. I don't know exactly what it is she does for you, but stick her for now in a motel, ship her off to someone, anything. And whatever you do, Mac-Manus, don't let her answer your fucking phone. You can self-destruct on your own time, not when you're working for me."

He hung up before I could say anything. For a moment I thought of calling him back and reminding him that I wasn't working for him, but then I remembered he was at a pay phone and, anyway, what would it bring except maybe a moment's pleasure. I hung up and checked my watch. It was already after five. I looked toward my windows and knew sunrise was now under way somewhere behind the shredded phantoms that moved past the fingery tops of the bare elms lining my street. I tried to think of what lay ahead. All I could do was sense the effort to come, the long nights and inevitable fear. We'd all been here before. I felt locked into something and didn't like it, but then I thought of Augie. I felt responsible, if not for him being where he was then for getting him out.

Tina spoke then, pulling me from my anticipations.

"It just kept ringing," she said.

I had been looking at her but not seeing her. I refocused my eyes. "What?"

"It just kept on ringing and I couldn't stand there and listen to it anymore. I'm sorry."

"Don't worry about it," I said. "Was he rude to you?"

She shook her head. "Is my father in trouble?"

I nodded. There was no point in trying to hide it. "I'll find out more what's going on tomorrow. I don't know much now. Listen, you should get some sleep. We can't do anything till morning. Take my bed, I'll take the couch. We'll be able to think better after we've gotten some rest."

I waited for her to move toward the bedroom then, but she didn't.

"It's just like last May, isn't it?" she said.

I looked away from her, through the center of my three front windows, out at the gray and muffled dawn that was rising up around us and enclosing us like a great cave of ice.

TWO

I drifted in and out of consciousness for an hour but never really fell asleep. Finally I gave up on the whole thing around six-thirty and sat up in the dim light and thought about what I knew of Frank Gannon.

He was married to a beautiful woman I had once glimpsed but never met. I had seen her behind a car windshield on a bright autumn day two years ago, through the stark reflection of the tree branches spread across the glass. Her thick hair was black and shoulder length, framing a broad and complex face. Her mouth was set in what looked like a serenely satisfied smile. I could not see her eyes through the expensive sunglasses she wore, but by the way her head moved as I walked past the front of her gold-colored Deville I could tell she was watching me. For a moment I did not know which to covet, her beauty or her wealth. It seemed that I should want one or the other. In the end I chose to desire both. It took me a few days to forget about her completely. She was beauty and wealth, everything my life wasn't, everything anyone would want. The memory of her remains in my mind, always willing to return under the right conditions and do a little dance through my head.

She and Frank had two daughters, both in college, and the house on the north side of Hill Street. Frank did well for a small-town private investigator, though just how well no one, not even Augie, knew. I didn't really care. His work brought him in continual contact with the powerful and influential, not just of the East End but of New York City, too, people who paid well to have their problems taken care of and their secrets kept. Frank knew the world well enough to make most situations work for him, one way or another. He kept the right people in his pocket—local cops, town committee members, businessmen, a town justice or two, anyone with money. He could pull in a half-dozen favors on a given day and still have clout to spare.

Years ago he had run for mayor and lost badly. The man who had beaten Frank for the mayor's seat had upon taking office tried to get Frank's license pulled. He sicked the Chief on Frank but nothing ever came of it.

I stayed out of things, or tried to. But when Frank wanted something from you, he had a way of getting it.

The only lighted window in town belonged to Frank's office, and for most of my walk along Main Street my movement was the only activity I could sense. Every now and then a car would pass, and as it did I would keep my eyes on the sidewalk but listen carefully for the sudden seizing of brakes and quick swinging open of doors. Last night's bout with my stun-gun friend was still fresh in my mind. My right kidney wasn't likely to let me forget for a while. But none of the cars that passed stopped or even slowed down. I followed the sound of their tires as they continued on behind me or ahead of me till I could hear nothing more but the sound of my own walking through the solemn morning.

The sound of the leaves crunching stiffly beneath the soles of my old sneakers never left me once. They announced my presence and direction with each step. I passed the Village Hall and wondered about Augie, where he was and if he was okay. I kept my head down and my eyes on my noisy feet as I crossed the alleyway that separated the Village Hall from the clothing store above which Frank kept his office.

The cold was pretty much well inside me when I opened the street door and started up the narrow stairs to his office. I knocked on his office door, then waited for his low voice before I entered. When I did I found him sitting behind his desk, under a single reading lamp, the phone pinned between his ear and shoulder. In his thick hands was an open file, and behind him one of the filing cabinet drawers was open, pulled out a little past halfway. I remembered again the night I got drunk and turned Frank's office upside down, pulling each drawer from its cabinet and scattering the contents across the room. It was after that night that I decided not to drink for a while. I made it a habit and kept with it till Tina came and stayed with me and all that nonsense between us started.

Frank looked up at me and gestured me in with a quick wave of his hand. His eyes stayed on me for only a second. I closed the door behind me and leaned on the wall near it, my hands in the pockets of my denim jacket. I let the warmth touch me and looked down the length of his office, toward the narrow window at the back that overlooked the parking lot behind the police station. Then I heard the sound of a car door closing coming up from the street outside the large front window. I went to it and looked down at Main. One of the patrol cars parked outside the Village Hall was backing out into the street. It paused for a moment, the reverse lights went out, and then it headed north, into the direction from which I had come. I didn't know which place was more unsafe for me, the street below or this office above it.

I half listened to Frank's side of his phone conversation while I waited.

"I don't care," he said. "It doesn't matter. Do what you have to do. Yeah. Just let me know. As soon as you can." He turned his hand and glanced at his watch. "Yeah, that's fine. Okay. Okay. Let me know."

He hung up the phone with his left hand and laid down the file with his right and looked at me.

"You look like shit, MacManus."

I ignored that. "What's going on, Frank?" I didn't look

at him, but from the corner of my eye I could see him close the file and stand and return it to the open cabinet drawer. He slid the heavy drawer shut, locked it and pocketed the key, then picked up a paper to-go cup of coffee from his desktop and took a sip.

"I don't know what you know," Frank began, "so if what I'm telling you is old news, bear with me." He paused a moment. "From what I understand two men tried to sack Augie at his house a few hours ago. He shot one of them in the chest twice. He's dead. The other took off. Right now there's a lab crew at his house, gathering evidence. All I know is they took Augie in for questioning, after which they booked him on the charge of manslaughter."

I thought of the trail of bloody footsteps I had left through Augie's house.

"Apparently, he shot from his front door an unarmed man standing on his lawn, twenty feet away."

"Augie said the man drew a weapon."

"Well, the Chief's boys are saying different. They found no weapon, nothing, not even an empty holster. I've sent a lawyer to meet Augie for the arraignment. I think we should be prepared for the worst, considering the personalities at play here, considering what's going on behind the scenes."

I turned my head and looked at him then. "Have you talked to Augie?"

"Briefly. He called me when they booked him. He said they questioned him for maybe twenty minutes and then the word came down to book him." He took another sip from his coffee and rested the cup back on the desktop. He was wearing dark wool pants and a densely knit fisherman's sweater and dark shoes. None of them looked cheap.

"Is he okay?"

Frank shrugged. "Yeah, he's fine. He's been in worse places."

"Do you know about the accident?"

"The girl, yeah. I was told Augie pulled her out of the water, but I assume you were there and just took off before the boys showed up."

"We went back afterward to look around. Augie was convinced the police did a half-assed job investigating the scene. He said it seemed to him that they were cleaning up more than anything else."

"What do you think?"

"I didn't see anything, except for what looked like the marks left by a spike strip."

"Anything else?"

"Not there."

"What do you mean?"

"After Augie dropped me off I got jumped by someone who tried hard to convince me to mind my own business."

"And when Augie got home the same thing was waiting for him. Except for him they thought to send two. How thoughtful."

"It seems so."

"Did you get a look at the guy who jumped you?"

"Not at his face, not enough to recognize him if I saw him again. He'll probably be walking with a limp for a while, that's all I can tell you. Do you have any idea who the girl in the Corvette was?"

"Not yet. From what I'm told they haven't notified next of kin. So they either don't know who she is or they're not saying just yet. Whatever the case, there's an awful lot of running around next door for what little seems to be getting accomplished. I'd like to find out why that is."

I turned my head again and looked back out at the sky beyond the bare branches of the old trees lining Main. I had no interest in town politics or benefiting from the suffering of others. To Frank every misfortune that befell another was a potential point of leverage for him to use as he saw fit. It was hard for me to think of the young girl Augie and I had tried to save as some kind of gift to Frank. I could remember clearly now the point I had reached last year, when I turned Frank's office upside down. I was a drunk then, and that contributed to my rage. It also explained what I was doing working for him in the first place. But I wasn't a drunk now. I could see things with bare attention, I could see things for what they were. I could see clearly where this meeting was going and that I had no desire to go there. All I had to do was tell Frank to go to hell and walk away and spend today washing dishes for an unhappy and ill-tempered boss.

But I also knew he wouldn't make it that easy for me

to do that. Augie needed help. Frank would know what to do. I wouldn't.

"One thing about the girl," Frank said. "She was wearing a high school ring. From Southampton High. The date on it makes her a senior. Maybe someone knows her. Flashy car like that, she probably doesn't go unnoticed."

It was obvious what he wanted from me. But I didn't see how using Tina to identify the dead girl would help Augie. I could only see how it might help Frank.

"You know that girl can only bring you trouble by the truckload," he said. "It doesn't matter that she's sixteen now. Maybe I'm all wrong, maybe you really aren't banging her, like you say. But when it comes down to it, it doesn't matter what I think. Whether it's innocent or not doesn't matter. You're still asking for a fall by keeping her around."

"What do you want me to do, Frank? Stick her in a motel?"

"Send her off to someone. Anything. Her being there is exactly what the Chief is looking for. You know that."

"I'm on top of it, Frank."

"Yeah, I bet."

"You've got a dirty mind."

"Me and everyone else in town. Just because you're known around here doesn't mean people won't be willing to believe whatever shit they hear. Trust me on this. You've made the papers, MacManus. The minute they put hero by your name, everyone began waiting for the first hint of that flaw which proves conclusively that in the scheme of things, you're really no better than they are. It's human nature; it's the way of the world. You might want to wise up to it fast."

A few years ago I had found the kidnapped daughter of an ex-girlfriend of mine, when no one else could. It was just luck. Since then people have sometimes come to me for help, mostly out of desperation. I was never comfortable with that, and I often wondered what freedom might come from having that status Frank spoke of stripped from me forever.

"I'm just a guy who washes dishes, Frank," I said. "That's all I am. It doesn't matter to me what anyone thinks."

He sighed, then shook his head. He eyed me skeptically for a moment. I caught the smell of him then, the smell of his expensive cologne and the fabric of his well-tailored clothes.

"Do you want to make trouble for yourself?" he said.

"Just the opposite."

"Do you want to keep living like a criminal, crawling around like a rat?"

"I didn't choose this life, Frank," I told him.

"I don't believe that. Not for one minute. You know, I take that back, MacManus. You don't live like a criminal at all. You live like a man who's got something to hide, like a man with a secret he's keen on keeping buried. That's what you look like to me. That's what you've always looked like."

"Believe what you want to believe, Frank. It's what you're good at. It's what you get paid for."

"We've all got secrets we want to keep, kid. We're all alike in that way."

"I don't know what you're talking about."

He shook his head from side to side. "You think no one knows what really happened on that boat."

"No one can know but me."

"But they can think they know, and in the end, in this town, that's all that matters."

"What do you want from me, Frank?"

"It's not just what I want. I'm fairly certain that if you had the chance to get rid of the Chief, you wouldn't pass it up. Even to your way of thinking survival is the top priority."

"What does the Chief have to do with all this?"

"Someone's pulling his strings. The whole thing looks too much like a puppet show to not be a fucking puppet show. Someone owns the Chief, that's common knowledge. We find out who, we get proof, and the Chief's history. And you get your life back."

"I didn't know I lost it."

"Knock off the Gandhi shit for a second, MacManus, and take a look at the big picture for once. The man is as corrupt as a man can get. We'd live in a much better town without him as chief of police. If you're looking for a higher road, I can't think of one any higher than that."

"What I don't understand is how my destroying the Chief is going to help Augie's case."

"I don't know what Augie's told you, but he's not all

that well off. He works for me because he has to, not because he's bored. His pension is enough to live on if he lived like you, but most humans prefer not to live like that. Tina's college-bound in a few years and Augie's scared, and rightfully so. I can put up his bail, but he's looking at some steep attorney fees, and I can't help him there. I've seen a lot of innocent people bled dry proving it. If Augie's going to win this case, he'll need a good lawyer, and a good lawyer's going to cost him everything he's got, and probably everything he will have for a long time to come."

I looked down at the street again. A second patrol car backed away from the curb and headed north, too. I hadn't heard its door close or its motor start up.

Frank said, "I've known Augie most of my life. He's not the kind of man to pop somebody for no reason, I don't care what happened to him last May. A temporary insanity defense will keep him out of jail, but I don't believe Augie shot a man just for standing on his lawn, not for one second. Find the man who jumped you. If all this is what I think it is, he'll lead us to the man pulling the Chief's strings and to the partner of the man Augie killed. Between them we just might be able to find the truth about what happened on Augie's lawn last night. If we're lucky maybe we can convince one of them that it's in his best interest to help Augie out. It's a long shot, but it's the only hope we have to keep Augie's life from going down the tubes. I'd dig under every rock in town if I thought it'd help. Wouldn't you?"

I glanced at Frank again, then looked out the window.

I wondered if Augie was next door still, or if he had been remanded already to Suffolk County Jail. I guess it didn't matter if he was near or far. Nothing mattered except that he was in trouble. The pieces were slipping out of place, and there was nothing I could do about that.

"What do I do exactly?"

"Find the man who jumped you, find out who he works for. He'll lead us to what we need."

"And that's all?"

"If that's as far as you're willing to go, yeah, that's all. I have to admit, I'm surprised. I thought you'd do anything for your friend. I would have thought that we were the same in that way."

I said nothing to that. I was tired of words and what they did. I was grateful that winter had come; I wanted the quiet that it brought out here, the harsh stillness. I craved silence, days of it, days of sitting at my chair by my window, watching Elm Street and the train station, listening and seeing but thinking of nothing.

On Main Street now a uniformed cop climbed into the third patrol car and backed away from the curb. He made an illegal reverse U-turn, paused, then started forward, passing below the window of Frank's office. The car turned left onto Meeting House Lane and headed in the direction of the hospital.

"Just find the guy who jumped you, MacManus," he said. "Find him and bring him to me, if that's all you're willing to do. I've never been afraid of doing what has to be done. Now's no exception."

I kept my eyes on the street and said, "I'd be, if I were you. I'd be very afraid."

"That's the difference between you and me."

"That's one of them."

"Is it really that cut and dried from where you sit, MacManus?"

"I don't spend my days thinking I've fooled everyone."

"Not all of us have the advantage of abject poverty like you do."

"You might want to give it a try sometime, Frank."

"I prefer my stomach full, thanks."

"It must be terrible for you when you get hungry."

"I do my best not to."

"Everyone gets hungry, Frank."

"If this is how you think, I can see why you hate me. It must be sad living in your ivory tower all alone."

"I don't hate you, Frank. And I'm not afraid of you. You hurt people, not because you need to, but because it suits you. I don't like what you do, but there's nothing I can do about that. Still, someday someone's going to put a shitload of bullets in you, and I want to be as far away from you as I can get then. I'll find the partner of the man Augie shot. I'll find him and tell you where you can pick him up. That's as far as I go. After that we're done. Do we understand each other?"

Frank didn't answer. After a moment I turned and looked at him. He nodded and said, "Perfectly." I waited a moment more, then turned toward the door. Once through it I went down the steep steps to the street. The cold air felt suddenly like freedom, something I had but Augie didn't.

Someone once told me that there are only three states of mind, those of greed, hate, and delusion, and that every action any of us makes has, as its origin, one of these three states. But I see it more simply than that. I see fear at the heart of everything we do. I see fear of not having at the heart of greed and wanting. I see fear of facing what is at hand at the heart of delusion. I see fear in the heart of hate and anger, prejudice and despondency. It's what keeps the TV on late into the night, the liquor stores in business, and it's what keeps us running blind from day to day.

Most of the people I know are too poor to be greedy. What they want they want out of need. There is no greed here, but there is fear. It's in Tina when she grasps, in Augie when he ignores facts that displease him, and in Frank when he stabs at an enemy. The Chief's desire for revenge against me comes from the fear of bearing in his heart the pain of a son crippled by a nothing like me. And when I face my own reflection in my dirty bathroom mirror, fear is what I see looking, cold and hungry, back at me.

This was with me as I walked back from Frank's office. I wondered about the state of mind of the men who attacked Augie and me and then of the mind of whoever had hired them. From what fear were they acting, greed, hate, delusion? Was there something they wanted to pull close to them or something they wanted to be rid of? Or were they just panicked and confused into recklessness, into frantic and desperate action?

This was the only line of thought I knew to follow. I knew nothing about investigations, nothing about the criminal mind, beyond what a nearly ten-year-old degree in criminology from a lesser-known college could offer. I barely knew my own. This philosophy was all I had to go on. It was the only way I knew how to help Augie.

Tina was asleep on the couch when I entered my apartment. I didn't bother to take off my jacket. She awoke when I picked up the phone. I dialed work. I should have been there fifteen minutes ago. I looked out my window at the train station and thought about everything Frank had said. My boss answered on the third ring. His voice was abrupt, unhappy.

"Pancho's."

"It's Mac."

"You're late."

"I should have called sooner."

"Don't even think about calling in sick. It's delivery day and I'm short a cook. I need you to prep."

"Something's come up," I said. "I'm not going to be in for a few days."

"I don't fucking believe this."

"There's something I have to take care of. I'm sorry."

"You don't come in today, you're fired, okay?"

"I only need a day."

He hung up before I finished. I waited a moment, then returned the receiver to the cradle. I was out of work again. I was broke and out of work and winter was here. Jobs were scarce. I looked down at Tina. Her eyes were glassy and red from sleeplessness, her face puffy from her short nap on the couch. She seemed to me almost surprised that she had in fact fallen asleep.

I sat down on the couch beside her. Somehow it didn't seem unsafe to be near her now. Or maybe I just didn't care anymore if the Chief walked in or not. We had dug past that strata of trouble and grief.

"Your father's been arrested," I told her. "He's being charged with manslaughter."

She didn't say anything, just watched my face carefully, as if she might see something in me that would help make sense of this.

"Frank's bailing him out. He'll be home later today. You okay?"

She shook her head from side to side.

"I'm going to do what I can for him. You should stay with him when he gets home, okay? Somebody has to keep an eye on him. Augie can sometimes be his own worst enemy. You know?"

"Yeah."

"It's going to be okay. If this goes to trial, he can beat it pretty easy, we think. But it'll cost him. So I'm going to do what I can to make sure it doesn't come to that, okay?"

"You've got troubles of your own, Mac."

"It doesn't matter. And anyway, I'm not convinced the two matters are unrelated."

"You think the Chief is trying to get to you through my father?"

"I'm not sure. In any case, I can't sit around and watch your father bleed dry. I've got to do something."

"What can you do?"

"The girl who died in the accident last night was from your school. She was a senior, she was driving an old Corvette. I need to know who she was."

A look came over her face fast. She said, "I know . . . oh my God. That's Amy Curry. She's dead?"

I nodded. "Was she a friend of yours?"

"Not really. I just knew of her. Everyone knew her. She was one of the prettiest girls in school. She's dead?"

"Did she have the Corvette at school yesterday?"

Tina nodded. "I saw her take off in it during lunch. The seniors just got their rings yesterday. They handed them out at lunch. She must have grabbed hers and ran."

"She drives a car like that to school every day?"

"It's her father's. When he's away she drives it." She thought for a moment. "She was a puzzle, you know," she said. "She got good grades, didn't date, didn't do drugs, all her teachers loved her, she was on every committee. But when she got in that car she'd go crazy. She was an accident waiting to happen. Everyone said that."

"The thing is, Tina, your father doesn't think it was an accident. Do you know of anybody who'd want to hurt her or maybe even kill her? A boyfriend, anyone?"

"I told you, she didn't date."

"Anyone who wanted to date her and she turned down, anything like that?"

"She wasn't like that. She didn't call attention to herself. She was pretty, that was it, but most of the boys go after the easy girls, not girls like Amy. She wasn't into anything, except her committees and her schoolwork."

"Do you know where she lived?"

"Halsey Neck Lane."

"Money."

"I think so, yeah."

"What else can you tell me about her?"

Tina seemed reluctant then to say what was on her mind.

"What?" I urged.

She shrugged. "I didn't remember till now, till you asked me where she lived. I don't know why I just thought of it."

"Of what?"

"There was a list that went around school a while back. Before last spring. Before . . . you know . . . I was attacked. Before you hurt Tommy Miller. It was a list of all the girls he was supposed to have done it with. On it were the girls he had . . . forced himself and the girls who had done it with him willingly. Supposedly Amy's name was on the list. I don't know if she was one of his victims or not. No one believed it, but then supposedly there was a video he showed to some people of him and her together. That's all I heard. No one said if he was hurting her or not on it. Anyway, there were supposed to be fifty names on the list. He was a monster, everyone knows that. He deserved everything you did to him, and more.

"Maybe this isn't so bad, what's happening to my father, I mean. If it's payback for what you did, then maybe this is a chance to put an end to this once and for all."

I said nothing to that, just looked at her.

"Let them see what they get when they mess with our family," she said. "When they mess with you and me and Augie."

"Is today a school day?"

Tina nodded. I got up and picked up the phone. Tina told me the number and I dialed it. It rang twice and was answered by a woman. I said, "This is Augie Hartsell. Tina's ill and won't be in today." I hung up and looked down at her.

"Stay here till you hear from your father," I told her. "Call Eddie for a ride home once Augie's back. Tell Augie to sit tight till he hears from me. Do you understand?"

"Yeah."

"Try to get some rest while you wait for his call. No shame in resting. Hartsells rest, too."

"Where are you going?"

"I need to find someone. There's nothing to worry about. I'll call your house by dinnertime, at the latest."

I went into the kitchen then and took a few gulps of rice milk from the carton in my refrigerator. It, aside from a container of yogurt and some leftover noodles and tofu, was all there was on its shelves. I had a few bucks in my pocket and nothing in the bank. I would need the few bucks for gas to look for the man whose knee I had popped. I put the nearly empty carton of rice milk back in the fridge, then went back into the living room and took the Galliano bottle standing by the door and left. Tina and I looked at each other as I closed the door behind me. I locked the deadbolt and then headed downstairs to George's apartment on the second floor. I knocked and it took him a moment to answer the door.

He was wearing the same clothes he had been wearing when I saw him a few hours ago. I could tell he had been sleeping in them. He leaned against the door frame, his eyes swollen. I smelled whiskey on his breath.

I handed the bottle to him and said, "What happened to my friend?"

George whispered, "He lay there on the porch for a minute, then got up and limped to an old LTD and drove off. That was all I saw. It was too far away. I didn't see any plates."

"Did you call the cops?"

"Yeah. They showed up about ten minutes after he left. I told them what happened, but I kept your name out. I figured that was the wise thing to do. They said there wasn't much they could do. Then they left."

"Did you notice what color the LTD was?"

"It was dark, maybe black, maybe blue, maybe green. But it was definitely a dark color."

"Anything else?"

"Yeah. The cops didn't seem all that interested. They

told me it wasn't worth their filing a report. Apparently some asshole zapping customers with a stun gun outside my business is something to be expected nowadays. I don't know. I pointed to our PBA sticker in the window but they weren't impressed."

"Listen, George, do me a favor. If you see this guy again, let me know, okay? Don't call the cops. If he leaves before I get here, just let him leave. Catch his license plate if you can, that's all."

"What's going on, Mac?"

"It's nothing. Go back to sleep. I'll see you around."

I left him before he could ask me any more questions. Even though it was daylight I took a good look around before I started toward my car. Once I was inside I cranked the ignition till the engine caught. As it warmed up I counted the bills in my pocket. Eight dollars. After a minute I shifted into gear and headed in my uninsured car toward the Texaco station on the corner of Sunrise Highway and North Sea Road.

Three

It was warm inside Southampton Hospital, the air dry and distinctly serene. I took in as much of the warmth as I could as I headed for the reception desk. The woman sitting in a low chair behind it looked up and eyed me uncertainly as I approached her. Being a gargoyle, a scarecrow, a grotesque, I was used to this. I gave her the warmest smile I could muster up, but I could tell it did little to ease her. By the time I reached the half-circle barrier-counter that separated us there was much in the way of defensiveness, even hostility, in her posture.

"Can I help you?"

I placed both my hands palms down on the counter-top. I did this sometimes to put people at ease, to show them that I was nothing much to worry about. But I don't think she even saw my gesture; she didn't take her eyes off my untended hair and the five-day-old stubble scattered across my face like some indication of class or nature. Some people just didn't like the sight of me.

I told her I was looking for a nurse named Gale Nolan. Her guard didn't lower in the least.

"And what is your name?"

"Mac."

"What?"

"My name is Declan MacManus."

"May I ask what this is in regards to?"

"It's personal."

"She's very busy right now. Perhaps you should come back after lunch."

"It can't wait till then. It won't take long."

"I'm sorry, but she's very busy working right now."

"Look, I'm a friend of hers, okay? I look like hell because I've been through hell. It's important that I see her right away."

"I'm sorry, unless you're here to see a patient—"

I moved around the counter, starting toward the bank of elevators behind it. The receptionist stood up fast, as much indignant as surprised. She was an authoritarian whose authority was slipping. "Excuse me, you can't enter without a pass."

I ignored her and headed toward the elevators. I didn't have the time or patience for this. Still, I moved slowly, in no real hurry, careful not to seem threatening or appear too crazy. Never run, never run. I had learned this a long time ago. From the corner of my eye I saw the receptionist reaching for her phone. She picked it up fast and called for security. Before she even hung up the phone a large uniformed black man emerged from the gift shop on the other end of the small lobby and moved casually toward us. I stopped and waited for him. He moved as slowly as I did, his eyes fixed on mine. The elevators were ten paces away.

The guard reached the desk and I recognized him then. He looked at the receptionist, then at me, then at the receptionist again and asked in a Georgia accent, "What's the problem here, Carol?" Her hand was still on the phone, poised, I knew, to dial 911 if necessary.

"This man refuses to register," she explained. "He would like to visit a nurse on duty and I told him she was busy now."

The guard looked at me. There was a smile at the corner of his lips, as if he were trying to suppress the expression of his delight.

"Why do you want to do that, Mac? Not sign in."

"It's good to see you, Reggie." A few years ago he had been a bouncer at the Hansom House for a summer. I had once pulled a drunk couple, punching man and clawing woman, off his back as he pinned their boozed-out, bottle-wielding friend to the hardwood dance floor. Reggie was a big man, easily two hundred eighty pounds, and could all by himself lift the front end of a car and turn it so it was facing the other direction. His hair was short, a few weeks shy of bald, and he would have been in the marines a long time ago if he wasn't on lithium for his mood swings.

That night I had pulled that couple off his back we sat at the bar after closing and drank till sunup. He was well read and knew more about Albert Camus than anyone I had ever met. He had always on him a tattered copy of *The Stranger*. We had talked for hours about Meursault and his way of living and taste for things—salt water, chocolates, Marie. When the summer ended and Reggie left for school I was sorry to hear that he had gone. That was maybe three years ago. I looked at him now and wondered if somewhere nearby lay something written by Camus.

"Someone you know laid up in here?" Reggie said.

"No. I'm looking for Gale."

"Hell, she's up on the second floor, where she always is. Go on up and see her. I'll sign you in."

"Thanks, Reg."

"How's Augie Doggie doing?"

"He's okay," I lied. I decided then not to wait for the elevator. I headed instead for the stairs at the far end of the corridor. I didn't look back at the receptionist, but I could imagine the sour look on her face. As I walked toward the door I heard Reggie say to her in a plain but accusing voice, "Don't you know who that is? That's the guy you go to when you got trouble." I cringed.

It wasn't easy being in this place. I don't know if it was the smells or the general, deadly silence, but I felt uneasy in hospitals. There is something almost supernatural here—men and women in white coats and green scrubs speaking a secret language all their own, colored pills, the assuring but vaguely ominous half promise of recovery and the ever-present threat of not recovering. It still seemed so medieval to me, polished on the surface but barbaric just beneath it, as much religion as science, as much faith as fact.

Augie recovered when no one said he would. A world-famous artist in for an appendectomy died on the operating table, fifteen minutes into the operation. A while back I had gotten shot in the shoulder when I tried to find the missing daughter of an old girlfriend. I spent almost two months in this hospital, observing as I lay and waited to heal. I learned not to trust hospitals, not to be lulled into the silence or distracted by the clean smells.

During both of these times, during my recovery and then Augie's, Gale had been our nurse—on the night shift during my stay and the day during Augie's. I knew really very little about her, though I remember lying up nights waiting for the sound of her sneakers in the hallway and guessing the details of her life beyond these walls. What I did know about her was that she was ten years older than I, that we had gone to the same high school, and that she was married to a veterinarian but had no kids. She had about her a tenderness I'll never forget.

She was tall and slender, built like a tennis player, and had short dark hair that I used to watch grow until she'd come in one night and it was cut back, and then I'd start watching it grow all over again. Her face was lined prematurely—she lived in the sun—but I think it only added to her looks. She was wearing nurse scrubs and the same short haircut as usual when I spotted her down the long, bright corridor. She was at the nurse's station, talking, and stopped midsentence suddenly and abruptly left when she saw me. She walked down the long corridor to meet me, surrounded by a glare that came in through the large picture window at the other end of the corridor. The light was almost blinding.

I started toward her, my hands in my pockets. We stopped just a few feet short of each other.

"What are you doing here?" she asked. Her reaction was a mixture of happiness and deep concern. "You look like hell."

"A long night."

She thought about that, eyeing me closely. She was never fond of the way I lived. I could smell her now—a mixture of rose water and hand cream. These smells grabbed at me like two powerful hands.

"You okay? What's going on?"

"Augie was arrested last night."

"My God, what happened?"

"He was attacked outside his house. He shot someone, killed him."

"I don't understand. It sounds like self-defense. Why . . . ?"

"Augie saw a gun but they couldn't find one on the scene. There's some kind of shit going on."

"When isn't there?"

"They're charging Augie with manslaughter."

"Jesus, Mac. Jesus. What can I do?"

"Around the same time he was getting jumped, someone jumped me outside the Hansom House. I cracked his right knee hard with a bottle of Galliano. I need to know if anyone came through the emergency room last night with a busted knee."

"I can find that out for you. Is Augie in jail now?"

"He should make bail and be home by this afternoon."

"You know, I've never seen anyone make the kind of recovery he did. He's a tough man."

"That's why we keep him around."

"It's good that you two stick together like you do. You need each other, I think."

"They're stacking the deck against him," I said, "and I need to find out why and who. The man with the limp is all I have to go on. He's my only chance at clearing Augie."

"I'll find out what I can."

"Thanks, Gale."

She reached up then and gently touched my shoulder with the palm of her left hand, touched it where the scarred-over bullet wound was. I remembered all those nights talking to her as I lay in bed, listening for her in the hallway, the smell of her lingering after she was gone, her presence in my room. I remembered staring at the ring on her finger and wondering why my luck was so bad. It was painkillers and sleeping pills causing my mind to rotate into a downward spiral of self-pity, but I spent most of my nights damning my life and waiting for her to walk in, and after she left, I waited for her to come back again and fought for sometimes hours against sleepiness and hopeless desire.

After a moment Gale removed her hand and said, "How's Tina?"

"She's fine. She's her father's daughter, I see that more and more each day."

"I remember how she'd come by every day after school, around the time Augie was getting out of physical therapy. Most of the time he'd be in a bad mood and try take it out on her, but she'd just give it right back to him, both barrels." She smiled and laughed at that. "They deserve each other."

"Definitely."

"Your taking care of her made it easier on him, you know. I think that's why he got better so fast. One less worry, you know. One less thought keeping him awake in the night. Where is she now?"

"My place."

"Once more unto the breach, huh?"

"Something like that."

Her eyes squinted, her lines colliding. She had once nursed me back to health and protected me from reporters and the eyes of the curious. I could only imagine how different my life would have to be to have her in it.

"Take care of yourself, Mac," she said.

"I will."

"On my break I'll find out what I can. I'll call you as soon as I know something."

I thanked her. A part of me wanted to stay there with her for a while longer, just to be near her, but what would be the point? We looked at each other, and then finally I turned and left her there in that long, sterile corridor. The only sounds to be heard were my own footfalls. I could feel her watching me as I walked toward the stairs. I could see in my tired mind that face of hers and all that white glare burning around her like the light that awaits at the moment of death.

I knew something Frank didn't. This was clear to me. I knew the identity of the dead girl. With that in mind, I steered my ancient LeMans through Southampton Village, down Hill Street, and onto Halsey Neck Lane, the part of town where the filthy rich lived.

I didn't like parts south of the highway and avoided them as much as I could. As beautiful as they were, I didn't much like these wide, tree-lined streets, tunnels running under a canopy of woven branches and green leaves. Nor did I like the great houses. I knew the arrogance that came with these houses, with the great wealth, the power and the inevitable seduction, the germ and the disease it wrought. I never knew someone with money who didn't expect, in the end, to be treated differently from those of us with little or none. I do better when I ignore this part of town. Amy Curry's home was a mere mile from mine and a whole world away.

I knew exactly where the Curry house was. I knew pretty much all the families in this part of town, at least by name and estate. If they had ever known me, if I had ever played with their children, I was forgotten now, and glad for it. One of the reasons why Frank wanted me to work for him was that I knew the East End at least as well as he did, and in some crucial ways better.

I rode down Halsey Neck Lane, careful to obey the speed limit, and then after a minute there was the Curry house before me, one of the few houses on that wide street not fortified by a hedge, as if it had nothing to hide. It was a turn-of-the-century nautical with a loop gravel driveway out front and a well-kept yard and ancient trees. The house ran nearly the width of the flat lot. There were no cars in the driveway, the house was eerily still. Most of the houses out here were like that this time of the year. I looked at it for a while and the still houses around it and then decided to push my luck a little and get out and take a look around. I still wanted to see it coming, whatever it was, to be ahead of Frank on this, and this drove me now like a compulsion.

I passed the house and pulled over to the shoulder of a neighboring yard and got out of my car and walked back to the open gate at the end of the hedge-lined driveway. I waited, studied the house a moment, then took a step through. It felt like stepping off the branch of a tree into darkness. I hated this work and always have. I didn't let myself think much about the risk I was taking; there was too much at stake not to take this gamble.

I stopped in my tracks and stood there, still, with my

eyes on the ground, listening, trying to get a sense of the neighborhood beyond the yard. Quiet was everywhere. The only sounds had been my footsteps on the gravel, and now that I had stopped there was nothing at all to hear but my breathing. After a moment I started walking again.

I followed the lawn around the left side of the house to the backyard. It was brighter there, the shadow of the house being cast on the front yard by the muted morning sun. When I got to the backyard I saw that the garage was on the right side of the house, across the lawn. I stopped again and listened and this time looked around. I could hear the faint hiss of the ocean, a half mile to the south. But that was all. The neighborhood felt abandoned, like winter was an enemy that drove everyone out.

I looked then up at the house. Up close it had the feel of a great wooden ship that had run solidly aground. I looked at the windows reflecting the November sky. There was nothing, no one, behind the ghostly reflections on the glass. I looked at them for a long time.

Maybe there I had found my reason not to proceed. Maybe it was the gray skies in those windows that spooked me, that eroded my resolve. For whatever reason, I felt suddenly too deep into enemy territory. The compulsion that brought me this far was diminishing fast. I still wasn't sure just what exactly it was I expected to find by being there. All I did know was that Augie was in jail and I had no leads. What was it I was hoping a look at this place would tell me about the Currys that their address already didn't? I had to do something to help Augie, but this suddenly didn't feel like it.

I felt the urge to bolt. I considered that the last thing I needed was to get picked up here for trespassing by one of the Chief's boys. I would be no help to anyone then, and so I decided fast that I had seen all there was to see— a great, empty house, nothing more—and was turning to get the hell out of there and back to the Hansom House and my part of town when something stopped me.

There was a wide set of stairs leading up to a back porch and a set of French doors at the rear of the house. One of the panes of glass in the French door was broken, punched in. When I reached the wide stairs I waited again, staring at the door, then started up them. When I was halfway to the top I could see that there was no broken glass under the shattered pane, no glass outside the door. I stepped onto the porch and walked to the door. All the broken bits of glass had fallen inside. It was then that I saw that one of the French doors was ajar.

Somewhere inside a phone started to ring. It rang seven or eight times, then ended. I looked through the French doors into a long hallway that ran straight down to the front door. It was wide and there was a long table against one wall. Across from it was an armoire. Paintings and antique mirrors were hung on the white walls. The hall had the look of a gallery, bright even in the pale morning light and a little sterile. Nothing, however, seemed to me to be out of place. There were no bare spots on the wall where a painting should be. Nothing but the window seemed disturbed.

The doors opened out, so I put my hand in the pocket of my denim jacket and gripped the handle, pulling the door open just enough for me to slip in. I was careful not to step on any of the broken glass or fine dust that covered the floor.

On the wall inside the door was a security system touch pad. The small red light indicating that the system was disarmed was lit. Whoever broke in had known the code. I wondered if maybe someone had forgotten or lost their key, but the door was left open and the house seemed empty.

I moved quietly, cautiously. My heart was pumping uncomfortably. With each step deeper into the gallery I thought of Augie and Frank and blocked out all thoughts of the Chief and his boys.

There was a Pollock on the wall. It was the first thing I saw. It was a piece of shit. Near it was a de Kooning. The Pollock was a large painting. I knew it probably carried a steep price. My adoptive mother had some paintings, most of them South American, but her true passion was antique rocking and carousel horses. You couldn't walk into a room in that thirty-room house without tripping over one. The Curry house wasn't like that; it was neat and cold and sparse, everything in its place. The house I grew up in was dark and cluttered and full of, like many of the old houses out here, secret rooms. Even in these there was some kind of representation of a horse standing about somewhere, some costing as much as a hundred grand.

Most of the art on these walls was New York or East Hampton art, most big names. I walked through the hall till I came to the table alongside the wall. There was nothing on it but a Tiffany pear tree lamp. There wasn't a hint of dust. With my hand in the pocket of my jacket I opened some drawers and found nothing but mail. Most were bills but some were personal letters addressed to James Curry. I checked the return addresses but saw nothing that seemed noteworthy. I closed the drawers carefully, quietly, then crossed the hall to the armoire. I opened its doors and found a bar stocked with expensive gin, Scotch, and a variety of cordials. Behind the bottles was a mirror. I saw my reflection and shook my head, as if to say to myself What are you doing?

I closed the doors and followed the hallway to its end. I was now at the front of the house, near the front door. To my right was the entrance of a side room and beside that a flight of stairs. To my left was another room. I paused to listen before looking into the room to my left. It was a family room, complete with a large-screen TV and a stereo system. Nothing was out of place. I stepped to the room to my right. A heavy oak table was preset with silverware. There were ten places set, dozens of pieces of silver there for the taking.

I looked up the flight of stairs to the landing above. It was a catwalk that looked down on the gallery. I waited and listened before starting up the stairs. The wide wood planks creaked little, but every sound, no matter how little, seemed too loud. At the top of the stairs I had the choice of turning left or right. I turned right and followed a hallway that led past several rooms, their doors opened. I walked down, passing each room, looking in. They looked to me like guest rooms. This hallway ended at another, smaller family room. Again, nothing was out of place.

I turned and crossed the catwalk to the hallway to my left. Nothing unusual: a study, a full bathroom, a small workout room, all perfectly ordered. I looked in each and then came to the room at the end of the hall. I stopped dead.

This last room was trashed, ransacked. The mattress was overturned and torn. Pillows were gutted. The bureau top and shelves were bare, their contents cast to the floor. It took a moment, but I could tell by the belongings that this was a girl's room, more specifically a teenage girl's room. There were stuffed animals and the remnants of pop star posters that had been torn from the wall. I scanned through the mess till I saw half lying under a heap of bedding a framed photograph of a smiling and tanned girl on a sailboat. It was Amy Curry. She was beautiful, radiant with life, maybe fifteen, maybe sixteen.

Downstairs, the phone started ringing again. I counted nine rings altogether. Once it was done, silence returned abruptly to the house. I waited a moment, looking over the room once more, and then I heard the sound of a car door close outside, coming from the direction of the garage. I went into the next room, which overlooked the right side of the house. Below a brown Mercedes sedan was parked outside the garage. A man carrying a briefcase and a suit bag was walking toward the house. All I could see was the top of his head, dark with flecks of gray that looked like splattered paint.

I broke then from my stillness and bolted. I took the stairs two at a time, reached the bottom, and turned toward the back door. Behind me I heard a key working the lock of the front door. It clicked, and then the door began to open. I was nowhere near the back door yet and had no choice but to duck through a side door. I found myself in the kitchen and waited there, panting.

I heard the man at the front door enter and pause. I figured he must have been at the keypad, which read "disarmed." Then I heard him say "What the fuck?" and I knew by this that he had spotted the French door with the broken pane. I heard heavy footsteps start then. He walked with certainty toward the door. I waited just inside the kitchen door, uncertain just where I was going to go now and not knowing how he couldn't hear me in such a quiet house. I listened to his footsteps approach and ignored my pounding heart beating against my ribs. He was about halfway down the gallery and I was in real trouble when the phone rang again. It stopped him. He turned and headed back through the gallery to the family room. I waited till he answered the phone and heard his voice, distant, muffled, but clear enough. "This is he," he said. "Yes. What? What . . . ? This must be a mistake. When? Oh, Jesus. Jesus. I'll be right there. Yes. I'll be right there."

I knew it was one of the Chief's boys on the other end notifying Amy Curry's next of kin. Amy's father let out a final denial as I slipped out the back door and down the steps to the brittle grass. I made it around the house and to my car quick. I got in and got the hell out of there.

Later I went out to the Texaco station and bought a newspaper with the change from my ashtray. I needed to look for another job and figured I could do that while I waited for Gale to call.

Tina was asleep in my bed, so I sat on my couch and laid the paper out on the coffee table and looked through the help wanted ads. There wasn't much to choose from. This wasn't the time of year to be looking for a job. But there was an ad for a dishwasher at the LeChef, the French restaurant on Job's Lane. I knew the owner's wife from the college. I circled the ad and closed the paper and glanced at the cover stories. A Hampton Bays teenager was arrested two nights ago and charged with running heroin from the city to Bridgehampton. An East Hampton businessman whose abandoned Lexus was found a week ago was still missing. As I skimmed the articles, I wondered if some night soon the mother of the teenager would come looking for me telling me that she had heard of me, asking for my help. Or would it be the wife of the well-respected businessman asking me to find him and bring him home safe since it was now painfully clear to her that no one else could, or would? I told myself that all that had nothing to do with me. I chanted it like a mantra. This wasn't me. This wasn't me. This wasn't me.

As I thought this I continued looking through the paper. It was always better to see it coming, even if, it turns out, it wasn't really coming at all, even if all it turned out to be was a close call. I liked the feeling of being prepared, even if that feeling was little more than an illusion. Sometimes all it took to get through to morning was an illusion. So I read on. But I could spot nothing, so I closed the paper and folded it and thought about the fact that I had rent to pay. Then I got tired, so I put the paper down and lay back on the couch with my arms folded across my chest like a corpse. I fell asleep easily and dreamed of my father, of him waving me to follow him into some unfamiliar woods. I did not follow him, just stood there and watched him go and felt the pain of his departure. Before anything more could happen I awoke to the sound of my phone ringing. I scrambled to grab, thinking of Tina asleep in the other room.

I caught the phone on the second ring. "Hello."

"Mac." It was Gale.

"What'd you find?"

"Nothing. No one came in last night or this morning with any kind of knee injury."

"Shit."

"Any news from Augie yet?"

"Not yet."

"You boys play too rough."

"Tell me about it."

"Keep me posted, Mac."

"I will."

I hung up and looked toward the bedroom. Tina was standing in the doorway. She was wearing one of my T-shirts, her long bare legs running like the two steep sides of a narrow triangle to the floor.

"Who was that?"

"Gale."

"From the hospital?"

"Yeah."

"What did she want?"

"She wanted to know if I'd heard from your father yet."

"Have you?"

I shook my head.

"What time is it?"

I didn't know. Tina turned and looked into the bedroom, at the secondhand windup clock by my bed.

"It's almost noon," she said. "Are you hungry?"

"You should put some clothes on, Tina."

"I went out and bought some food. You had nothing. You know, you need to keep up your strength, especially after last night."

Tina didn't move from the bedroom doorway. "You're home now. Do you want me to leave? Do you want me to go back to Lizzie's?"

"I'm going back out," I said. "I need you to wait for Augie's call."

"Okay. Did you find whoever it was you were looking for?"

"Not yet."

"You look tired."

"Tina, put something on, please."

She waited a moment before turning impatiently and going into the bedroom. A minute later she came out with jeans on and the T-shirt tucked in. Her limbs were lanky, her torso narrow, like a girl's, but in places she was a woman, the worst place being her mind. I ignored her obvious bralessness. My mind had wandered back to my dream and for now I was stuck there.

She looked at me for a moment, studying my face closely.

"You were thinking about your father, weren't you? I can tell by that look on your face."

We had gotten to know each other too well during our three months crowded together under the same roof. I had taken lately to acting a little cold toward her, to keep at a distance. It seemed the more my guard was up, the more she needed to try to bypass it.

"I was just remembering a dream I had."

"About him?"

I nodded.

"You miss him?"

"I never really knew him, Tina. I mean, I have a few memories, but I have no real idea who the man was."

"Why didn't he . . . keep you? Why did he send you to live with that creepy family?"

"I don't know. I'm sure he had his reasons."

"You know, you never talk to me about how you grew up, except that it was hell."

"I don't talk to anyone about it."

"Why not?"

"It's just not something I talk about."

"Did he hurt you?"

"Tina."

"Is that how you learned to fight, defending yourself against him?"

"Tina."

"Why don't you talk about it? He was your father."

"He wasn't my father. My real father wasn't my father, as far as I'm concerned. I had no father, just two men who are no longer a part of my life, okay?"

Tina looked away. "I don't know what I'd do without Augie," she offered.

"You won't have to worry about that."

She took a step toward me and looked at me square, as if searching out an opening in my guard, and said, "Are we ever going to be normal? You and I, I mean. Are we ever going to be like we were before all this started?"

"Let's get your father straightened out first," I told her, my eyes locked on a distant, bare wall.

"I can't pretend I don't feel what I feel, Mac."

"No one's asking you to."

"You don't want to even look at me, let alone hear what I'm feeling."

"We're allowed all the feelings, Tina. We're just not always allowed to act on them."

"I gave up trying to seduce you a long time ago, Mac. I'm not after you anymore. My schoolgirl crush is way over."

"You know my concerns," I said. "You know my situation with the Chief."

"If he's your enemy, then vanquish him."

I looked at her and laughed. I had never heard her speak in that way before. "You are your father's daughter."

"We're reading *Julius Caesar* in English."

"Finish it, then we'll talk all you want about that particular school of thought."

"Sometimes I just don't understand you."

Deeply tired, not wanting this at all, I muttered, "Yeah, well, join the club." I rubbed my eyes with the heels of my palms, digging in deep.

"You never used to be like this, Mac. You used to be someone people could count on. When the Chief's son and his friends tried to rape me, you went through them like they were nothing."

"And look where it got us."

"My life would be shit right now if you hadn't been there, if you hadn't done what you'd done."

"You don't get it, Tina. I don't regret having saved you. I'm just tired of it all. When I did what I did to the

Chief's son, after you were safe, when we were free to go, I kept going, out of rage, out of greed, and I set into motion events that resulted in the deaths of three people. I have blood on my hands. I want the blood off and I want to keep it off."

Tina looked toward the windows and the November gloom beyond them. She was thinking something through. I could tell this by the look on her face. I'd give her whatever time she needed.

Finally she said, "After they killed Caesar they washed their hands in his blood."

"Wasn't very bright of them, was it?"

"No. Marc Antony walked in and took one look and knew exactly who killed Caesar."

"There are consequences to every action we make."

"Yes."

"Everyone around here is so reckless, Tina. Frank, the Chief, even your father. Even me. I don't want to be that anymore. No one dies because of me again. No one. So the pieces stay in place, and once your father calls, you go home to him and you stay away from here, okay? I'm going to help your father, I promise, and everything's going to be fine, as long as the pieces stay in place. Will you help me keep them there?"

"I'll do anything you want, you know that."

"Good. I'm going to go out for a while," I said. "You probably won't be here when I get back. If I don't see you before, I'll see you Thanksgiving, okay?"

"Okay."

I pulled on my sneakers and then put on my jacket. Tina stayed where she was in the bedroom doorway. We looked at each once again, and then I left her.

I went down the two flights of stairs to the bar below. There was a good lunch crowd at the bar. George saw me as I slipped into the antique phone booth and closed the door. I dialed Eddie's number. His wife, Angel, was working dispatch and answered on the third ring.

"It's Mac," I said. "I need Eddie to meet me."

"Where?"

"Outside the Hansom House."

"What time?"

"As soon as he can."

"He's on a run to Water Mill. He'll be there in twenty minutes."

"Thanks, Angel."

"Take care, Mac."

We hung up. I sat in the booth and thought things through. I was tired. I had no idea where to look now for the man Frank thought could help us clear Augie. I felt helpless and frustrated. I wanted more than anything to be up in my warm bed, but of course Tina was there. I looked through the narrow panes of glass in the booth door and saw the bar and the people seated at it. I recognized a few faces. I wanted to be among them, drinking Jack neat and not caring about anybody or anything. I didn't want Augie's fate in my hands; I refused on a good day to carry even my own. I had made my choice long ago, when I decided not to enter the police academy, not to follow my father, and stepped off into the fringe of life and was content to stay there, if only people like Frank would let me. The first trouble I got into was when I saved a neighborhood girl from being mauled in the street by a mastiff the summer I was ten. It seemed someone always turned up in need of some kind of help or another every now and then since. It was, a girlfriend of mine told me once long ago, my karmic debt. Some I saved, others I didn't. Was that all part of some cosmic checks and balances? Would failing to save Augie diminish or increase some debt? I wondered as I sat there in that booth if it was possible to be someone else if you wished long enough.

I hadn't had anything to drink in a while—months—and a part of me missed the way it relaxed me, the effect it had that nothing else in the world had. Every time I drank I could see why people drank. If every machine has its friction, then booze is the oil to the human machine. Things go easier, friendships seem deeper, strangers are welcomed. For a while anyway. I always drank for free at the Hansom House, when George was behind the bar, and that didn't make it any easier to practice restraint. I was never an ugly drunk, or a sloppy one, or even a sullen one. I was simply inebriated, impaired, useless. A girl named Becky once died because I was too drunk to pull a sawed-off double-barreled shotgun from the hands of her irate boyfriend, my old house-painting partner and longtime friend, Jamie Ray. She had been cheating on him, and when he cornered her and demanded to know who, she lied and told him she was cheating on him with me, thinking he wouldn't dare make trouble. He dragged her to the Hansom House one morning and sent George to get me. When I came down, still in the bag from the night before, I found them on one of the overstuffed sofas in the parlor room off the bar. Jamie Ray sat beside her with his arm around her and the shotgun to her head. He wanted to hear it from me that she and I were lovers. But there was no talking to him. He was drunk, spitting mad. I stalled him and stepped closer to them and waited for the best possible moment. It never came, and when it became clear he had reached his end, when he rose up on his knees beside her and pressed both barrels against the side of her head, I moved as fast as I could, grabbing the gun with both hands. But I wasn't any use. I felt the shot rush through and I felt the heat swelling within my grip. The next day Jamie Ray hanged himself with his shoelaces in his cell at the Suffolk County Jail.

Drinking makes it easier, makes the failures easier. I could forget them for a time after a few tumblers of Jack. I could be free of it for a time, free of the weight, and awaken in the morning on my living room floor with holes punched in my memory and more pressing concerns with which to deal, like the collapsing star just behind my forehead and the ringing anvil in my ear. I've chosen each drink I had. I've chosen this life I live.

This was the deal:

Augie and I, while waiting for a sports car to tail, see

a man in the dark alongside the road a few hundred feet behind us and witness a car wreck in which a high school girl, the daughter of a wealthy man, is killed. According to Augie, the Chief's boys do more of a clean-up job than document the scene. Augie and I go back for a look later, hear a sports car gearing through the back roads in the distance. Augie finds what seem like the marks of a spike strip, a device police use to blow out the tires of cars. Back at our homes, Augie and I are sacked, told to mind our own business. Augie shoots a man who was armed but no weapon is found by the police. Frank suspects the Chief is up to something and coerces me into finding the man who had sacked me so he might lead us to a man who might clear Augie of manslaughter charges and might give Frank something to use against the Chief. I enter the girl's home and find her room ransacked but priceless artwork and top-of-the-line appliances untouched. The door to the house had been broken into but the alarm wasn't triggered.

This was what I knew, this was all I had. It was noon and all my leads were exhausted. All but one.

I left the phone booth and walked out of the bar without making eye contact with George. It wasn't long after I got outside that Eddie's cab came down Elm and stopped. I opened the door and got in.

I told Eddie what I needed. A dark late-model LTD, a man with a limp. I told him where I'd be. He nodded and listened, watching me in the rearview mirror. The conversation only took a minute, and then I got out again into the cold and closed the heavy door. Eddie drove away, and I went to my car and got in and drove back to the hospital to wait.

I sat in my LeMans in the parking lot and thought of Gale close to the end of her shift inside. A little after two I saw her come out and get into her Jeep Cherokee and drive off. She didn't see me. I thought about the envy I felt, how maybe life would be better if she was mine. But that's not the way things were. At some point after she drove off I fell asleep sitting up. When I awoke it was dark and I was disoriented for a few long seconds. The parking lot lights were on but there was no LTD to be seen. It was cold in my car, so I started the engine and turned on the heat. It didn't take long for me to convince myself that this was a waste of time.

When I got home my apartment was empty. There was a note from Tina telling me that Augie was home and to call when I got in. But I didn't call. I guess I just wanted to be free of it for a while. I made something to eat and then got into bed with my clothes on.

I awoke sometime later to the phone ringing. It felt like the middle of the night. I felt disappointment at my return to consciousness. I let the phone ring three times, lingering in what was left of my slumber, then got up and staggered into the living room and picked up the receiver in the middle of the fifth ring.

"Yeah," I muttered. I expected Augie's voice, or Tina's, but instead I heard the musical accent of my Jamaican-born friend.

"I got him," he said.

"What?"

"I got him. I found him. The man you wanted. Old LTD, limp. I got him."

"Jesus, Eddie," I said. "Where are you?"

Four

Bars in New York close at four in the morning, and that always seemed to me a particularly soulless time of night. When I worked as a bartender for a few years in Sag Harbor in my twenties, it was, in the summertime, dawn by the time I got back to the Hansom House. I drove west on the back roads, along the rim of Peconic Bay, and watched the sky fill with light shades of gray and blue till it was finally light. I quit the bar business because I grew tired of getting people drunk and taking money for it. I grew tired of the knowledge that people I had gotten drunk were on the roads of my town. In the wintertime, when my ride home was through darkness that spread out around me without hint of end, I would think of kids waiting for school buses and my customers, reeling as they left, virtually handicapped, out on the roads.

Now it was November, and as black as ever outside my windshield. I could barely see the bare branches of the trees that flickered past my driver's door window. I was alone on the long road to Sag Harbor. During my entire ride out there I didn't pass one car. I saw nothing at all that resembled human activity or life till I turned onto a side street on the backside of town and saw Murph's Backstreet Tavern through my windshield.

It was a small tavern, like something out of the American Revolution, painted green and falling apart. Beams sagged, the stone foundation was crumbled out in places on one side, gnarled trees surrounded it as close as framework. I remembered Murph's well from my drinking days. It was known to some as an after-hours bar, sometimes serving drunks like me till seven in the morning.

I saw Eddie's cab right off, parked across the street in the lot of an auto shop, just where he had said he would be. His lights were off and his cab was parked perfectly in line with the other cars in the lot. He was hidden well enough from the casual eye.

Before I pulled into the lot I looked to my right, into the long dirt, tree-lined drive that ran past Murph's. In it was only one car, a dark LTD circa 1975. I hit the blinker and turned into the lot and backed my car in between two wrecks.

I walked across the crowded auto shop lot to Eddie's cab. He wound his window down, and a burst of cloves and cigar smoke raced out at me on the steady current of heated air that fled his cab.

"He's in there," Eddie said. He nodded toward Murph's.

I looked around, surveying the scene. I focused on the ramshackle bar. A few dull lights were on inside but I could hear no voices or music, nothing. The LTD was the only car anywhere to be seen, beyond the contents of the auto shop lot. It was late, it was past late.

"I was dropping off a fare in Bridgehampton when I spotted him. He was coming out of that bar on the corner, the one that changes names every year, what's its name?"

"Winston's," I said. A light went out inside Murph's. I watched the windows.

"Yeah, that's it," Eddie said. "He's been here about an hour. He looked drunk enough to me when he limped in. I can only imagine what he's like now."

I didn't take my eyes off the bar. "Thanks, Eddie."

"You want me to wait?"

"No, go home."

"You want me to call anyone?"

I thought about having him call Frank and tell Frank to meet me somewhere in an hour. But I thought it would be better to have the man with the limp in my possession before I did that. As much as I wanted to remain an amateur, I didn't want to look like one in front of Frank.

"I can take care of this, Eddie," I told him. "Get out of here. And thanks."

"We do what we do, Mac. I'll see ya."

I walked back across the crowded lot to my LeMans, opened the passenger door, and leaned in. In the glove compartment was my Spyderco knife. I removed it and clipped it inside the right hip pocket of my jeans. Then I started across the street to the LTD.

I went to the passenger door of the LTD and saw at once that it was unlocked. I opened the door and climbed into the backseat. It was as cold in the car as it was outside. I thought of the laws I was breaking and the laws I was about to break, and then I thought of Augie and the shit storm he was in and knew there was nothing else I could do.

One good thing, I was in Sag Harbor, not Southampton. I didn't have to fear the Chief here. Still, a felony was a felony, no matter what town I was in. And I wasn't convinced that, one way or another, the Chief wouldn't get his hands on me no matter where on the East End I was busted.

I tried to keep my mind focused on Augie, on his needing my particular help, on the trouble he was in. Now and then, though, Tina would cross my mind. It was hard to think of him without thinking of her. I remembered the warm nights last summer when Augie was still in the hospital and Tina was staying with me. I remembered us spending late-weekend nights sitting in my living room and listening to the radio and speaking Spanish. She had studied it for two years at school and wasn't half bad. Of course, this was before her attentions turned dangerous and I started hiding from her in the bar downstairs, drinking myself senseless and making myself impervious to her attempts at getting me to want her.

I don't know how long I had been there waiting when I finally heard the sound of a door open and close, followed by footsteps on the dirt driveway. Even though I could hear him make his approach it seemed almost sudden when he appeared at the driver's side and opened the door. I slid the Spyderco out of my pocket and held it tightly. I waited while the driver's door opened. A hinge squeaked. The man with the limp more fell into his seat than anything else. He closed the heavy door and fumbled with his keys. After a moment, the ignition cranked and the engine caught. He switched the heat to high, shifted into drive, clicked on the lights, and, after a long pause, started down the dirt drive to the street.

The car moved forward with a jolt. He turned left, then left again, heading toward the bridge to Northhaven.

I waited as we crossed the bridge. A minute after we rolled onto ground again the LTD began to slow for a stoplight. I could hear the heater fan running up front but felt nothing but cold around me still. When the car came to its stop, I drew a breath and made my move.

I jumped up and wrapped my left hand around the man's forehead, pulling his head back. I placed the closed knife against his throat so he'd feel metal and said, "Pull over." I could see his eyes in the rearview mirror, half opened, the eyes of a man well past drunk.

"What the fuck?"

"Pull the car over."

"Who the fuck . . . ?"

I flipped open the blade with my thumb. It clicked loudly. I pressed the four inches of serrated metal against his throat. Even though it was a bluff, we were clearly well across the line now.

"Pull over."

"Where?"

"Turn left onto Long Beach. Beside those bushes and trees. Start too fast or stop too sudden and you cut your own throat, got it?"

He turned left on Long Beach, then pulled the LTD over under an ash tree. The man with the limp did everything slowly, more out of drunkenness than caution.

He shifted into park, one gear at a time. His clothes reeked of cigarettes and sweet whiskey.

"Kill the motor and the lights," I said.

He turned the key and the engine cut off. Then he switched off the lights.

We sat there together in the dark. I looked to make sure there were no other cars around. I could see the night sky clearly through the windows. It looked as cold as a pile of coal ash.

"I don't have any money."

"I don't want money," I told him. "Move over into the passenger seat. Now."

"What?"

"Just do it, now."

"Why?"

I said nothing more. Our eyes met in the rearview mirror. There was a moment of cognition when I looked into the calm eye at the center of his drunken storm. Somewhere in there was a sober man. "Okay." He climbed over the console into the passenger seat. He moved clumsily. I kept my hand on his forehead and the knife to his throat, moving behind him. Once in the passenger seat, I pressed his head against the headrest, my left hand clamped tight on his forehead.

"If you want the car, take it. Take it."

"I don't want your car," I told him. "Remove your belt."

He tried to look at me out of the corner of his eyes, but I was directly behind him, out of his peripheral vision.

"Who are you . . . ?"

"Just remove your belt."

He reached down and undid his belt and slowly pulled it off.

"Hand it back to me."

He held it up. I took it. I held the knife against his throat with my right hand and made a loop out of the belt with my left. Then I tossed the loop over his head and around the headrest till it made a noose around his throat. I pulled it tight. He gagged but I didn't loosen it. I made a hole in the belt with the knife, then closed the knife and clipped it back in my right hip pocket. I used the new hole to fasten the belt buckle. I quickly double-checked my work. His head was pressed even harder against the headrest. His body seemed pulled rigid, as if slouching would lynch him.

I reached around and searched through his overcoat pockets. I found a blackjack and stiletto. In a shoulder holster was a 9mm Taurus semiautomatic.

"You carry a lot of tools, don't you?" I said into his ear. "Can't decide if that's the sign of a craftsman or a hack."

He said nothing. I could tell he was sobering up fast.

"You like hurting people?" I said.

"It pays the rent." He swallowed hard, his Adam's apple bobbing slowly. It looked like a snake swallowing an egg whole.

"What do you want with me?"

I removed the Taurus by the butt, holding it between my thumb and forefinger. I removed a handkerchief from the pocket of my denim jacket and used it as a glove as I removed the clip and the chambered shell from the gun. I emptied the clip and placed the bullets into my jacket pocket, then wiped down everything I had touched, including the clip and the gun. Then I placed everything on the handkerchief, tied its corners together, and tossed the bundle out the window and into the road-side scrub outside. The bundle landed noisily in a patch of overgrown winter grass.

"Lift your feet up onto the seat and place them beside each other, ankles touching."

He hesitated, straining to breathe. Finally he lifted his feet one at a time to his chest. His knees came to his chin. He was wearing black dress shoes, oxfords.

"Untie the laces, then tie them together tight, in a knot," I said.

He did what I told him. I watched him as he worked. The belt around his neck prevented him from looking down without cutting into his breathing, but I didn't care. He gagged and took shallow, panicky breaths.

A distended artery crossed down his forehead like a slash of lightning. Even in the dark I could see that his face had reddened significantly.

When the laces were knotted together I moved across the backseat and out the door. I got into the driver's seat and removed my belt from around my waist and bound his hands together by the wrists. His eyes were on me but I didn't care if he saw my face. When I was done I sat and looked at him for a moment, then turned on the interior light and leaned across the seat till we were face to face. The distended vein in his forehead looked ready to burst. He strained to look at me from the corner of his eye.

"Remember me?"

He said nothing. His strained breathing was the only sound. After a moment of this foolishness I flipped off the overhead dome light and sat back behind the wheel and cranked the ignition till the engine caught.

I switched on the headlights and saw in their long beams a swirling of white flakes. The storm I had been sensing all day was here. I could imagine the bulk of it still to the west, past Peconic Bay, past the Pine Barrens, past Queens, pouring heavy and silent onto Manhattan.

We rode the back roads toward Southampton. I kept my eye out for cops when I wasn't glancing over at limper. He kept perfectly still, watching the road ahead, his breathing short and measured, his eyes bulged. Fear was sobering him up fast.

It was still a good hour and a half till dawn, till we lost the cover of dark. In the village of North Sea I stopped at a deli and dialed Frank's beeper number from a pay phone outside. All the glass in the booth had been smashed in and the cold night air flowed through it, carrying snow. On the floor of the booth was a pile of bits of broken glass that looked in the dark like diamonds. But they crushed into powder beneath the toe of my sneaker.

When I heard the tone I punched in the number of the pay phone. Then I hung up and waited. I watched the man strapped to the headrest in the passenger seat of the warm LTD. I looked at nothing but him, or the shape of him, which was all that was visible in the dark. I could barely feel the earth beneath me; I could barely feel anything but the wind that moved through the booth and the snow that touched my face. I think if I had looked at my own reflection then I would not have recognized much of what I saw. I was glad it was dark.

Five minutes went by and then the phone rang. I picked it up on the second ring. I could hear what I always heard when I spoke to Frank on the phone: the hiss of a pay phone connection. He was probably at the one near Cameron Street, in the village by the camera shop. His house wasn't far from there.

"I've got it," I said. "Where do you want to take delivery?"

"Road D, off Dune Road."

"When?"

"How soon can you get there?"

"Ten minutes."

"I'll be waiting."

I drove around the village to avoid being seen. I passed the hospital and then followed Gin Lane till it became Dune Road. Here was where the road changed from a coastal road to a peninsula that ran for a little over a mile and separated Shinnecock Bay from the Atlantic Ocean. Across the bay to my right was the Shinnecock Indian Reservation and, in the low hills above it, Southampton College. To my left were the dunes and the fantastic homes built upon them. Beyond the dunes was the beach and the Atlantic. I could hear the sound of the surf, faint like a whisper over the engine and through the closed windows.

It was a dark, inky morning, made even more so by the heavy storm clouds. There were no streetlights on Dune Road. The snow was falling heavier now, in straighter lines. I wondered if inland it had begun to accumulate. Here by the ocean nothing would last long enough to amount to anything.

I turned left into Road D, which was really just a

hundred-foot-long parking lot cut into the tall beach grass. Frank's Seville was the only car there, and he was waiting beside it when I parked.

He was dressed for the weather in a heavy black leather coat and black gloves. His pants and shoes, too, were black. He moved quickly toward the LTD and yanked opened the door.

The interior light came on. In Frank's fist was his .45 semiautomatic Colt. He leaned in and with one sudden, violent motion, smashed the dome with the butt of the gun. The light blinked out fast. For a second I wasn't sure what to expect.

Frank's moves were certain and swift, like those of a man on a mission, or caught up in an obsession. He leaned back out of the LTD then and pressed the muzzle of the pistol hard against the head of the man.

Frank wasn't here to play games, and he wanted everyone present to know it.

"We're taking you for a walk," he said. "Do you understand?"

The man nodded once, his eyes straining to see Frank. He seemed more drunk now than before. Strands of wet hair were matted to his forehead. Frank held the gun steady and said to me, "Undo him."

I leaned in and undid the belts and cut the laces of his shoes with my knife. Free of the noose, the man leaned forward, his body relaxing, and drew in deep breaths. Frank allowed him little time to enjoy his freedom. He pulled the man out roughly, dragging him by the collar of his overcoat, spilling him onto the pavement. I heard then for the first time the familiar sound of heavy waves breaking over the shore. I had heard that sound most every day of my young life, a steady hiss spilling over the sill of my bedroom window. That house sat not far at all from here, but it was, now and always, the last thing on my mind.

"Get up," Frank ordered, his hand still on the man's collar.

I walked around the car to them. Frank pulled till the man scrambled to his feet. I watched but did nothing. It was Frank's show now. I had done my part and was free to go. But something, maybe a sense of dread, made me want to stay.

The man with the limp looked at Frank, then at me, then back at Frank. He was almost too drunk to stand. I don't think he knew anymore where he was.

"Toward the water," Frank ordered. He stood behind the man, the gun pressed into the base of his skull. With his left hand on the man's collar, Frank steered him off the narrow lot and onto the sand and between two dunes. The man fell more than once, and each time he fell Frank would yank him back up to his feet.

There was frost on the surface of the sand, but it was broken through easily, and once you broke through it you sank heel and toe deep into the softness. I walked behind Frank, hoping to hide my presence. My gut told me not to be here but I continued to follow him. The snow was falling heavy and fast, swirling crazily. It was a squall, blinding and chaotic. Cold shards hit my open eyes, caused a quick chill, and then melted. I blinked continuously and tucked my chin into my chest. It did little good.

I followed Frank into this storm, between the two dunes, and stopped at an overturned boat and waited as they continued down the beach to the water's edge. It was high tide, a frigid mist in the air. I sat on the boat and took a look around.

The man went to the water's edge and stood facing the turbulent Atlantic, his back to Frank. Frank took a few steps back and aimed his .45 square at the back of the man's head. Even from this distance and through the wild snow I could see the man's eyes shifting frantically. Always the badly slurred question, "What did I do?" I knew this question well: I had asked it with wild eyes just before a bullet tore into my shoulder a few years ago. The half-dollar-size wound itched now, just as it always did before and during snow and rain.

I watched from the safe distance of a hundred feet and kept still on that overturned boat and said nothing. I watched what I could see of the side of the man's face, hoping to see something to hate. All I saw was a man afraid for his life.

I could not hear Frank speak over the sound of the ocean. Occasionally I heard the sound of a raised voice, but no word. The man with the limp held both his hands high in the air and Frank remained behind him by a few paces, the .45 aimed at the back of the man's head. They were discussing something now. I heard curses, mainly from Frank. Things seemed to be reaching a pitch, and then Frank took several fast steps forward and placed the muzzle of the gun against the man's head and shoved him with his left hand toward the water.

The man stopped, refused to move, and then Frank shoved him again. I saw Frank cock the .45. The man seemed aware of this, hesitated, then proceeded to wade into the heavy surf.

I didn't move from the overturned boat, just sat there and watched. It was Frank's show and had nothing to do with me. This was as far as I agreed to come.

The man took several steps forward, then was hit by a wave and stumbled and fell into the water. He struggled to keep his head up but to no avail. Frank yelled at him again and the man got to his feet and paused. He embraced his torso with his arms as if to keep warm and began to turn his head back to look at Frank. Frank fired the .45 once, into the ocean, and the man turned forward again.

I stood up from the boat then. The gunshot was a momentary crack in the broad night sky, and then it was gone, swallowed up by the sound of the incoming waves.

Frank yelled at the man again and the man started forward, wading in up to his waist. He got past the waves and stood chest deep in freezing water.

I had no idea what Frank was doing. I stayed by the overturned boat and called, "Frank," but he didn't hear me. I just didn't see how a man dead from exposure could help Augie any, so I started down the beach toward Frank. He was calling something to the man but I couldn't hear what it was. I could see though that Frank was caught up in something almost wild.

"Frank."

He was fixated on the man in the water, telling him to stay there till he was ready to talk. His outstretched right arm seemed locked at the elbow.

"Frank."

He acknowledged me but did not take his eyes off the man in the ocean. "Stay out of this, Mac."

"What the fuck are you doing?"

"I'm finding out the name of the man who hired him."

"Looks to me like you're drowning him."

"He didn't want to talk."

"Maybe he didn't know."

"I don't think he'll die to keep that secret."

"Put the gun down, Frank."

"Stay out of this, Mac. You've done your bit, now go home."

"Not like this, Frank."

"What?"

"I can't let you do this. Put down the gun." I called to the man in the water. "Get out. C'mon, get out."

He didn't take his eyes off of Frank. He was chest deep in the icy water, battered by relentless waves, but still he was unwilling to move.

"Frank, he doesn't know anything. Let him out."

"Stay out of it, Mac."

"Put the gun down, Frank."

"Stay the fuck out of it."

"You can't do this, Frank."

Frank called to the man, "Who hired you?"

The man could not answer. He would barely remain above the water. He slipped under once and came up again immediately. He was coughing, hacking seawater out of his lungs.

"You can't do this, Frank."

"Stay out of it, Mac."

"If he drowns, whatever he might know goes with him."

"He knows. He'll tell us."

"Frank, I'm telling you for the last time, put the gun down."

"This is Augie's life, MacManus. Don't you want to save Augie's life?"

"Not like this."

"You piece-of-shit pussy. I had you pegged from the start. You're a loser, MacManus. You're the worst kind of loser. You're not willing to do what it takes. You're a pussy and you'd rather fuck Augie's daughter than keep him out of jail—"

He was facing me then, his mouth twisted with anger and rage. The first thing I threw was a head butt, smashing his nose. I leapt forward and clung to him and dug my thumbnails into his eyes. Then I went straight for the .45 in his right hand. I grabbed the barrel and peeled the gun from his grip, securing it in my left hand. With my right I slapped him in the balls and he dropped to the ground. I kicked the clip out of the .45 and tossed it down the beach. I ejected the chambered shell and threw it in the opposite direction. Then I dropped the empty .45 into the sand by my feet and ran to the edge of the water.

I ran into the ocean. The water that splashed up stung my face, but that was the least of it. I grabbed the man and held him as I walked back on rubbery legs toward the shore.

The waves pushed us forward, and we collapsed side by side on our backs on the sand. My clothes were soaked again, brutal cold pressing against every part of my body. The man with the limp looked over at me. There was sand on his face and he could barely breathe. He was only slightly more sober now. Neither of us said anything. Then he pulled himself up, took one more look at me, and limped toward the dunes beyond which lay Road D. He moved desperately, as quickly as the sand and his limp and his hardening clothes would allow. He moved without once looking back.

I lay in silence for a while. I started to count the sound of the waves and then lost count. I was freezing, but it was all so familiar now. After a while Frank was standing over me, aiming a gun at me, a .380 Llama, his backup. I was more tired than I thought I should be. The man with the limp had gotten up and fled, so why was I still sprawled out and panting? I looked up at Frank. His nose was bleeding and his eyes were inflamed from where I had raked them. It must have taken him a while to get to his feet. He was breathing hard. I didn't need to look close at his face to know how pissed he was.

"You more than anybody should know better than to cross me," he said. You could tell by the way he spoke that he had taken one in the groin. There was a grunt after every word, as if he ran suddenly short of breath. That knowledge brought me a degree of comfort. Not many people slap Frank Gannon in the balls, one way or the other, and live to tell about it.

"What's going on, Frank?" I said between gasps. Nothing of what I had seen tonight had made sense. Nothing I had seen since the accident had made sense.

"You let our only lead go, MacManus. You've washed Augie's chances right down the gutter. You're his friend, at least he thinks you are. I'll let you have the pleasure of telling him."

"He wouldn't have let that man drown. He wouldn't want it like that, either."

"An innocent girl drowning in a pond is one thing. Your enemy is another. That man was your enemy. And now that he knows we're after him, there's no way he's going to let us find him again. Right down the gutter, MacManus. Right down the fucking gutter."

Frank holstered the .380, then picked up his sand-encrusted .45. He put that in the pocket of his leather coat, then started to walk away. "I'd offer you a ride, but my seats are leather."

"Call Eddie," I said. "Please."

"You'll find your way home. You always do."

"I'll die out here, Frank."

Frank stopped. "Call the cops."

"Don't be a prick, Frank."

"Maybe your friend will come back."

"I'll do a job for you. Whatever you want. Just get me someplace warm."

"You're a fuck-up, MacManus. I used to think you were just unlucky. Now I see just how hard you work at failure." He reached into his pocket and tossed a coin into the sand.

"There's a pay phone in the lot on Road D. You can call whomever you want from there. If it works, that is. If not, maybe some of your former neighbors'll take pity on you and take you in." He looked me over then. "You might want to get a haircut first."

He was gone then. I knew I didn't have time. I felt through the sand with aching fingers and found the coin, then pulled myself up and started toward the dune. I made it by sheer will between the two dunes onto Road D. Both the LTD and the Seville were long gone. I was alone in a stretch of nowhere. The pay phone was by the road. It felt as if my ear shattered when I put it to the earpiece. I didn't want to risk Eddie being out on a fare, and I didn't want to have to explain to Augie or Tina what had happened. There was only one other person I could think to call. I dialed the number with reluctance.

He answered on the fourth ring, his voice groggy.
"George, it's Mac," I said. "I need your help."

I got three hours' sleep and woke with a headache. My
clothes lying on the floor just inside my door had thawed
and were still wet and covered with sand. I placed them
on the radiator to dry. The snow had long since stopped
and there was little accumulation to speak of along Elm
Street. Because of the salt in the air snow rarely stuck on
the East End, except in the case of a nor'easter, but we
hadn't had one of those in years. As I slowly awoke it became clear to me that the abuse and sleeplessness were
beginning to take their toll on me. I rose slowly, like a
mountain. Before breakfast I called Eddie and had him
take me to my car in Sag Harbor. We didn't talk much
the entire trip out, except for when he wished me a
Happy Thanksgiving. I had no idea up till then what day
it was. When I got my bearings I wished him one, too,
and said nothing more. I thought about dinner at Augie's
around one. I had no clue what I would say to him about
the man with the limp.

On my way back with my LeMans I stopped and got
a paper. Back in my apartment I took my Spyderco knife
out of my pocket and tossed it into the top drawer of my
bureau. Then I sat in my chair at my living room window and drank cold tea and searched the want ads for
jobs. There weren't any; I knew there wouldn't be, not at
this time of the year. I've lived out here all my life and
spent the last ten years hiding as best I could from the

heart of things, in these crowded rooms of mine two floors above an out-of-the-way bar. I've lived here in my precious self-exile, trying to matter as little as possible whenever possible. It was the life I've chosen, miserable and empty and, I had determined a long time ago, all I deserved, and I wanted it back.

As I closed the paper I glanced at the headline about the Curry girl being killed in an auto accident. There were quotes from the Chief expressing his sympathy to the family and his frustration at the senselessness of it all. I read all that I could stomach and then put the paper down and placed my feet up on the sill and drank my tea till it was gone and tried not to think about anything, especially Amy Curry dead in my arms.

At one I showered and dressed and left for Augie's house. I was expected to bring nothing and had exactly that.

Inside Augie took my coat and offered me a drink. It was, despite my concerns, good to see him. He walked with his cane less than before. He was wearing jeans and a sweatshirt. Part of his physical training had included weights, and he looked larger than I remembered. I sat on a couch and nursed an apple juice. I couldn't really look Augie in the eye.

Tina was in the kitchen, putting together the dinner. Every so often she'd come out and place something on the table and I would see her. I had never seen her in a dress before and stared at her. Her boyfriend had yet to arrive but was due any minute.

"You okay?" Augie asked. He was holding a tumbler of straight Jack.

"Yeah," I said. "Sorry I didn't call last night. I got in late."

"My lawyer says the D.A. won't deal. He's going for manslaughter two. It's going before a grand jury beginning of next week. He's pretty certain it's going to go to trial, unless something new pops up."

I looked down at my drink.

Augie said, "He had a gun, I saw it. It was aimed right at me. I'm no greenhorn. I took him down and went down for cover. The other guy, his partner, took off. I could have shot him in the back but didn't. There was a gun, I know it. It had to have disappeared sometime between the shooting and the cops arriving."

"You called for the cops from inside?"

"Yeah."

"So the partner was out of your sight for a while."

"You think he came back for the gun?"

"It's possible."

"So when we find this fucker we'll find the gun."

Tina came out of the kitchen, placed a small plate of cranberry sauce on the table.

I glanced toward Tina as she moved back into the kitchen. Augie followed my line of vision. He watched me for a moment; I could feel it. Then he said, "This could go bad for me, Mac. We both know that. All I seem to do is impose on you. But I was wondering if things don't work out for me if you'd take care of her. I have no one else, and it would mean a lot to me, knowing she was safe. No one can keep her from harm better than you."

I said nothing.

"Will you do that for me, Mac? Will you take care of Tina again, if this goes bad?"

I lifted my head and looked at him. I didn't know what to say. Augie read my face and his expression shifted quickly to one of concern.

"What's wrong, Mac?"

My mouth opened but nothing came out, not even air. Finally I muttered, "Frank thinks the Chief is behind all this, that he's covering something up. I think he thinks these men were working for the Chief."

A moment went by, and then Augie said, "You're hiding something, Mac. What is it? What's wrong?"

I closed my eyes tight, then reopened them again.

"Mac?"

I shifted in my seat. There was no way out of this. I managed to look at Augie, but only briefly. "I went to look for the man who sacked me. I was hoping he would lead me to the man who sacked you. I found him and brought him to Frank." Augie watched me, looking puzzled. "But before Frank could get anything out of him I let him go."

"What?"

"I let him go."

"Jesus Christ, why would you do that?"

I said nothing. I had nothing to say for myself.

"You let him go. You let the only man who could save my ass go. You chose his fucking life over mine?"

"That wasn't the choice I was making, Aug."

"What choice were you making?"

"It seemed like Frank was more interested in killing the guy than finding out who the second man was."

"You're not Gandhi, Mac. In fact, you're far from it."

"We don't kill people, Augie, we don't do that, not unless we have no choice. And it seems that even if it is in some way justified, something bad always ends up coming out of it."

"So you're going to let me go to jail?"

"No."

"Then what exactly are you going to do to stop that from happening?"

I shook my head. "I don't know."

"You know, in jail, when people find out I'm ex-DEA, I won't last very long. I could do the time; I've been in worse places. But if I go to prison I won't live to finish my sentence."

"I swear to you, Aug, I won't—"

"—Get out, Mac."

Tina came to the kitchen door then and looked at us. She had an oven mitt in her hands.

"What's going on?" she said.

"Get out."

I looked at Augie. I could feel the rage moving along his nerves as well as if it were moving along my own. It caused some places in me to throb with currents of electricity and others to contract, as if gotten by snakes. Augie and I looked at each other, wordless. I had taken us over a line. When it was clear there was no point in me staying, I put my glass of juice on the coffee table and stood. Tina came through the door and into the room and placed herself in the middle of it all.

"Mac's staying for dinner, Augie," she told him.

I have seen them stand toe to toe many times before. I have yet to see her concede or back down.

I started toward the door. Tina came after me and put her hand on my shoulder. I turned and looked at her. She opened her mouth to speak but said nothing. She knew my face almost as well as she knew her father's.

I continued toward the door, leaving them both to their silence. I walked out and hit the cold air and started across the lawn. At the halfway point I realized someone was approaching me. I glanced up and saw a well-built teenager walking full stride toward the house. He startled me from my thoughts. I assumed he was Tina's new boyfriend, the one Augie had told me about, the one she tortured with stories about me, of what I did for her and how much I meant to her, of admiration and heroics and other such shit. I knew by the way he looked at me, with something close to the deep hate Augie had just thrown my way, that she had done a good job making me a threat to his budding ego. I actually felt bad for the kid.

We passed each other without a word. We were all hard stares. But really I wasn't in the mood for this, so I looked away and passed him by and headed for my Le-

Mans. The radio, like so much of it, didn't work. I drove home through the cold in silence.

I sat in my chair at my living room window and watched the November sky darken and night rise up like a flood of black water. I fought the urge to go downstairs and have a drink. I tried not to think about much but it wasn't easy. Augie was the only friend I had. He and Tina were the only family I knew. I had let him down, but I knew if I had to I would do the same thing again. Nobody dies. When it reached full night out I thought of all of them out there: the man with the limp, the dead man's partner, Amy Curry's father, whoever had ransacked her room, Frank, the Chief—all of them out there with their feet touching ground somewhere on the East End. I could almost sense them moving around, feel the waves their motions caused in the cold night air. I sat there in my chair for hours, not moving, staring at the train station and thinking. I thought of Augie extending his cane to me just as I was about to go under in that icy pond. I thought of the afternoons back when we first met that we spent drinking Jack at his house. Then I remembered Tina after the Chief's son and friends had tried to rape her, when Frank had come by to tell us that Augie was out on a job and long overdue. This was the night I found Augie almost beaten to death in his study. I remembered the look on Tina's face after Frank left. I remembered telling her I would find her father.

I knew nothing, only that something was going on in

my town, that a girl was dead and that Augie had gotten caught in the worst of it. I felt helpless, and you would have thought I would have gotten used to that by now.

I had my own life to get back to, my own problems with which to deal, so sometime after midnight I lay out on my mattress and caught some sleep. When I awoke it was just after nine in the morning. I drank some rice milk and ate a pear, then showered and dressed and drove to Job's Lane. I went around to the back of LeChef and found one of the owners, a thin Frenchman with black curly hair and frowning mustache. His name was Bernard. The other owner, whose wife I had known in college, was not in yet. The Frenchman interviewed me on the back steps leading to the kitchen. It was warmer than it had been the days before, a springlike chill in the air. The only cloud in the sky now was a menacing mass to the south, a dark bank of unfinished steel riding the low East End horizon.

"You've washed dishes before?"

"Yeah."

"Prep work?"

"Yeah."

He looked me over, thinking about it. "Minimum wage and staff dinners."

"That's fine."

"We cater, too, so there's a lot of prep work."

"I know how to cut," I said.

"Can you work doubles on the weekends?"

"Whatever you want."

"Do you speak any French?"

"Yeah."

"How much?"

"I'll understand what I hear."

He eyed me closely. After a minute he said, "I've seen you in the papers. I don't want any trouble in my restaurant."

"I'm just a guy who washes dishes," I said.

He nodded as if that was what he wanted to hear. He seemed content with my assurance. "When can you start?"

"Right away."

"Be here at six tomorrow morning. We're catering a party for some real estate people. We'll be busy."

"I'll be there."

"Expect to stay till around midnight or one. If you have a problem with that tell me now."

"I need all the hours I can get."

"Don't worry, we'll feed you. We treat our staff like people. I started out as a dishwasher in Paris. They treat you like shit there, but I tell you there is no kitchen that wouldn't fall apart without a good dishwasher. And who knows, maybe over time we will teach you to cook."

"When's payday?"

"Saturdays. Can you make it till then?"

"Yeah."

"We'll see you tomorrow, then."

I nodded. "Tomorrow."

I rode home with the driver's door window half down. It must have been fifty degrees out. I didn't need a jacket at all. The air that blew in smelled clean. But it was the air that rides ahead of rain.

By four the rain began. One minute there was nothing, the next it was pouring heavy and fast. Often I would see a little sleet bouncing off the roofs of the cars lining Elm Street. I sat at my window and watched the mixture of rain and sleet fall, listening to it drill through the leaves on the ground and patter off windows and spill from the leaky gutter. From above me I heard a deep and steady hiss of the rain and sleet falling on the roof. I watched the rain till night came and the streetlights came on. The drops that smashed onto the light covers burst into a mist that hung suspended around the lights, a grainy presence that churned slowly under the bright white glow.

I kept thinking of calling Augie. After a while I decided that I had to go back and talk things through with him, and I was on my way out, pulling on my sneakers, when someone knocked on my door. I answered it. George the bartender was standing in the dark hallway.

"What's going on?"

"There's someone here to see you."

"Who is it?"

"Some guy."

"Did you get a name?"

"Cory. Cor-something. He's wearing expensive clothes, he's clean shaven."

"Curry," I said.

"That's it."

"What does he want?"

"He just said he wants to see you."

"Is anyone else with him?"

"No."

"Are you sure?"

"It's dead down there. Everyone else there I know."

"Did he say why he wants to see me?"

"He said something about his daughter."

I didn't say anything to that. I could feel George watching me.

"Do you want me to tell him you weren't home, Mac?"

"No, send him up. Do me a favor though, wait five minutes and then give me a call."

George nodded. "Gotcha." He left and I closed the door. I went to my living room window and looked down on Elm Street and wondered what it could be Amy Curry's father wanted from me, or how he even knew about me, or where to find me.

After a few minutes there was a knock at my door. I stayed with my back to the window. I said, "Come in," and waited as the door opened. A man in a Brooks Brothers shirt and L.L. Bean trousers stepped partially in and stopped.

"I'm looking for Declan MacManus," he said. He was

polite and well mannered. Over his arm was a brown leather jacket, slick from the rain.

"You found him."

He slipped the rest of the way in and closed the door behind him. He glanced at me for a moment, then took a quick look around.

"Have we met?" I said.

"No. Sorry. My name is James Curry."

We nodded to each other. I stayed by the window and he stayed by the door. For some reason the room between us felt necessary.

"Is there something I can do for you, Mr. Curry?"

"James, please." He hesitated, then said, "Do you know me? I mean, have you heard of me?"

"Yeah. You live out on Halsey Neck Lane. You're rich."

"I'm rich," he repeated. He looked around my living room again. "And you're not," he said. "No offense."

"It's plain to see."

"Maybe we can help each other, then."

"I'm not sure I'm following you."

"Sorry. I'm not myself." He took in a breath. "The other night my daughter was killed in an auto accident. You might have heard about it."

I nodded.

"Her mother is ill. She's in a hospital in Westchester. She's not . . . well. Amy was all I had in my home. She was beautiful. She was a good student. Popular. The worst thing you could say about her was that she took my Corvette out for a spin every time I left town." He smiled at that, but it shifted quickly into a kind of grimace.

"A friend of mine's daughter is a junior at the high school. She knew Amy. She said she was a nice girl."

"I should have sent her to a boarding school, like her mother wanted, but I wanted her near. I can guess how you feel about the rich, Mr. MacManus, just by the way you're looking at me, but no amount of money can protect you from pain."

"Call me Mac. And I never thought money could protect a person from anything, except cold and hunger. And I don't hate the rich."

"I don't think that's true, Mac. I've heard things about you. I've been asking around. I heard how you grew up on my side of town, that you lived with the Van Deusens on Gin Lane."

"I'm familiar with the story."

"He was a madman, you know that. He was a son of a bitch, but I guess you probably know all about that, don't you? His boat sank, didn't it? He and his wife and their crazy son were lost at sea, wasn't that what happened?"

Curry took a step toward me. "I guess what I'm saying is, I see maybe why you can hate the rich the way you do. Van Deusen and his Pittsburgh crowd, well, let's just say they were bad news. They bought and sold people. And they were the worst kind of capitalists. Some say they had too much coal dust in their lungs, that it chipped away at their sanity. I don't think I've met a more cruel man in my life than your father."

"He wasn't my father."

"I mean your adoptive father. If I were you I'd probably think twice about crossing south of the highway, too."

"I'm sorry, I should have told you, I'm on my way out."

Though I didn't move he held up both hands as if to stop me. "Please, hear me out."

"Whatever you have to say, leave my biography out of it."

"You help people, I've been told."

"You've been misinformed."

"You found a town justice's son when no one else could, you found that Mary Anne Rose girl, you found the Bishop girl. I've seen the newspaper clippings in the morgue at the *Southampton Press*."

"Those were favors for friends." It was a half lie, and I could hear the falsity clear in my voice.

"Well, I'm willing to pay you for your time."

"I'm not interested."

"I'll pay you ten grand right now. And another ten if you find out what I want you to find out."

I looked away from him. "Sorry. Sorry, I'm not your man."

"You're the only one in town who can help me."

"You want help, go to the police."

"That's the thing. I think the police are the problem.

And I know, too, you are about as fond of them as you are of rich people."

"There's a private investigator here in town, he'll help you out."

"I'm not all that interested in landing in someone's pocket, if you know what I mean. From what I hear this gentleman to whom you refer more often than not works as much for himself as for his clients. I'd like to hire someone I trust."

"What makes you think you can trust me?"

"You didn't jump at the money. That says a lot to me."

"I wish I could help you. Really."

"You're a dishwasher, right?"

"Right. Yeah."

"How much do you make an hour?"

"I make minimum wage."

"Do you get by on that?"

"No. But I sleep at night. And come bedtime, I'm alive. I like that."

"I'll throw in another ten thousand dollars in stocks. I'll have my broker put together a prime portfolio, for retirement."

"I'm trying to be polite here."

He took another step forward. "Mac, my daughter is dead, and the police are saying it was an accident, but I don't believe it was an accident."

"It's none of my business. Really. I'm sorry."

"Then why did you jump into that freezing pond and try to save her?"

"What?"

"You went into the water, you pulled her out of the car. You tried to revive her. You almost drowned trying to save her."

"Who told you this? Tina? She tends to shoot her mouth off about things she knows nothing about."

"It wasn't the Hartsell girl. It was her friend, Elizabeth Cole."

"Lizzie."

"Lizzie. When I heard you were friends with Augie Hartsell I asked some people who was friends with his daughter. Lizzie sold you out for five hundred bucks."

"She got you on that one, James, because it never happened."

"She said you almost froze to death running from the scene. I won't say anything to the police or the papers. Like I said, I think the police are the problem."

I looked at the floor, at a point about halfway between us.

"You have to help me."

I'd been skirting the issue, but now there was no avoiding it.

"What is it you want?" I said.

"The morning after Amy was killed someone ransacked her room. They were obviously looking for something."

"Do you know what?"

"No. But I know *who* it was."

"You know or you think you know?"

"I'm fairly certain I know. I lied when I said the worst thing you could say about Amy was that she took my Corvette when I was out of town. The worst thing about her, as far as I was concerned, was that she was involved with a man much too old for her. An adjunct professor at the college. Concannon. Phil Concannon. He lives out there by that pond, out in the middle of nowhere, on the edge of town. He's a married man. I suspect he was searching through her room for something that would connect him with her. The room was a shambles. The police didn't seem to take much interest in that, either."

"They are rather indifferent by nature, it seems. So what is it you want me to do?"

"Find out who killed her. Find out who killed my daughter. Find out why. You saw her, you held her body in your arms, you know how beautiful she was. Someone just blew her out like a candle, and I want to know who and I want to know why. I'll pay you whatever you want."

"I don't want your money."

"No, sorry, this is supposed to be a job for you, not a hobby. I want you out there, around the clock, if necessary. I insist on paying you. I'll cover your expenses, I'll give you money to buy information. You do an honest job and you keep the ten grand, whether you find something or not. You find out who killed her and why and you get another ten in cash and the ten in stocks. You kill the son of a bitch, and I'll give you a hundred grand."

I could almost hear the alarms in my head. "Put your hands up," I said abruptly.

"What?"

I started toward him, fast. "Put your hands up."

Uncertain, he stood there frozen. When I reached him I threw his arms up and started to frisk him. I was searching for a wire, a bug, a microphone, anything. I handled him rough. I checked him thoroughly but found nothing. I still didn't trust or like this. We stood face to face. He was waiting for me to speak. I took my time, studying his face.

"First, I'm not killing anyone. So start dealing with that right now. Nor will I tell you who killed your daughter, if I find out who, if your plan is to kill him. That would make me an accessory. Do you understand?"

"I want justice for my daughter."

"Then I'll try to get enough evidence to get him or her put away for a long time."

"I told you, I don't trust the police."

"Then you and your lawyer take it to the FBI. That's what it's there for. Are we in agreement on this?"

"Yes." He looked at me. "Why are you doing this? I mean, I'm paying you, don't even think about not taking it. But you're clearly not doing it for the money. So why are you doing it?"

I shrugged. "If I couldn't save her, then maybe I can at least do this for her."

James looked at me for a moment, then nodded once, absently. He reached into his jacket pocket and removed his checkbook. With a pen that cost more than I made in a month he wrote out a check to me for ten thousand dollars. He tore the check out of the book and offered it to me.

"You can put it on the table by the door," I said.

He looked at me and smiled at that, then stepped to the table and placed the check on it. He turned back and looked at me.

He removed a business card from the pocket of his shirt and handed it to me. I took it.

"All possible ways to get ahold of me are on this. Call anytime, day or night." He reached back for his wallet, opened it, and removed ten one-hundred-dollar bills. He put that in my shirt pocket. "For expenses and whatnot. That car of yours must eat up gas. And your tires look about as bald as a tire can get. Don't want you following a lead and sliding off the road into a tree."

I looked at him but said nothing.

"You're probably one of those people who have a hard time accepting things from people. Maybe if I were a woman it would be different for you, but I'm not, I'm a guy, so it's hard for you to say thanks. Don't worry, I understand. I'm the same way."

I ignored that as best I could. "I'll call you when I find something."

"Please. If possible, I'd like to hear from you every other day. So I know you're not dead in a ditch somewhere."

"That's fine. You might want to get some surveillance people to come out and check your house for bugs."

"Is that necessary?"

"If we're going to be talking on the phone, yeah. And when you talk to me, no cell phone, no cordless phone. It has to be a corded phone."

"I don't mean to smile, but this strikes me as more than a little paranoid."

"I learned from the best," I said. I wondered then just what Frank was up to.

"You learned well."

"And don't swing by. If you need to see me, call me and I'll meet you somewhere out of the way. It's best if we're not seen together."

James nodded. "Okay. Whatever you say."

"I'll call you as soon as I know anything."

He extended his hand. I took it. We looked each other in the eye.

"I was starting to think I was the only person in town who cared about Amy," he said. "I'm glad to know I was wrong."

We shook hands for a moment more, let go, and then he was gone. I went to the window to see what kind of car he got into. It was a black Mercedes Benz sports utility vehicle. It glimmered in the rain and under the lights like stone in a stream.

I went then to the table by the door and looked at the check for a moment. All those zeros told me that there was now ten grand toward Augie's defense. Not enough, but something, a start. I was pleased. Unwilling to touch it, I left the check where it was and grabbed my jacket and left my apartment and started down the stairs. I didn't want to waste any time.

The night sky was in constant flux, like something in the throes of metamorphosis above us. It was unclear whether what was evolving in shreds of tattered clouds and patches of dark sky was good or not, but I knew there was no point in looking for such distinctions in something still playing out.

In the phone booth I looked up Phil Concannon's address. It was familiar to me. Then went to George at the bar and asked him to break a hundred. I ignored the look on his face and took the money and left.

I drove my LeMans to the gas station on North Sea Road and filled the tank to the top. I couldn't remember the last time I had done that. The back of the car sat a little low because of the weight. But it felt like a sturdier drive, like the earth was holding onto me tighter, maybe even closer.

As I sat in my car on Seven Ponds Road I kept thinking how there was a feeling that came with having money in your pocket and a tank so full of gas that the headlights aim up into the trees as you drive. I would have to admit I liked it, that I liked the feeling of it. It felt like being part of the game. This thousand dollars could easily last me a month and give me everything I'd need—rent, food, new boots and a coat, and time to sit in my chair and watch the train station. I even imagined that somehow it would even keep others from me, keep me safe from those who come looking for me, for my help or to do me harm. Maybe all this would be worth a month of peace, a month of shelter, of living like the Buddha or maybe even Boo Radley. I didn't care which.

The night was clearer than the last night I was here but still dark. I had driven past the pond, past the spot where Augie and I sat in his truck at the side of the road, past the tree where we had seen the mysterious man, where the spike strip had been laid out for Amy Curry.

I rounded the corner that she had rounded too quickly and saw the only lights to be seen—a contemporary house with a small lawn set right in the middle of a potato field. Several of the long vertical windows were lit, and in the driveway was a sports car. As I got closer I saw that it was a Fiat.

I parked on the shoulder, under an oak tree whose lower branches reached not upward but downward, for the ground. I cut the motor and the lights and watched the house. Its covering wood was plank, painted gray, and its driveway was gravel. The stones were white and caught what little light the night sky had to offer. The house was angular and not very large. It seemed to me like a piece of a child's toy left out in the yard.

I cracked my window and let in the cold and the smell of farmland. It was subtle but I could sense it. It felt just like November to me. In town leaves would tumble across Elm Street and the smell of leaves that burned in the afternoon would still be lingering in the air. The Hansom House fireplace would be lit, and that smell would be in the air, too. Out here on Seven Ponds Road the only smells were that of near-dormant earth and cold, smells that moved on a steadily blowing wind.

I watched the house for an hour, feeling the inside of my car turn from warm to cold, but nothing more than that happened. Then around one in the morning a man exited through the garage and got into the Fiat parked in the driveway and started it up. I could hear the distinctive sound of its motor, more of a power tool than an automobile. When he pulled out of the driveway and started toward me, I could hear him move through the gears fast. He drove by me quickly, and when he was out of sight I cranked the ignition and hit the lights and made a U-turn and went after him.

I sped till I caught sight of him, and then I backed off. I kept my distance as I followed through the winding back roads. He headed toward town, then rode east through the village, often jumping lights. I didn't want to get busted for a traffic violation, so I kept to the traffic laws. Each time I lost him I'd press the speed limit as much as I dared till I caught sight of him again. Once we cleared the village he continued east on Sunrise Highway. I followed him through Water Mill and Bridgehampton, past the street on which Gale lived. By the time we passed East Hampton I had been following him for half an hour, keeping my distance, letting him get ahead of me, then pulling up behind him at stoplights, only to let him pull ahead again after they turned green. I had no idea where he was going or what my following him would tell me. I had no idea what I would bring back from this trek, if anything. After East Hampton we passed through Amagansett and were then headed toward Montauk and the road's end.

I followed it onto Old Montauk Highway, where the road narrowed and ran close to the primary dunes and the ocean beyond them. It was a stretch of no-man's land where only grass and sand bordered the road on both sides for long stretches at a time. Once we were on this road the Fiat all of a sudden took off in a burst, racing down the highway, its engine whining. My engine was a 327, fast, and the road immediately ahead was long and straight, and I felt my foot press down on the gas, heard the deep groan of the exhaust tumbling down the pipes below, and watched the Fiat go from pulling away from me to coming closer.

I knew that the smart thing to do was let the Fiat go, but I wasn't in the mood for smart. I wanted to press the issue, to force him to act in a way that would give something up, something I could use.

Ahead I could see the curve that ended the long stretch in the road. I had to press my advantage while I could. I held the accelerator to the floor, my right leg almost completely straight. I was closing on the Fiat but knew I would lose much of the ground I had gained in the turn. I held the accelerator down and gripped the wheel firmly and watched the curve get closer and closer. It came up fast, almost as if it and I were both in motion, almost as if it and I were both racing toward each other and not just me toward it. I heard the Fiat downshift and the pitch of the engine change from baritone to tenor. It screamed through the corner as if it were on tracks. I dropped a gear and pressed the brakes, though I knew it was much too late. I knew I would cross onto the shoulder and maybe even eat sand as I moved recklessly into the turn. I turned the wheel to the left and felt the right side of my car dip. My suspension was for shit, and my bald tires chirped like four frightened birds. The steering wheel tugged and jerked as if I had pushed my whole car into spasms. I was flung into the turn and it seemed for a moment that my car would flip and I would roll, kicking up sand and grass, into the dunes.

Then headlights filled my car. I looked down at the speedometer and realized I had dropped from eighty to forty, and was still dropping. I was on the shoulder, halfway through the turn; I heard sand shifting under my tires. Then it seemed that all there was were headlights, that the interior of my car was entirely lit up, that I saw my dashboard and console and knobs in such stark detail that it fascinated me for several seconds.

Then I realized what was happening, and every muscle in my body flexed in anticipation.

A black Ford Explorer had been waiting just around the turn. It came at me, headlong into my driver's side door just as the right side of my car was dipped to the point of turning over. It struck at me hard, right on target, and I felt first the jolt, the sudden transition from forward motion to sideways motion, and then I felt the left side of my car rise upward. It felt so much like a carnival ride, a combination of bumper cars and the corkscrew of a roller coaster. I heard glass break and metal fold, and then I was airborne, tumbling down a drop just off the shoulder of the highway.

Now it didn't feel so much like a carnival ride. Now I was in two tons of steel that was being rolled like a toy, unable to find my bearings. I was facing upward, then upside down, then upward again. My seat belt was on but I was still getting banged up pretty good. My arms flailed with the spinning motion, hitting the ceiling and the door. I felt sharp pains in my ribs and a heaviness on my chest. I couldn't breathe. I prayed for each turn to be the last, and when finally it stopped, I was hanging upside down.

I felt nauseated, and too many hurts were checking in with my brain for me to keep track of. I hung in the seat belt, the crumbled door against my side, my head against the ceiling. I seemed heavier upside down.

I felt around till I found the buckle and then pressed the button. The force against the locking mechanism made the button hard to push, but I got it finally and slumped from the seat onto the roof—first my shoulder, then my side, then one leg. The other was caught between the door and the dash. I stayed that way for a moment, then tried to work my leg free. There was pain but I didn't think that it was broken. I strained, my hands cupped behind my knee, and pulled till it came free.

I lay still and heard the sound of someone approaching across the sand. I turned my head as far as it would go and looked out the passenger's door window. The glass was gone; bits of it were everywhere. I saw the SUV up on the road, its headlights aimed down at me. I saw in the light the shape of someone. He moved slowly. I remembered my mad dash down to the pond where Amy Curry's car was sinking. He had no such urgency.

I pulled myself toward the driver's door window. Its glass, too, was gone. I could feel blood coming from my head, I could feel its warmth spreading over me in an oddly comforting way. I pulled myself through the window and onto the sand. My car was between me and the man who was approaching. I tried to stand but couldn't. I pulled myself on my stomach away from the car, but there was nowhere to go. Ahead of me was a dune I couldn't possibly climb, and beyond I could hear waves hissing. I rolled onto my back. I was breathing hard, shallow breaths. I couldn't get enough air. I reached for my pocket, but my knife wasn't there, and anyway, what did I think I was going to do with it? I lay there in the sand and heard the man getting closer. Then the footsteps stopped. I looked through the windows and could see feet.

The man crouched down and looked inside the car. Then he saw me and stood. I watched his feet as he moved around the back of the car. The minute he was visible I saw the gun in his hand. It was a chrome-plated revolver. The lights were behind him; I couldn't see his face, just the shape of him, dark and towering.

I looked up and I couldn't hear the waves anymore, all

I could hear was my own breathing, short bursts through my nose. My brow tingled and I broke out in a fast sweat. The man came around the car and approached me and stood over me. He looked at me for a moment, then raised the gun and aimed it at me.

I don't know if I could see the barrel or just imagined that I did, but either way it seemed as big as a well and it pulled me into it. I felt as if I were falling. It was hypnotic. The gun was level with my head.

And then it rushed ahead again just as suddenly. I heard a gunshot and felt my body flinch violently. A burst of mist sprayed from the man's head. It was colorless in the poor light. The man's body dropped to the ground. It fell fast and landed in a heap at my feet, and then I could see another figure, standing at the foot of the drop from the highway. I saw a gun in his hand. The gun was aimed at me now. And then whoever was holding it lowered the gun and limped toward me.

He knelt beside me and held up four fingers and asked me to tell him what I saw. I could hear the ocean clearly now. The headlights from the SUV up on the road stabbed my eyes, but I was able to count the digits and answer him correctly. His hands clamped on my thighs and he asked me if I could feel anything. I told him I could. He moved his hands down to my knees, then my shins, then to my feet. I could feel each place his hands came to rest. Then he ran his hands over my ribs. I winced at his touch. When I breathed it felt as if tissue were rubbing against metal, as if something sharp and broken was shifting inside me. He looked at my face and studied my reaction, then moved up to my neck, then my head.

"You're bleeding," he said. "Can you sit up?"

I nodded. He took my arm and helped me up to a seated position. My lips drew tight and I grunted.

"I think you cracked a rib or two."

"It's okay. Help me up."

"How's your head feel?"

"Just help me up."

He braced himself under my right arm and lifted me to my feet. I could sense the world moving, rotating at a thousand miles an hour. The sand on which I stood felt like mud, though I knew it was dry. I couldn't get footing.

"Go easy," he said.

I had to concentrate to stand. I felt drunk. I looked down at the body lying in a heap. Blood was flowing fast from its head, sinking down into sand. It was hard to imagine that just moments ago that heap was a walking, talking living being.

"He's dead," I said. I slurred my words. There was no reason for my statement, but I said it anyway.

"Yeah."

"Who was he?"

"There isn't time. Montauk cops have nothing better to do than cruise these roads."

I nodded and we headed side by side up the slope to

the road. We both moved with a limp; it was in the same leg. I looked at him as we climbed toward the pavement, studying the side of his face. The back of my jacket and shirt were soaked with blood. There was a chilled tingling in my forehead.

"Why? Why'd you help me?"

He looked ahead as he spoke, at the crest of the hill and the bent beach grass that lined the road. I could smell his breath.

"You saved my life," he said. "Now we're even."

"How did you know?"

"I heard they were going to move against you. I picked up your tail just after East Hampton. I gotta tell you, you took the bait well."

"You said 'they.' Who are 'they'?"

We crested the hill and reached the pavement. The earth didn't feel any more stable for its solidity. The LTD stood at the side of the road, its engine running. The man with the limp moved me quickly toward the passenger door.

"Just forget about them. Do us all a favor and just forget about them." He opened the door and helped me into the back. He swung my legs carefully in and closed the door. I lay on my side across the seat, facing forward.

"My plates," I muttered.

"What?"

"My license plates. They can trace the car by the plates."

"They can just as easily trace it by the serial numbers on the engine and dashboard."

"I filed those down. The plates are all they'd have to go on. I need the plates. I can't have any trouble with the law."

He hesitated, then leaned the seat back and opened the glove compartment. He dug through it and removed a screwdriver. Then he disappeared for a few minutes. During that time all I could think about was the tank full of gas. When he returned he had the two plates in his hands. He tossed them behind the front seat and climbed in and closed the door. He shifted into gear and made a U-turn, heading us back toward Southampton. It was now the last moments of night.

He reached into the backseat and handed a rag to me. I put it to the back of my head, where my skin had split.

He glanced back at me quick. "You okay?"

"Who are they?"

"Don't waste your breath. I've stuck my neck out as far as it can go."

"Who was that man back there?"

"Just an asshole."

"Who hired him?" My own voice sounded weak, as if I were hearing it from across a distance.

"They don't tell you the name of the man who pays, and I don't ask."

"I have to find someone."

"Listen to me, man, I can only take you as far as Bridgehampton. You'll have to get to where you need to go from there. Do you understand?"

I felt myself slipping toward unconsciousness. I

wanted to ask him more but I lost track of words. I blacked out then, and when I came to, my left arm was wrapped around his neck and he was beside me like a crutch, walking me. I felt cold air, and it took me a moment to realize that we were on the platform at the Bridgehampton train station.

"You can catch the train to Southampton from here," he said. He moved me behind the tiny station house and leaned me up against the wall, facing the tracks. We were out of sight from the street there.

He stepped away to see if I would remain standing. I did, but barely. I looked at his face then. It hurt my eyes to focus.

"Why was the Curry girl killed?"

"Look, the biggest land deal this town has seen in four hundred and fifty years is about to go down. The Shinnecock Indians are selling their reservation, and it's got a lot of people in town worried."

"What does this have to do with the girl?"

"This makes us more than even, kid. Next time we meet, it's business as usual. Understand?"

He turned then and walked around the corner of the station house and was gone. I never learned his name.

The westbound train came in about a half hour later. I got on with my plates in my hand and rode to the next stop, Southampton. The conductor didn't have time to come by and collect the fare from me. I got out and made my way down the platform and across the street and headed for the Hansom House. It was less than a block away.

Parked out front was Eddie's cab. I saw him talking with George. When they saw me they started toward me. They helped me up the two flights of stairs to my rooms.

Inside Eddie lay me down on my bed while George stood by the door. I didn't know much anymore and liked it that way. All I knew was what the man with the limp had told me. Eddie asked me if I wanted a doctor. I told him no. I had him bring me silver duct tape from a drawer in my kitchen. I removed my shirt, exposing bruises the color of sunsets, and had him wind the tape several times around my ribs, tight. He watched my face each time I winced.

I lifted my feet up onto the couch and propped my head up with several pillows. I had slept on this couch for three months when Tina lived here and for countless nights when I was too drunk to find my bed.

"Do you think you should sleep, Mac?" Eddie said. George was still by the door.

"I'll be fine."

"Maybe I'll have George check on you every once in a while."

"Maybe that's a good idea."

"Is your car somewhere? We could get it for you."

I shook my head.

"Do you want anything, my friend?"

"Just leave me alone."

"Okay."

"Wait. Ask George if he would go over to LeChef on Job's Lane and explain to a guy named Bernard that I've been in an accident and would still like the job when I'm better, if they haven't already replaced me. Tell him I should be up and around in a day or so. Can he do that for me?"

"Yeah, I can do that," George said. He took a step into the room. "No problem."

"Good."

"What's going on?" Eddie said. He leaned close to me.

I didn't answer. Despite the fact that it was morning, darkness was closing around me, my eyes weakening. Somewhere inside of me some part of me was still in that spinning car.

"Any word on Augie?"

"Not that I've heard. You want me to call him?"

"No. Just leave me now."

He and George left then and I lay motionless except for my breathing and counted the aches and pains that rushed my brain like children eager for attention. I fell asleep gradually, one stage at a time, as if I were falling through a series of floors, downward and downward. I dreamed of Southampton Village in a light spring rain. I dreamed of a world made by Camus and Hemingway. When I awoke again it was night and the only light in my apartment was what spilled in from the streetlights outside. I lay awake, listening patiently to each ache and pain, till I realized gradually that there was someone else in the room with me.

Five

He was a tall man, long legged and wide through the shoulders. He was well over six feet and occupied a corner of the room much as a Christmas tree would; his head seemed just inches from my plaster ceiling. I used to think as a child that he was like one of those mountain men out of the movies, all power and self-reliance. As I grew he did not seem to shrink at all. In high school we feared him as much as we had in grade school. He was a physically imposing man, with wisps of thinning gray hair and a face deeply lined and gaunt, the grim face of a lifelong outdoorsman, or maybe that of a man trapped in grief that he held on to as much as it held on to him.

His eyes were green and flinty, like two wet emerald stones. I could see them even in the dim light coming from the streetlights outside. I could see, too, that he was in uniform—he was rarely out of it. Under his hunter's jacket his leather belt creaked once as he shifted his weight from one foot to the other.

I sat up fast, my ribs protesting sharply. But I didn't dare wince. I had no shirt on. The silver duct tape Eddie had wound around me showed up brighter than anything else in the room.

I stayed there in the seated position, unmoving, and looked at him. He was standing by my front windows, looking down at me. His baton hung from his belt, sticking out at an odd angle. He turned on the standing reading lamp by my chair at my window.

I took several shallow breaths and said, "Chief."

"When I saw your car I had hopes you were dead. I hoped you were twisted up like a pretzel inside it."

I tried to ease my pain by adjusting my posture. I checked the tape, just to keep from looking at him. "What are you talking about, Chief?"

"Oh, you don't know?"

"My car was stolen two days ago."

"Sure it was."

I swung my legs out and placed my bare feet on the cold floor. The bruise on my left thigh was spread like a tattoo that had faded from exposure and time.

"Still breaking into people's homes," I said. "Find anything useful?"

I reached for a T-shirt. The Chief took a step toward me.

"You have your father's build," he said. "A lanky middleweight."

I pulled the shirt over my head and looked at him. Before I could make any kind of response to the Chief's comment, he took another step toward me and held up a slip of paper for me to see. I recognized at once the check for ten grand that James Curry had given me, which I had left on the table by the door.

I looked at him, then started to tuck my shirt into my jeans. "You want me to endorse it over to you, Chief?" I said. "Is that what all this is about?"

"Is this why you've been tailing the geologist?"

"I'm not tailing anyone, Chief."

"This is my town, MacManus. Don't think for a second that I don't know what goes on in it. Sorry to break it to you, but I'm not the fool you think I am. So I'm going to ask you again. Why did James Curry give you a check for ten grand?"

I stood up to finish tucking in my shirt. I could barely breathe. Even though I moved slowly the Chief's other hand went fast to rest on the handle of his nightstick. It seemed less of a blind reflex and more of a hope than anything else.

"I'm his new groundskeeper and house sitter," I answered. "In case you haven't heard, he got busted into recently."

"You're telling me this is an advance for some yard work?"

"Something like that, yeah."

The Chief thought about that for a moment. "So how'd you get this job to begin with? Last I knew you didn't want anything to do with the Halsey Neck Lane crew."

"I got it through Augie."

"I didn't know Augie knew James Curry."

"I don't think he does. But their daughters went to school together, that is, of course, before the Curry girl was murdered."

The Chief smiled at that and looked around the cluttered front room. "What makes you think she was murdered?"

"What makes you think she wasn't?"

"I never said she wasn't."

"So then why the shoddy police work?"

The Chief looked around the room and then said, "You're working at that frog place on Job's Lane, aren't you?" He looked at me squarely. His jaw was set hard, like it was ready to snap. I could see his hate for me in his eyes, in the way he stood, in the sound of his breathing. I could smell it on him. I had maimed his son for trying to rape Tina the summer before.

"I just got hired there, yeah."

He nodded at that. "You know I hate you, MacManus," he said. "You give me the excuse, I'll arrest you. As you know, once I arrest you there are about a half-dozen cops with nightsticks waiting for you in the basement of Village Hall. We take care of our own. So, you jaywalk in this town and I'll bust you. You take up with another fifteen-year-old, and believe me, I'll know before the night is over and I'll be here to bust you before she kisses you good morning. I'd prefer a big mistake, like what Augie did, but I'll take what I can get. All I care about is seeing to it that you have to learn to walk all over again, just like my son, that you kiss whatever putrid dreams you have, if a lowlife like you has any, good-bye, just like he had to. My boy could be playing for Michigan. He was that good. Now he can barely take a bath without help."

I could sense that he was flexed under his clothes, flexing to keep his rage and hate from spraying out of him. The Chief was the kind of man who made an art out of sitting on his feelings and waiting for the right time to strike.

"Do you want to take a swing at me, Chief? Is that what you came here for?"

"Don't tempt me."

"It's just you and me here. You've got the stick, you've got the gun. I've got nothing."

He tossed the check on the couch. I left it there.

"I grew up with Augie, you know that," he said. "Frank Gannon, too. And, believe it or not, your father. The four of us were best friends. We played football together in high school. And your father was quarterback. He played in the Empire State Games. You didn't know that, did you?"

I knew little of my father, of my real father, of the cop from Southampton who left me with strangers after my mother died. I knew even less of her—shadows, smells, the sound of her voice but no words. I cannot remember her whole presence, but I can remember close to most of his—chain-smoking in a tiny hotel room in Riverhead on his afternoons off, sitting by the window in silence, in chinos and a white T-shirt, looking out, me watching him from my cot, smelling fried food from the restaurant below, hearing the voices of strange men in the hallways, men's voices and only men's voices except for Saturday nights when I heard the laughter of drunken women and words I did not understand.

I was seven when he left me in the care of a man with eyes like the sea. I do not remember my father dropping me off, I do not remember us saying good-bye. I have lost those memories, lost them a long time ago. I used to allow myself to imagine what it was like, but at some point in my life I gave that up. At some point.

I thought of the Chief's devotion to his son, however blind and misguided it may be. I tried to imagine a world in which the Chief and I were family, where Tommy Miller was my kid brother, where we all lived under the same roof and protected each other with fierce loyalty. It was too hard to imagine, nearly as hard as it was to try to imagine what my father was beyond the handful of memories, beyond what I've always heard and what the Chief just told me. I wondered if Tommy Miller looked at his father and saw his own reflection, or some distorted aspect of it. How much of Tommy's meanness was a reaction to his father, and how much was it a reaction against?

I didn't like that the Chief could do this to me, that in some ways he knew more about me than I did. He was my enemy. And yet he was one of the only two men in town I knew of who was present when my father disappeared, who maybe had seen my father the day he dropped me off, the tears in his eyes or the look of relief or maybe even heard in his voice second thoughts.

The Chief sized me up for a moment, then said, "Is that what's eating you up inside, MacManus? Is that what makes you the creep you are? Your daddy gave you away to strangers and skipped town. You must think about it all the time. Maybe he's alive, maybe he's not. Maybe he's a bum, sleeping on a heating grate somewhere and drinking Thunderbird out of a paper bag. Maybe he started a new life, with a new wife and a mentally balanced kid, one he doesn't mind being father to. Maybe he thinks about you. Maybe every day he's glad he shook a little shit like you off his shoe. But the not knowing must kill you."

I took a step toward him and said, "What do you want, Chief?"

He matched my step forward and said, "I'm here to warn you. I'm here to tell you that both of our lives are in jeopardy right now."

"What are you talking about?"

"The man you're looking for is named Townsend."

"What man?"

"The partner of the man Augie shot. I assume that's what this is all about. His name is Townsend. He's part Shinnecock Indian. He lives on the reservation. On Cemetery Road. Number 54."

I looked at the Chief but said nothing.

He said, "I've done something for you, and now I want you to do something for me in return."

"What?"

"I can't enter the reservation unless it's an emergency. Nor can any of my men. I want you to go there and keep an eye on Townsend. If he's not home when you get there, I want you to search his place, find out whatever you can."

"Like what?"

"I want you to find out who's paying his salary. You need him to save Augie. If he disappears, neither of us gets what we want."

I felt my face twist and my head cock slightly with surprise.

"Just don't let Townsend go far. You'll figure out why sooner or later."

Something deep inside me reacted to that. This seemed to me too much like bait to be anything else.

"Everyone needs to be careful on this one, Mac-Manus, even me."

His leather belt creaked. I could hear his breathing, I could smell the mints on his breath, feel the warmth of it, he was that much into my apartment now. He was that close to me.

"As unpleasant as it is for both of us, it seems we're bound together till all this is over."

"How different would things be if I hadn't been on that road when Amy Curry crashed into the pond? There'd be no one right now bothering to try to find out

THE BONE ORCHARD 171

who killed her. We're all bound together in a town like this, Chief. In a small pond you feel every ripple."

The Chief had nothing to say. He just looked at me.

I said, "You'd think a man as rich as James Curry wouldn't have to come to someone like me for help. As I've always seen it, the people with all the money in this town get preferential treatment."

"You have no idea what's going on."

"Why should I do this, Chief?"

"Because I know how much Augie means to you. And because you have no choice."

"What are you talking about, I have no choice?"

"There was a dead body near your car. A male Caucasian. Shot in the back of the head. Leaving the scene of an accident is bad enough, MacManus, but this, this is a whole different thing. The Montauk Police are going to want to talk to you. They're going to take one look at you and your story about your car being stolen two days ago will be shot to shit. That is, of course, unless someone was to come up with a police report that corroborates your particular take on things."

Even though I had taken the plates and the serial numbers had been filed down, my car was the only thirty-year-old shitbox LeMans on the East End. And the Chief was right; one look at me and it was all over. It was as simple as that.

I knew there was something he wasn't telling me, though I wasn't really surprised by that. I had no way of seeing just what he was setting me up for, if he was in fact setting me up at all. Everything I had left was telling me not to go. But he was right. I had no choice. The trouble I had left behind in Montauk could burn me bad. I'd be just as useless to Augie there as I would be in Village Hall in Southampton. I had to keep one step ahead, even if that step brought me that much closer to the edge.

"Well?" he said finally.

"Okay, you write me out a report and I'll do what you want."

The Chief nodded. "It's already done. There's a copy in my car. I'll leave the report downstairs with that bartender friend of yours on my way out."

The Chief walked past me then. I didn't move, even after I heard the door close, even as his footsteps faded down my hallway. I just stood there and let everything fall away till only one question remained.

In all the time I had known Augie, why hadn't he said anything to me about having known my father?

I borrowed George's Volkswagen Bug and in it drove to the 7-Eleven on Sunrise and bought a pair of cloth work gloves. Then I headed west on Sunrise Highway, turned left at the college onto Tuckahoe Road, and turned left again at the end of that, heading east on Montauk. The reservation was on the right.

The muffler on George's Bug was shot, and it sounded more like a Harley than the tiny car it was. I kept telling myself that this wasn't my game, that this wasn't the kind of thing I did, but it didn't seem to make much of a difference. I felt like a stranger to my own life. The Volkswagen felt powerless compared to my old Le-Mans, and that seemed only fitting.

Somewhere in the dark East End, under the broad sky, in one of those contemporary houses built on potato fields or one of those great mansions standing on the primary dunes of the long stretch of beach between Southampton and East Hampton, the rich were playing their game. I knew all too well the cruelty that can come with wealth.

My adoptive father had made it clear often enough that I was more servant than a son, more playmate and protector to his troubled son than brother. I was free labor, trapped in a world I did not belong in, and it took a boating accident and more than I'll ever care to talk about to set me free of them. I was twenty when I finally escaped, a criminology major at the college and broke. I turned my back on that unreal world and never looked back. I worked my way through my senior year tending bar at an Irish pub in Hampton Bays. I slept on the couch in a professor's office in the Humanities wing of the Fine Arts Building for a month till I moved into an apartment over a real estate office across from the IGA in Hampton Bays with a dark-haired and beautiful business major named Catherine. At night we slept in a tangle of limbs and blankets in a room that overlooked Main Street. The only furniture we had was a kitchen table, three folding chairs, and her bed. We stayed together for almost a year, till she took a job in New York and moved to Queens with a girlfriend of hers who had never liked me all that much. During that year everything took a dive. My grades slipped and I began to drink. I barely managed to graduate and was accepted into the police academy, though I never ended up making it there. I'd learned the hard way that I was the last person who deserved to carry a badge and a gun, let alone much else.

The reservation was mainly wilderness, the least affluent part of the East End, though the property, south of the highway bay front and undeveloped, was probably worth a fortune. Its roads were narrow, some of them just packed dirt, and there were no streetlights, just rows of cottage after cottage. Townsend's place was small and set on a treed-in lot of land on Cemetery Road. It was a single-story, box-shape nautical with a glassed-in front porch. Its windows were dark and looked to me like a row of blank faces staring back.

There was a small pickup in the driveway, new. The hurting business always did pay well, and Frank Gannon wasn't the only one who prospered by it out here.

I passed the cottage and parked on the shoulder of the tree-lined road three houses down. The sky was overcast with clouds, and the darkness outside the windows of the Bug was complete. I turned off the motor and the headlights and waited for my eyes to adjust to the blackness and my heart to stop its violent spasms in my chest.

When I was ready I put on the gloves and stepped out, closing the door quietly. My denim jacket was nowhere near enough. I backtracked up the dark street and stepped onto the lawn, then walked carefully toward the cottage. I reached it and took a look through one of the front windows. All I saw was a narrow porch cluttered with old furniture and piled cardboard boxes.

I could see that the front door to the house was blocked by an upended and battered couch. I looked behind me to see if anyone was passing on the road, then I walked around the side of the cottage to the back door. I took another look around, then tried the knob with my gloved hand. It turned smoothly and the door eased inward.

I stood there and listened. I could sense nothing, no movement, no breathing, nothing. The cottage felt empty to me. I took a few steps inside. I was in the kitchen. It was clean and neat, so much so that I began to wonder if anyone had been here in a while. Everything seemed too ordered to be lived in.

The air was stale and smelled sharply of must. I walked through the kitchen and down a narrow hallway, past the bathroom, and into the front room. I moved slowly, a step at a time. The floorboards creaked several times. I winced at each one. When I reached the end of the hallway I stopped. I could barely see through the darkness, but after a moment I made out the shape of someone lying on the couch.

My eyes were better in the dark now. I saw on a coffee table near the couch a near-empty bottle of Cutty Sark. On the wood floor beside the couch a plastic glass lay on its side, as if dropped. I got close to the figure and took a smell of his breath. It reeked of Scotch. But I realized then that the smell was coming out his pores. There was no breath. I could see the shape of a small lamp in the corner of the room, and I went to it and switched it on. The bulb was dull, the lamp shade thick. Yellowish, muted light filled the small room.

I looked down at the man lying dead on the couch. He had short black hair and a broad face. He looked no different from anyone I had met in the past few days. I guessed he was maybe a light-heavyweight and not much taller than I. He was lying on his left side. The cushions beneath him were soaked with blood. It looked fresh. It was clear that his throat had been cut. I could see the bulge of his wallet in his right back pocket. I reached for it with my gloved hand and pried it free with my fingers and opened it.

He had a New Jersey driver's license. His photo, and the name William Townsend, was on it. I put the license back and looked through the wallet for anything else. Nothing, no business cards, no scraps of paper with names I recognized, nothing. I counted his money; there was well over eight hundred dollars in cash. I thought of the nine hundred in my pocket and only realized then just how far into this world of hurt for hire I had gone.

Suddenly I wanted out of it. I was hit with the urge to bolt. I looked at Townsend's face and saw hints of Frank and the Chief, even Augie. I began to wonder if I really looked any different.

I took one last look down at Townsend and then

turned to get out of there. I moved fast, my strides long, my feet light on the linoleum.

I was halfway through the kitchen when it burst out of a side pantry. It was to my right, parallel to me, a sudden blur of noise and motion and force. It knocked over a chair as it rushed to intercept me, and then we came together like two cars at an intersection. The figure crashing into me was in dark clothes and knit mask and gloves. He lifted upward and sent me sideways, heaving me against the refrigerator. I felt as if I had been caught by a wave. My body folded like a doll and I smacked the refrigerator door with back of my head. I heard glass tumbling off shelves and shattering inside.

Then the man in the mask was all over me. He moved in quick, crowding me. I saw his right arm come up suddenly. I saw a flash of metal in his hand. I saw the hand and the metal in it move and come down, making a sweeping half-moon arc, angling toward the left side of my face like an outstretched hook punch. It was all a blur and was coming at my neck. I raised my left arm and folded it back till my fist touched my shoulder, and then I ducked behind it. It was all I had time to do. The knife caught me in my left shoulder, and I felt the blade zip open my jacket sleeve and the skin beneath as it moved in one quick motion across my deltoid. I felt a deep, lingering pinch and was instantly aware of blood running down the inside of my jacket sleeve. I winced but held back the grunt that rose in my throat.

The man in the mask swung at me again, but my

knees had buckled enough for me to slip under the blade. The man immediately wound up for a third swing, but this time he paused and grabbed at my left arm with his, trying to trap it and leave an open shot. We tangled, and in that brief delay I had enough time to launch a short stomp kick to his forward shin. I scraped downward and struck his foot close to his ankle. It wasn't much, but it took his mind off his attack and made him play defense, and that was all I wanted from it.

I grabbed his knife hand with my right and clawed at his eyes with my left. In the process I pulled up his mask, exposing his chin. The mask rose more and I saw teeth, perfect teeth. But his power was too much for me, so I lifted him off the ground with a knee to his gut. But the instant he landed he grabbed on to me and spun and flung me across the room. I was airborne, and then I hit the opposite wall hard and slumped to the floor. I heard plaster raining down behind the sheet rock. My legs felt weak. The wind had been knocked out of me. I turned and looked at my attacker. He had paused to pull down the part of his mask I had managed to peel up. I looked fast at the knife in his hand. It was four inches of serrated steel, smeared with my blood.

I searched for anything that I could use as a weapon. The only thing I could see was the overturned chair, but it was out of my reach. Once his mask was set my attacker started to move toward me again. He walked with fast, determined steps, one right after the other. I crawled up the wall as quickly as I could, scrambling to my feet.

Standing was like trying to climb stairs after a long run. I needed the wall to keep me up. There wasn't anywhere to go, there wasn't time for anything but to stand and face him and the blade in his gloved hand.

We were maybe three feet apart and I was ready for the worst of it when he suddenly stopped short and turned his head as if startled. I saw it just a second after he did: flashing red-and-blue lights filling the living room. He looked in their direction, then looked back at me. I could see that his thick chest was heaving under his black sweater. He studied me for a quick second, frozen, then turned away and bolted toward the back door.

He burst through it and out into the night. I listened to him go, then looked up the short hallway to the front room. Police lights danced on the walls. I could tell by the uneven patterns that there was more than one cop car out front. I thought of what the Chief had told me about entering the reservation in an emergency. I looked at my bloody shoulder, then looked once again down the hall, this time at Townsend's body on the couch. I was on my way through the back door, out into the cold night, running with everything I had left.

The police lights caught in the bare trees looked like madness. My heart pounded with each flicker. I had nowhere to go but to run blind, my right hand cupped over my bleeding shoulder, into the woods behind the cottage. I ran with all I had across the back lawn. I ran through the woods as branches grabbed at my face. I ducked my head and kept moving till I could no longer see the chaotic blue-and-red lights in the trees and the only sound in my ears was my own frantic breathing.

I was losing blood and had to do something about that soon. I could only think of one place I could go.

I came to Montauk Highway and crossed it quickly. No one saw me. I made it to the campus and hid in a cluster of trees behind the library. I tore my T-shirt and made a compress for my cut and waited till first light. Then I made my way to the campus train station and waited on the platform for the first train. When it came a half hour later I got onboard and took a seat. As the train began to move I kept my head at an uncomfortable angle against the vibrating window to keep from passing out. I rode like that to the Southampton stop and stared through the streaked window at the Hansom House. Then the train moved again, and when it stopped at Bridgehampton I got off. When the train pulled out I stepped onto the tracks and walked as straight as I could along its wide beams. I was heading east, into the cold morning sun.

Eventually I made it to her house, though I had no idea how long it took me. I was more tired and cold and wracked with pain that I would have ever guessed was possible. All I wanted to do was lie down and sleep. I craved my empty bed like it was the better part of me I had left behind. Her house was a hundred feet from the tracks, through a narrow line of trees. I was half-way across her backyard when she spotted me from her kitchen window. She came running out the back door to me. At the sight of her my strength started giving out. But I kept moving toward her, my eyes locked on her. I wanted to make it to her, but by then my legs were rubber and I could feel one knee buckle, then the other.

She caught me just as I began to fall. I had nothing left. She struggled to hold me up but I was just dead weight and too much for her and ended up taking her down to the ground with me. She landed on top of me. I felt no pain, just her warm breath on my face. She felt as light as a feather.

Then I smelled dead leaves and heard her voice but no words. I could see her face and she was talking to me but I heard nothing. Her hands were on me and I felt something inside me burst softly. Warmth spilled through me.

I lost some time then, and the next thing I knew I was being carried into her house and placed on the kitchen table. I felt on me two pairs of hands. I looked up at her finely lined, tanned face as she unbuttoned my denim jacket. Above her head the ceiling-mounted light burned brightly, and my eyes ached as if someone were rubbing their knuckles in them.

I heard her say, "You boys play too rough."

I nodded, and then my eyes closed, pinching out tears that ran down my temples to the table.

A male voice said, "I'm going to get my kit out of the car."

I heard a door open and close. Then my eyes opened again. She was holding my right hand with one hand and wiping the trail of tears from my temples with the other.

I just looked up at her beautiful face and the bright light behind it. I remember wishing then that I had had a different life, a life that would have allowed me her. I remember opening my mouth to speak. But of course I said nothing, and my silence was the last thing I knew for a long while.

I welcomed the nothingness.

Six

My eyes opened to the muted light of dusk. Or was it dawn? I couldn't tell for sure. I was under blankets on a bed in a room I didn't recognize. The mattress felt and smelled new. The only other piece of furniture in that room aside from the bed was a Chippendale chair to the right of the door. There were two windows, one of which was open a few inches. The curtains moved slightly and I smelled smoke from burning leaves and crisp November air coming over the sill. The walls were bare except for a few small framed prints, the details of which I could not make out. The door was opened to a lighted hallway. Eventually I realized there was a cold compress on my forehead. I touched it with my hand. It was a folded washcloth.

I tried to figure out if it was day or night that was

coming our way. Somewhere in the middle of that thought I slipped into unconsciousness again. When I came to it was full night out and the hallway was dark and someone was standing beside the bed.

I thought of sitting up but knew I wouldn't get too far. The brief euphoria I had experienced had long since gone. I could feel the sharp edges of reality pressing into every part of my body now.

It came to me that I was in my jeans and a clean T-shirt that was too large for me. Her husband was a big man, six foot something, and athletic. It must have been his.

"You're awake," she said.

I found her face and muttered, "Gale."

She touched my forehead with the back of her hand. "Your fever's down. How do you feel?" Her voice was a late-night whisper.

"I feel like shit."

"That's a lot better than what I thought you were going to say. You're in pretty bad shape. You've got a few cracked ribs, and you've obviously taken some blows to the head. And the cut on your shoulder is pretty deep."

I became aware then of a bandage over my left shoulder cap. I looked at that arm; there was no blood on it.

"That's a knife wound, isn't it?"

I nodded.

The only light in the room was what came in through the windows, from the broad sky of stars and from the moon. The night must have been a clear one, the first clear one in a week. It gave just enough light to see her face by.

"You were smart to come here, Mac."

"I can feel stitches."

"Gary sewed you up."

"Your husband?"

"Yeah."

"He's a veterinarian," I said. "Right?"

She nodded. "You took eleven stitches."

"Thank him for me."

"What's going on, Mac?"

She was dressed in jeans and a red flannel shirt over a blue turtleneck. I could see the veins in her long, athletic hands. Her legs were crossed at the ankles, one foot flat, the toe of the other touching the floor. Her legs, too, looked long. She was leaning on one hip, her arms folded under her breasts. She looked concerned, even a little bit nervous. Out of her nurse's scrubs she seemed somehow taller, or maybe that was because I was lying down.

"I'm not sure what's going on yet, Gale."

"I thought you were out of this line of work."

"I never was in it."

"Well, you're out of it for a while now. You're not going anywhere. You need to rest."

"What time is it?" I said.

"It's almost midnight."

"How long have I been out? I mean, have I been out just a day or days or what?"

"Just today. You've been here since this morning. Don't worry. Just try to rest."

I looked up at her. Neither of us said anything. In the silence I became aware of the house around us. It was completely still, but from somewhere down the hallway I heard faint breathing. The stillness made me tired. I could feel my body sinking into a smothering sleep.

"You can stay here as long as you want, Mac. I'll take care of you. All right?"

I nodded. "All right."

"Good. Now get some rest. If you need anything, I'll be right here."

I felt my eyes close as if at her command. I gave myself over to her, as I had done before, at Southampton Hospital, when she kept me company on sleepless nights, when all I could do was lie there in bed and think of her and close my eyes and smell her when she had gone.

I fell asleep now to the sound of my own breathing. When I awoke again before dawn the bedroom door was closed and Gale was asleep beside me on the bed. She was on top of the covers, an afghan over her. She was on her right side, facing me, her hand on my chest. Her left leg was bent and draped over my knee so that her knee was between my legs. I wondered where her husband, the man whose life I wanted, was. I listened but could only hear our breathing. I kept still and looked at her face. Our breathing was in sync, though her breaths were deeper than mine. The silver duct tape had been replaced by surgical tape.

Gale's head was resting on a pillow that lay just inches

from mine. I could smell the sweet and stale smell of sleep on her breath. Her mouth was closed, her lips parted slightly. She was breathing through her nose. Her eyes were still beneath their lids. I felt such peace all around me, and within me. I could feel it move through my broken body like a hit of morphine.

I didn't fall back to sleep for a while. I lay there beside her with her body against mine and watched her as the room gradually filled with light. It wasn't till daylight had come that I felt the need to sleep come over me. I closed my eyes and drifted off. I knew when I awoke this moment would be gone, but there was nothing at all I could do about that.

We awoke together at a little before nine. I opened my eyes and turned to see if she was still there. It seemed to me that she had not moved at all. Her eyes were open now and she was looking at me. We said good morning to each other but did not move. Her hand was still on my chest and her knee was between my legs. The thought of kissing her crossed my mind but I knew better. She asked me how I felt and I told her I was okay and that was close enough to the truth.

Augie was still in trouble, and out there somewhere was the man who had killed Amy Curry. I couldn't stay away from that even if by some miracle I could remain in Gale's life, if I could sleep every night with her hand on my chest and her leg between mine.

She helped me down the stairs, my right arm draped

around her neck, her shoulder wedged hard against my torso. She said I should have stayed in bed but I knew I needed to move and see what I could and couldn't do. I needed to know how far I could go when the time came.

Gale made a breakfast of eggs and toast, but all I could eat was part of a nectarine and some red grapes. I felt exhausted but tried my best to hide that from her. My thoughts were clouded, fragmented. I felt like a hand in a loose-fitting glove, separated, distanced, a little lost.

After breakfast Gale rolled up the left sleeve of the T-shirt she had given me and removed the dressing from my shoulder. We both studied the wound. It seemed, oddly, the least of my problems, till I remembered that it had come from a knife. The black, bristly stitches looked good to me, and there was a green stain on the skin around it where an antiseptic had been applied. Gale dabbed some vitamin E lotion as carefully as she could along the crease of the wound, then applied a fresh dressing over it. I felt a fever tingle behind my forehead again but said nothing to her about that. It was probably just from the sight of the tear in my skin and from her touching it, from her inadvertently moving the stitches and the freshly split flesh around as she tended to it.

Sometime after lunch I thought I'd better call George and let him know where to find his car. After that I called Eddie to let him know that I was okay and where I was. Chances were he was probably looking for me. I didn't see myself leaving Gale's anytime soon and I knew he would get word of my resurrection out to the few people who would care. As usual Eddie's wife, Angel, was working dispatch and answered on the second ring.

"Eddie's Cab Company."

"Angel, it's Mac. I need you to get a message to Eddie."

"Mac, oh my God, you're alive. For the love of God, where have you been? Eddie spent all night looking for you. He's out there now. He hasn't taken a fare since yesterday. He's been worried sick. Where have you been?"

"Angel, I'm sorry, I should have called sooner. Radio him and tell him I'm okay so he can get back to work. I'll call him in a couple of days—"

"Mac, you don't understand, there's trouble. You're in trouble."

"What?"

"He told me to find out where you were if you called. He says he has to talk to you, in person."

"Angel, what's going on?"

"I don't know the whole story. Eddie'll tell you when he gets there. Where are you?"

I glanced at Gale. She had stopped in the middle of washing dishes and was looking at me. The water was running from the tap, a low-pitched, steady hiss. Gale looked both concerned and uncertain.

I told Angel the address. Then I hung up and turned and looked at Gale. Neither of us spoke. I went out to the glassed-in porch and sat in the rocking chair and waited. After about a minute Gale came out and sat in her chair. Together we sat and watched the driveway and waited.

"What is it with you two?"

"What?"

"With you and Eddie. What is it with you two? He does whatever you ask him to. Why?"

I shrugged. "He left Jamaica for America because he was in trouble. The trouble followed him here. I helped him out of a jam. I just happened to be there when he needed help. I was a kid and ran in blind to help a stranger. I used to do that a lot."

"You saved his life."

I nodded.

"And that's how you two became friends?"

"It didn't happen overnight," I explained. "Just over the years we ended up for one reason or another doing things for each other. Most of it was probably chance. For some reason our paths just seem to keep crossing. We aren't even friends really, not like Augie and me, not in the conventional sense. We don't hang out together. He doesn't pry into my life and I don't pry into his. The daughter of an ex-girlfriend of mine was kidnapped a few years ago. No one could find her. Out of desperation she asked me to see what I could do. I went out looking, but it was Eddie who told me where to find her. On one of his fares through Hampton Bays he had seen a man and a young girl go into a house that was up for sale, that was empty. I wouldn't have known where to start looking for her if it wasn't for him. But that's the kind of man he is."

"So you found her? Your ex-girlfriend's daughter, I mean."

The answer was there but I wasn't sure how to speak it.

"I found her body, yeah. My ex-girlfriend had come to me at night and asked me to look for her daughter. I told her I would and had a few drinks to work up the courage. A few drinks turned into a few drinks too many. I didn't end up going out till late the next morning. When I found her she wasn't even an hour dead. Anyway, I turned to run out of the house to call the cops and came face to face with her killer. That's when I caught the bullet in the shoulder that brought me to you."

"You have three cracked ribs," Gale said flatly. "God knows how many blows you've taken to your head. You're covered with bruises. And then, of course, there's that cut in your shoulder and all the blood you've lost. I just want you to know that if you go back out there and start playing this game you boys play . . . well, I don't want to begin to count all the ways it could go bad for you." She waited a moment more, then said, "I just want you to know that."

I didn't say anything, just looked ahead through the windows at the driveway at the end of her yard. A minute later Eddie's red cab pulled in and stopped less than halfway down. Gale watched, then after a moment she rose from her chair, went through the porch door, and went down the steps and strode with those long tennis-player legs of hers across her lawn. She stopped suddenly halfway between the house and Eddie's cab and waited for him to come to her.

Eddie walked toward her on legs so bowed he was almost hobbled. I had forgotten how odd he looked, how he seemed, in his baggy trousers and shirt, so small outside of his cab.

He walked stiffly, as if years of sitting had weakened him beyond all reason. He reminded me then of a man come back from space, burdened by gravity. When Eddie reached Gale he stopped, and they faced each other for a moment on the leaf-covered lawn. Gale left the door opened, and the cool air smelled crisp and felt good on my face. They spoke to each other briefly, but I didn't hear what they said. When they were done Gale turned and led Eddie across the lawn to the porch.

As he entered he looked at me in a way that made me think Gale had told him what to expect as far as my condition was concerned. He stood above me and tilted his head to get a better look at my face.

"Jesus, Mac, where you been? A war?" He tried to joke, but his smile was less than convincing.

"Have a seat, Eddie," I said. He sat down and leaned toward me in that way people do when they address the infirm. My mood was dropping fast. I wanted to be alone with Gale, in her home, safe. Eddie brought the outside world into my hiding place.

"What's going on, Eddie?" I said.

Eddie spoke softly. "The cops are looking for you, Mac," he said. "They're everywhere. Patrol cars everywhere you turn. I've never seen so many cops out in my life."

I was confused. "What are Montauk cops doing in Southampton?"

Eddie wasn't sure what to make of this. He glanced up at Gale, then back at me. "What Montauk cops, my friend? I'm talking about the Southampton cops. The Chief's boys. They've been to the Hansom House, they've been to Augie's house, they've even been to my house. They are serious about finding you, my friend. They are looking everywhere for you, calling on everyone who knew you. They made poor George piss his pants." He glanced at Gale again. "Sorry, ma'am." Gale shrugged.

"You say it's the Southampton cops?"

Eddie nodded. He was still speaking low, leaning toward me. "They've pulled me over twice already today."

All machines have their friction, and my brain was beginning to heat. It turned like a motor without oil. Thinking was a physical thing, like lifting heavy rocks and moving them from one place to another.

"Eddie, why are they looking for me?"

He glanced at Gale again, then back at me. Even in my confusion I could read him.

"It's okay," I assured him.

"I guess you haven't heard. It's been on the radio."

"What has?"

"The geologist."

"What about him?"

"He's dead, Mac."

"What?"

"That geologist, the one from the college, he was murdered."

"Concannon?"

"Yeah, that's the one. He was killed last night. Someone tied him to a chair and cut his throat. They say the cut was so deep his head was almost half cut off. I guess he was cut more than once. Whoever killed him must have been really pissed off about something."

I glanced at Gale. She looked puzzled in a way that reminded me of Tina the night she was attacked by the Chief's son.

Eddie said, "If you don't have any money, I can give you some, Mac. You'd better leave town as soon as you can. Not right now, it's not safe on the roads during the day. But tonight. I'll take you wherever you want to go."

"I don't get it," I said. "Why are the Southampton cops looking for me? Are you telling me they think I killed Concannon?"

"From what I hear the knife they found on the scene was a Spyderco, just like the one you carry. There are prints all over it, from what I'm told."

"A lot of people carry that knife. It's a popular knife. Why are they so certain it's mine?"

"I don't know. Apparently, someone in the department has got it in their head that it belongs to you."

"I need to get to my apartment," I said quickly. There was a touch of panic in my voice. "I need to check something."

"What?"

"I need to check something."

"The Chief could be making his move, Mac. It's time for you to get out of town."

"I have to check this first. I have to know something first. Take me there tonight."

Eddie looked up at Gale again, then back at me.

"Please don't fight me on this, Eddie. I need to get into my apartment."

In a warning tone he said, "If we can't get you in, if we see one cop car parked outside, anything, we don't stop, I take you straight out of town. Agreed?"

"Agreed."

"If it is a setup, Mac, if this is the Chief finally getting his revenge, then I'd think he's probably got you good. He's not a stupid man."

"That's what I hear."

"I'm serious, Mac."

"I just have to know that for sure, Eddie. I just have to know exactly what it is I'm running from and for how long I'll have to stay away."

Eddie nodded. He understood that. He had fled his country twenty years ago after a rival for the woman he loved dropped cocaine in Eddie's car and turned him in to the cops.

"Okay," he said. "You look and we leave, no matter what you find, right?"

"Right."

"I'll come back for you when it's dark."

Gale followed him outside. She spoke to him as they walked but I didn't hear a thing she said. Then, at the edge of the driveway, she stopped and waited as Eddie got into his cab. She waited till he was backing down the driveway before she turned and crossed the lawn again.

Gale stepped up onto the porch but remained in the doorway and looked at me. In the light I saw threads of gray in her hair. I had to look away, she looked that good.

"You have no intention of leaving town tonight, do you?"

"Is that what you and Eddie talked about?"

"No."

"I can't just abandon Augie."

"He'd be the first one to tell you to go."

"And I'd tell him to go to hell."

"Touching."

"I need to get to my apartment."

"And after that?"

I wasn't thinking that far ahead. My life hinged on the contents of a bureau drawer. It was too absurd to dwell on.

We looked at each other in silence, and then after that I got up from the chair. It was a struggle. She just stood there in the doorway with her arms folded under her breasts and watched.

Gale said in a flat voice, "What is it exactly you're looking for?"

"I keep my knife in the top drawer of a bureau in my living room. If it's still there, I know the Chief is bluffing."

"Do you really think the Chief bluffs?"

"If he isn't, then all hell's going to break loose."

I suddenly became very tired. I let out a short breath and said, "I should get some rest, Gale."

At first she didn't make a move. Then she nodded and said, "I'll help you upstairs."

She eased me down on the bed in that sparse, dim room. The two windows on either side of the bed were half open. A breeze lifted the curtains. Gale went to close them.

"Please don't," I said.

She looked at me. "It's cold."

"Cold feels good right now."

She looked away from me, toward an empty corner of the room. She thought about something for what seemed a long time. I waited. Finally she looked toward the open bedroom door and went to it. She closed it, turned the lock, and paused with her hand on the knob. She let go of it and turned and faced me.

She was near the foot of the bed, her back against the door, her hands behind her. I didn't know what was going on. She looked both puzzled and relieved all at once, like someone who suddenly accepts a dark fact of their life and is to their surprise made free by it. She stayed there for a while, looking at me, and then all at once, decisively but without urgency, moved away from the door and approached the other side of the bed. There she removed one shoe, then the other, but left her white socks on. Then she unbuttoned her jeans and pulled them down her hips and stepped out of them. I looked at her bare legs. Then she removed the flannel shirt and did that trick women have and removed her bra without removing her shirt. All that remained was her blue turtleneck that stopped just below her navel and lavender panties with a white flower trim. I could see the impression on the cotton that her mound made.

Her long legs were smooth and still tanned, tight from her tennis playing. She pulled open the covers of her half of the bed and climbed in under them. She lay on her side beside me. Then she draped her left arm and leg over me. Her left hand lay flat on my chest.

Her face was inches from mine but I didn't dare make a move. We looked at each other for a while, and then she lowered her head and rested it on my chest, settling into me.

"Get some sleep," she said. "If I'm not here when you wake, I'll be downstairs. But I won't leave, okay? I won't leave. So go ahead and get some sleep."

But I didn't sleep, not for a while anyway, and neither did she. We did a good job of lying still, but there was no fooling each other; our breathing gave us away. Still, we just lay there together, unable for a dozen reasons not to act. I ran through them all in my head, but she was still there, beside me and awake, when I was done. Then my physical state got the better of me and I started to drift off. The last thing I knew was her breathing, which still held the element of consciousness to it.

He lies propped up on pillows in tan chinos and a white T-shirt, the perfect middleweight, on his back, smoking. He is a young man with sleepy eyes and a sharp jaw, and I am a boy of seven, motherless in a world bigger than I can comprehend. He is smoking on a bare mattress by an open window in a room of a hotel that has never had a heyday. I remember the crack lines in the plaster walls and the smell of overcooked grease coming up through the floors. It is his day off and I watch him smoke, all day, watch the curls of dirty white that look somehow almost liquid rise to the yellow-stained ceiling. It disappears and I wonder where it goes but never ask. His eyes squint as the smoke rises past them, drifting lazily from his nose and mouth in puffs, like smoke signals. I think that maybe they mean something but cannot figure out what. I sit on my cot and watch him for hours as he smokes and looks out that window at whatever comes and goes on the main street of Riverhead. After a while he naps for a bit, and so do I. When he awakens, I wake. I feel safe and entertained and contented. He shrinks the world down to this single room and makes clouds with his mouth. Even then I take the silence between us as a good thing.

Now we are in a dark room, maybe a bar. He approaches me from the other end of the room as if he has come back for me. He walks on the balls of his feet. I can barely see him in the dark. Now he says something I cannot hear. His hard, bony face hangs long. I wonder if this is concern. I do not know him well enough to tell. It hits me now that I am not a child but an adult. I see that he has aged, that there are lines in his face that remind me of the cracked plaster. His eyes are focused over my head and behind me. I turn but see nothing.

I hear sounds, the rush of someone coming up to me quickly. Before I can look to see who it is, I hear a long-forgotten voice whisper in my ear. It is my father's voice, urgent but assured.

"Wake up, son," he says. "Wake up." I feel his breath in my ear, I feel its warmth spiral into me. "Wake up, son, we're in trouble."

I awoke to the weak blueness of twilight. I had lifted my head off the pillow before I was even completely conscious, and I knew at once that was a mistake. For a moment I couldn't breathe. I lay my head back down and stared at the flawless ceiling above. I felt for a while like I had a foot in two different worlds. I wasn't sure which one I wanted. When my mind cleared I thought of how I could not remember the last time I had dreamed of my father and the hotel room we had called home after my mother died. It didn't dawn on me till just now that it was then that my father became so silent. Of course I see now how lonely he must have been. Death has a way of depleting us of life bit by bit by taking those we hold dear.

There was a rim of unpolished metal along the horizon, and above that, like strata, were differing shades of night. Gale was not in bed with me, so when I could I got up and made my way assisted only by the railing down the stairs. There were few lights on in the house, and I went from room to room till I found her on the glassed-in porch, in her rocker, under an afghan. Her feet were on the seat of the rocker, her knees to her chest. She hugged them.

She didn't look at me when I entered, just kept her eyes ahead and looked through the windows at the dark shape of an oak tree in her front yard. It looked like a hand with countless narrowing fingers.

She knew I was there, I knew that, but I waited a while, and when she didn't speak or show any signs of speaking, I said, "What's up?"

"Eddie called a few minutes ago," she said. Her voice was monotone. She continued to look straight ahead. "He's on his way to get you, to take you out of town."

I nodded. "I should get ready then."

"Yes," she said. "By all means, get ready."

"I'm doing what I have to do, Gale. You know that."

A pair of headlights swung into her driveway then, long beams scanning her lawn. I knew they belonged to Eddie. I looked and saw his cab move slowly down the driveway. I could hear leaves crumbling under the tires.

Gale stood, wearing the afghan like an embrace, and faced me. She said nothing. Then she turned away from me and went into her house.

I stood there on her dark porch for a minute, dazed, then joined Eddie in his warm cab. Together we rode in silence toward violence.

"You sure you want to do this?" Eddie said.

We were parked across the street from the Hansom House. There wasn't a cop in sight. I looked at Eddie's tired eyes framed in the long rectangle of the rearview mirror. I wondered when was the last time he had slept.

"Yeah. I'm sure."

"I'm giving you five minutes, then I'm coming in to get you, okay?"

I reached for the door handle. "Okay," I said. I looked up and down Elm Street but saw nothing out of the ordinary. Train station and Mexican restaurant on one end, a long row of middle-class houses on the other. I walked up the path and through the front door. I looked down the entrance hallway and saw George behind the bar. I saw the backs of a handful of regulars. To the left of the hallway was the stairs.

I paused at my door to listen, then opened it and stepped inside. Nothing seemed out of place. I left the lights off and made my way across my living room by the light from the streetlamps outside my front windows. The floorboards squeaked twice under my feet. I went to the bureau and pulled open the top drawer. There were just a few things in there, bits of mail and a photograph of Catherine and newspaper clippings, but no knife.

I stood there in the half dark and wondered just how

long the Chief had been in my apartment the other night before I woke up. Long enough, it seemed. I picked up the photograph of Catherine and looked at it, then put it back and closed the drawer fast and ran into my kitchen.

I grabbed a paper napkin off my eating table and a pen from the countertop and wrote "Sorry, Eddie" in big letters. I searched through a kitchen drawer and found a thumbtack, then grabbed a fork from the dish drainer and my roll of silver duct tape and went out into the hallway. I tacked the napkin to the door, then went down one flight of stairs to the second floor.

George's door was locked, but I could tell by the way the door gave when I leaned against it that he hadn't thrown the deadbolt. I slid the fork between the door and the jamb and pried back the smaller bolt at the knob. It took about a minute for me to catch it just right and pull it back enough for the door to swing open. Once inside I grabbed the keys to his Bug from a dish on a table by the door. I left four hundred dollars of James Curry's money where the keys had been. I put the fork into my back pocket and moved through George's living room to his bedroom. His bedroom window, like mine, looked out over the yard behind the Hansom House. It was for me the only way out.

I opened the window, tossed out my roll of tape, then made my way out onto the sill. I sat on its edge and brought my knees to my chest and swung my legs out. I could feel my ribs giving too easily, as if they were about to fold. I ducked my head and leaned forward so my head was outside the window and I was sitting on the sill with my legs dangling. I reached behind me and grabbed the sill with both hands. I took a breath, closed my eyes for a moment, and then slid off the sill and let my body fall.

I dropped fast and hit the ground within what seemed less than a second. I let my knees buckle to slow my fall. But it did little. When my body hit the ground it was as if I had set off dozens of tiny white-hot fires inside me.

I lay there on my side for a moment. The cold ground felt good on my face. For a few sweet minutes I didn't know anything. Then I thought of Gale, of her sleeping beside me, her body tangled with mine, and the feel of her face against mine. I knew then what I had to do. If I would kill a man just to survive, how much farther would I go to finally really live?

Just one man stood between me and the life I now wanted. I had no room to move, nowhere to go but through him. There was no choice to make but the wrong one. Wrong was all there was now.

I grabbed the roll of tape and pulled myself up to my feet and lumbered around the side of the Hansom House to the front. I peeked around the corner. Eddie was still in his cab, waiting. Every once in a while he'd glance up at my windows. I looked for George's Bug. It was parked at the end of Elm Street, outside the Mexican restaurant where I used to work, maybe four or five car lengths behind Eddie's cab. I could see its two new tires against the curb.

There was no route I could take to it that would hide me from Eddie. So I just stood up as straight as I could and started walking to it. I looked at Eddie as I went out of the corner of my eye. He was looking at the Hansom House, sometimes at the front entrance, others at my windows above. I kept my eye on him till my path turned and I could no longer look at him without turning my head. Then I just looked ahead and walked toward George's Bug. When I reached it I opened the door and slipped in. I was looking forward then. I could see Eddie's cab through the windshield. I could see him still waiting and looking.

I slid in the key and cranked the ignition. The motor was still as loud as a Harley. I flipped on the headlights, shifted into gear, then made a U-turn. I stopped at the end of Elm and looked into the rearview mirror. I saw Eddie climb out of his cab and pause, looking up at my windows. He leaned into his cab and killed the motor and the lights, then started up the path to the entrance.

I looked ahead then and made a left turn on Railroad Plaza. I passed the train station, lit up but abandoned, then made a left turn onto North Street, heading under the row of bare elms toward the heart of the village.

His house was a modest Victorian on Moses Lane, north of Hill Street. It was somehow smaller than I expected. Only the second-floor lights were on, the windows glow-ing yellow behind curtains. The rest of the house and the property around it stood in blackness. That suited me fine. I parked the Volkswagen several houses down, killed the motor and the lights, grabbed the tape, and got out and opened the trunk. I removed George's crowbar and then backtracked to the house and made my way down the driveway, past his black Crown Victoria, so shiny in the dark it looked almost liquid.

I reached the back of the house but didn't bother with the back door. I was looking for something else, a ground-level window into the basement that I could tape up to keep the glass from falling when I broke it with the crowbar. But instead I found something better below the utility meters at the far corner of the back of the house.

It was an old-style coal chute, the double doors locked from the inside. I looked around the backyard, more out of habit than caution, and then felt around till I found the hinges. The bolts felt like a quarter inch at least. I put the flat end of the crowbar against the top knob of the bolt, then began to work it back and forth as I pressed forward. I was careful not to push too hard and risk sliding off and announcing my presence by hitting the door with the bar. It took a few moments but I broke through the rust and worked the bolt free. Then worked on the lower bolt. It was more difficult, but once it got started it came out easily enough. Then I pried the unhinged door free of the jamb and lifted it as far as it would go. It was barely enough for me to squeeze through. I used the crowbar to prop it open, tossed the tape aside, and got down on my stomach and made my way on sore elbows and knees into even more blackness.

Once inside I found nothing to grab hold of and rolled down the chute to a hard basement floor. I stood and kept still for a few minutes, listening to my breathing, which was the only thing to hear. The air that touched my face was cool and watery, like the air that rushed up from the bottom of a well. Disorientation screwed with my inner compass. I quickly lost sense of where the coal chute was, or where I was in relation to it.

Finally I picked a direction at random. After a few steps I found a wall and felt my way along it. The wall was made of rocks and was damp. It felt like the walls of a cave. A residue of moisture was applied to my palms with each touch, a dank film that evaporated when I removed my hand and reached for another part of the wall farther down when the toe of my right sneaker hit something solid.

I felt around till I felt something made of wood. I ran my hand across it till I finally made out the familiar shape of a staircase.

The door at the top of the stairs led into the kitchen. Even though the lights were off it was nothing compared to what I had just stumbled through. I could see the appliances and the kitchen table and white cabinets and countertops.

I stood there in the doorway and listened. I heard nothing but I knew I was not alone. I remembered my experience in Townsend's cottage and went to the back door and unlocked it, in case I needed to get out fast. Then I backtracked through the kitchen and moved through a narrow dining room into a living room. Off the living room was a study. Below the furnace kicked in, the low, irritable grumble of a waking animal. I felt a slight rumble in the floorboards.

I reached the door of the study and looked in. There was enough light to see the gun safe and the desk and the glass showcase filled with trophies behind it. The walls were covered from ceiling to floor with framed photographs. I thought of one of those old European estates where paintings of all sizes cover every inch of a wall like pieces of some kind of screwed-up jigsaw puzzle. The door was halfway open. I eased it the rest of the way with the back of my hand and took a step in.

You can tell a lot about a man by his study. In Augie's, like this one, there was a desk and a fireplace, but the walls held only a half-dozen framed photos. Hanging directly above his safe was a photo of Tina at the age of thirteen, at the firing range, orange ear protectors over her tiny head and safety glasses on the end of her nose and a .45 caught just in the first split second of recoil in both her hands, a puff of gray smoke in the air above the hammer. Standing just behind her, looking toward the target that was well out of frame, was Augie, beaming proudly. There were no photographs of Augie's late wife anywhere because he said it just hurt too much.

Though I wasn't here to get to know the man better,

I was curious what photographs were hanging on the walls. I felt around to the right of the door for the light switch and found it, but before I could throw it I heard the sound of someone rushing up behind me, a rustle of clothes and quiet footsteps. I turned and bent my knees to lower my center of gravity and out of sheer luck managed to duck under a swinging stick. It hit, and the knuckles of the hand holding it made little divots in the wall. I shot up fast and hit the stick with a hammer fist, knocking it to the floor. Without missing a beat he moved toward me faster than I would have thought possible for him. I braced myself to accept a charge, but it did little good.

He came crashing into me, driving me across the room and into the wall opposite the door. Frames fell, glass shattered around my feet. My back crushed the few that remained hanging; I could feel the broken glass piercing my denim jacket and pricking my skin. I arched my back out of reflex and his shoulder slammed into my ribs. My body had nowhere to give and my ribs nothing else to do but pop under his weight. The sound was almost metallic, like a pin shearing, and the pain caused my eyes to roll back for a few seconds.

He grabbed my jacket and lifted me off the floor, pressing me against the wall. Only then were we face to face. Frames were falling around me, smashing on the floor. Our eyes met. There was a brief cognition, and then, still holding on to my jacket, he dropped me to my feet. The instant they touched the ground he spun around, pulling me with him. I actually felt Gs. I crashed into another wall, into another collection of framed photos. Plaster cracked where my shoulder landed.

Before I could do anything I was off for another ride again, my feet racing along the floor, trying to keep up. His legs were so much longer than mine, and anyway he was the axis of our little circle, he barely had to move at all, no more than a few strides toward the wall of his choice. He carried me like a child but I didn't resist. His long arms were bent, holding me close to him. I knew I didn't particularly want another run-in with a wall, but there was nothing I could do. He either let go of me or lost his grip on my jacket. I flew into the wall and hit it hard, harder than before. I felt my kidneys shift and blood rush to my head, pounding as if I were hanging upside down. I slid to the floor.

He scrambled for the stick then, broken glass cracking under his shoes. Then next thing I knew he was over me. The first blow landed just above my temple. My head almost flew off and I saw a blue light with a dense core of orange. A second shot, a backhand, clipped my jaw. It rang the bone. I lifted my hands blindly for cover, and the third shot hit my left wrist. A fourth struck my right shoulder.

He towered above me, taking wild swings, looking for that clean shot at my skull that would crack it open. He grabbed me then out of frustration and lifted me to my feet. The instant my feet touched the ground I reached out and grabbed for his throat, catching his larynx between my thumb and four fingers. I dug around it till my fingers and thumbs were close to touching. The Chief's mouth opened then and his tongue stuck out, flat and motionless. I kept my hold on his throat with my right hand and trapped his right arm with my left. I locked the crook of my elbow under his and then pulled my arm into my ribs with one swift motion. His elbow snapped and he tried to scream but all that came out was gurgling.

The stick hit the floor but I held his throat and broken arm a moment more, then released him. He dropped to the floor, coughing and cradling his arms. He lifted his head and looked up at me. His face was white and there were beads of sweat on his upper lip.

I looked for the nightstick then and grabbed it off the floor, then found the light switch and flipped it on. I turned back to the Chief and raised the stick above my head. I was about to bring it down when something caught my eye and stopped me frozen in my tracks.

On the wall directly in front of me, in a narrow rimmed silver frame with a cracked glass, hung a photograph of Tommy Miller, in his football uniform, in a time before I had crippled him behind the Southampton Library the night he and two friends tried to rape Tina.

I looked at the photograph and couldn't move. I looked around the room. Every frame on the wall contained a photograph of Tommy at various times in his life, all before I got to him. In the showcase were his trophies, dozens of them and, too, a letter congratulating him on his full scholarship to the University of Michigan, which of course he never got to use. I lowered my hand and saw on the desk a photograph of Tommy and his mother, after the fact. His joints were all turned—a knee twisted almost halfway around, an arm that could not straighten and seemed now almost mechanical, like the arm of the Tin Woodsman. In the photo Tommy didn't smile, and the one on his mother's face was so forced and brave that she really shouldn't have bothered at all.

I turned back to the Chief. He looked at me, his face ashen, the edges of his eyes red and raw.

I was still dazed, breathing fast, shallow breaths. I didn't bother to check if my head or face was bleeding. It was beyond all that now.

"What is it you want, Chief?" I said.

His breathing, the swelling of his mountain man's chest, reminded me of a heaving ocean.

"What do you want from me, Chief?" I said again. I was out of breath. Words were wisps.

"What are you talking about, MacManus?" he muttered.

"You set me up for Concannon's murder, didn't you?" I gasped as I spoke. "First you tried to kill me in Townsend's house. And when that didn't work you set me up for Concannon's murder. You took my knife from my apartment, didn't you? When you were there, waiting for me. You set me up good, Chief. My life's in your hands. So just tell me what the fuck it is you want and get it over with."

He adjusted his position against the wall, rising from his slouch to more of a seated position. I kept a close eye on him. He winced and drew in air through his teeth. I thought of how I reacted the same way to similar pain.

"You're scared, aren't you?" he said.

"Yeah. I'm scared. Is that what you wanted? To scare me? Well, you got it, job's done, you got what you wanted, so call off your dogs."

The Chief shook his head. It seemed more a gesture of correction than disagreement.

"It's not what I want, MacManus," he said. "It's never been what I wanted. It's what *he* wants. It's been that way for a long time now."

I watched his words as carefully as I watched his movements.

"What are you talking about, Chief?"

"He's wanted you dead for a few days now, actually. He's hired people to kill you. Professionals. But you don't seem to have enough sense to die when you're supposed to. Montauk, the reservation, it was all him. Since you wouldn't die, he came up with this instead. Concannon had to die anyway, so why not get two for the price of one? He's always been one for a bargain. Christ, he's the cheapest son of a bitch I've ever known."

"Chief, what the hell are you talking about?"

He looked down at his arm for a moment. He seemed

to be gathering the strength he needed to continue. Finally he shook his head in almost amused disbelief and looked up at me. His face was white, but dirty white, like newspaper.

"You don't even know what you're in the middle of, do you, MacManus?"

I took a step toward him. "Why don't you enlighten me, Chief?"

"He's the reason why I didn't just walk into your place and drag you out by your collar and beat you like a dog right there on Elm Street. He's the reason why I didn't do a lot of things."

"Who?"

"He told me that he needed you, and that was that. This was after what you did to my son. I wanted to kill you, but he wanted you around, and in good health, in case he needed you for something at some point down the road. So I sat on my hands, I did just what I was told. He assured me that once you were no longer of use to him, I could do what I wanted. I'll tell you, it was a day I lived for."

"You're saying Frank was—"

"He always likes to tell people that someone is pulling my strings. That *I'm* the corrupt and evil one and should be run out of town on a rail. He makes a big deal of saying that he needs to know exactly who it is pulling my strings, that he's determined to find out. You've probably heard the speech. Looking out for the good of the town, he's the only one who can do something, that kind of thing. He's the one who runs my department, not me. He has half of my men in his pocket. They do what he tells them. Christ, they've even murdered for him." The Chief sighed through his nose, short and brisk, and shook his head regretfully. "You don't know what's going on here, do you? You live here in this town with your head in the ground and you don't see a damn thing that's going on."

I felt like I was doing math in my head. It was exhausting me just to listen to him, just to try to keep up. I could put the numbers together, just slowly. It took a minute for the bell to ring. When it did my jaw went slack.

"Chief, are you telling me what I think you're telling me?"

"Too many blows to the head, MacManus?"

"Yeah. Something like that."

"All this time he's been telling you I'm the monster. He's been telling you, I bet, that any day now I was going to bust down your door and slap a made-up charge on you. He wanted to keep you scared and in line. You could be more easily coerced then. Meanwhile, I'm at my desk counting the holes burning in my gut. I wasn't even allowed to go anywhere near you, and there you were in constant fear of me. The man knows what he's doing. He played you like a plywood violin."

"You're just telling me bullshit, Chief. Frank's clever, but he's not that clever." What I was really saying was I wasn't that stupid. I heard my voice and it sounded exactly like what I was, a panicked man clinging to his fixed perspective of a suddenly changing world. The floor had been yanked out from beneath me, and I was afraid to look directly at all that might now lie below.

The Chief said, "Who put you and Augie at the scene of the accident? Frank, right?"

"Why would he do that?"

"He wanted you and Augie there to witness the crash, to tell everyone that it was a terrible accident and nothing more. There was no errant son-in-law you were tailing. You were there to see a murder disguised as an accident and tell the papers and everyone who cared that that's just what it was."

"Wait, what does Frank have to do with the accident?"

"You still haven't figured it out. Frank killed the Curry girl. Frank blew out her tires to make it look like an accident, and my men covered it up. Jesus, MacManus, Frank's been running this thing all along. He killed Amy Curry, and that was just for starters."

I stared at the Chief. It was all I could do. I wondered why I felt as much betrayal as anger. Frank was not a friend, or a colleague. Frank was what I didn't want to be—greedy, mean, blind. He was the mirror reflection by which I judged myself. And now that reflection had deceived me. It had deceived me all long.

The Chief was my enemy, and I was his, and that had kept my world simple. He was the extent of evil in my town, he and only he held my back against the wall. But now I was to accept that there was another whole world beyond that wall, and in it roamed free the man who held both of our chains.

"What do you mean, 'for starters'?" I said.

"He ordered the hit on Augie."

"Hit?"

"The two men that came to his house, they were sent there to kill him."

"Why?"

"Because he was taking pictures, getting nosy. Frank got nervous."

"So the man Augie killed had a gun."

"Of course he did. My men removed it from the scene, locked it away. Augie survived two tours of duty as a marine in Nam. He spent twenty-five years working undercover for the DEA. It's impossible for him to panic and shoot an unarmed man." He smiled then. "I can only imagine those two fools not knowing what hit them. Augie's a tough son of a bitch. That's why Frank sent two."

Hearing of the existence of the gun gave me a burst of hope. It was like a rush of adrenaline. It was almost enough to matter. I felt that I had to do something with that information.

"How are you doing so far, MacManus? Still with me?"

I didn't answer that. I was onto another thought upon which I had only a casual grasp at best. I didn't want to lose it.

"So the man who sacked me outside the Hansom House, he worked for Frank?"

"Yeah, at that point you weren't a threat to Frank. He didn't think you could come anywhere near him, so there was no reason to kill you. He felt he could still use you. Augie was the seasoned investigator. But then you got close, Frank got nervous, and that's when he decided to have you killed."

I tried to keep up but couldn't. My mind snagged on something. The man whose knee I popped, whom I found and brought to Frank, whom Frank sent walking into the freezing Atlantic—this man worked for Frank. By finding him, I had without knowing it surprised and threatened Frank. By trying to kill him, Frank was tying up loose ends. I thought of my old overcoat, of going that cold afternoon—how long ago was it now?—to see what the hell it was Frank Gannon wanted.

"When that failed, he went to plan B. If he couldn't kill you, he'd have the State of New York do it for him. He got your knife and killed Concannon with it. You were lucky you were wherever you were and not home when my men came to your place looking for you."

I thought about that, about where I was and how I had come to be there. Had the Chief inadvertently saved me by sending me to the reservation? Could he live with himself if he knew?

And then I thought of Gale, on her porch, wrapped in her afghan, maybe scanning the dark night, looking for me. After a while I looked at the Chief and said, "Why kill Concannon?"

"Because I think Concannon found the truth."

"What truth?"

"I think he came across what someone's been trying to keep secret. What someone's been killing to keep secret."

"What are you talking about?"

The Chief looked at me, waited a moment, then said, "In the past thirty years Frank Gannon has murdered or has had murdered close to fifteen men, mostly political rivals and men who found out something about him that he didn't want to get out. And I'm sure that in his early days, when he was just starting out, he killed for money. None of the bodies of these men has ever been found. Not one of them. Not a trace. And, in most cases, Frank was the man they were last seen with. I'm no genius, MacManus, but even I can do that math. I've thought about this a lot, and over the years I've come to conclude that Frank had to have been hiding the bodies in one place, in his own private graveyard somewhere out there, right under our fucking noses."

"Why do you think that?"

"If he scattered the bodies around the East End, with all the development that has occurred out here over the past thirty years, we would have found at least one of them. If he dropped the bodies in the ocean, one had to have washed ashore by now. No, Frank has his own burial ground somewhere, and by what's been going on these last few days I've got a pretty good idea for the first time where it is."

"The reservation," I said.

"I can think of several good places to hide bodies,

places no one would ever build on—or, rather, no Shinnecock would build on."

"You're saying Frank killed Concannon. Because Concannon found out about the bodies."

"The environmental group opposing the sale hired Concannon to research the effects future construction might have on the ecology. They wanted to block the sale entirely, or at least have the land declared a wildlife refuge. Anything to prevent construction. The town was behind them. Of course, Frank was all for this, too. It would solve a lot of his problems. He watched closely, staying out of things. But Concannon must have found something that made Frank nervous, and so Frank had him killed."

"The girl, Amy Curry. Why did Frank kill her?"

The Chief shrugged. "To warn Concannon, maybe."

"To warn him of what?"

"To keep his mouth shut. To do what Frank told him to do. To write his report the way Frank wanted. I don't know. Maybe it was all that. Maybe it was something else."

"And in between he tried to kill me and Augie."

"Yeah."

"Just my luck to have an overachiever for my enemy."

The Chief nodded. "I've never seen Frank this reckless. He's running scared. I don't see how he'd be able to sleep at night, knowing that a few hours after the first bone is found the FBI will come crashing down on our little town. A lot of people have a lot to say about Frank, if only someone would just ask them. But he's in a panic now. And there's going to be a lot more killing before this is over, you can count on that."

"So do something about it, Chief. Now that you know where his victims are, call the FBI, get them over there now. Be the one who brings down Frank Gannon."

The Chief was silent for a moment. I could hear a faint wheezing deep in my lungs when I exhaled.

He shook his head and said, his eyes wincing as if he was in pain, "Frank would just take me down with him."

"What does he have on you?"

"I wasn't always corrupt. Don't get me wrong. I was corrupt when Frank nabbed me, yeah, I was corrupt for years before that. But I wasn't always. Once upon a time I was an honest cop. Just like your father. And see where that got him."

"I don't know where it got him, Chief. He disappeared, remember?"

"I guess that's my point. It got him nowhere."

I said nothing to that.

"I was at their wedding, you know. Your mother and father's. So was Augie. So was Frank." The Chief laughed. "One of the gift envelopes disappeared, and everyone just assumed Frank took it."

I waited a moment, then said, "You should get your arm taken care of, Chief."

He looked at me again, this time as if he were summing me up. He looked skeptical, unsure about me—or maybe unsure about what he was about to do.

"We don't have much time," he said. "Open my gun safe."

I didn't move.

"Go ahead. Go. We don't have time to fuck around. Open it. It's unlocked."

I turned and went to the safe. It was as tall as I. I turned the lever down. The door swung back slowly, moved by its own weight. Inside the safe were four assault shotguns, two hunting rifles, and six handguns of various kinds mounted on pegs. On a series of narrow shelves were boxes of ammo, several for each type of gun, some cleaning kits and a pair of gloves, and, tucked in one shelf, what looked like clear plastic.

"On the second shelf from the top there are some baggies," the Chief said. "Can you see them?"

"Yeah."

"Take the one closest to the edge of the shelf out."

I looked back at him, then back into the safe.

"Hurry," he urged softly.

I reached into the second shelf and grabbed the plastic baggy between my thumb and forefinger. I pulled it out carefully and slowly, as if whatever it was might at any minute bite me.

But when the baggy fell free of the shelf and I held on to it and stopped it from falling to the floor I felt a weight I recognized immediately. I held up the baggy and looked through the clear plastic to its contents, then looked back at the Chief.

"It's the gun that belonged to the man Augie shot," he

said. "Yesterday I removed it from its place of safekeeping at the station house and brought it here."

I didn't know what to say. My mouth hung open slightly. A part of me wanted to hold the gun to my chest and laugh. Augie was free. Augie was free. Augie was free.

The Chief said, "Tell Augie to give this to his attorney. Tell him to tell his attorney that you found it in a storm drain. Then tell his attorney to call the DA. The dead man's prints are all over it. It's as simple as that."

"And what happens when they find this missing? What happens to you?"

"I don't plan on being here to find out. My wife and son are safely out of town. I'm leaving tonight to join them till this whole thing blows over."

"What whole thing?"

"Frank's cleaning house tonight. He's got his own little death squad, his own SS, and they're on the march. I imagine they'll come here. I imagine they'll come to your place. And I imagine they'll come to—"

"Augie."

"I'm not sure how much of this Augie's figured out. If Augie has a fault, it's that he's loyal to his friends. Even a friend like Frank. Frank could knock on his door and Augie'll let him right in."

"Shit," I said. I turned to leave.

The Chief said, "Wait. There's just one more thing."

I stopped and turned my head to look at him. "What?" I said quickly.

"There's another bag on that shelf. Pull it out."

I went back to the safe, put the baggy with the gun in my left hand, and reached into the shelf with my right. Again I grabbed hold of the plastic between my thumb and forefinger. I pulled the bag out.

I held it up, though I didn't need to look at it to know what it contained. Inside was my Spyderco knife, the blade opened. It was stained with Concannon's blood, and a light talcum on it showed that it was covered with fingerprints, most certainly my own. The blood had dried, but not before it had smeared the clear plastic. I looked at the Chief.

"Help me up," he said.

I squatted beside him. I wrapped his left arm around my neck and stood. I was more something he could push against than something that lifted him. He was a giant of a man.

We were face to face then, closer than we had ever been. I saw that the crow's feet around his eyes were dark furrows that wedged themselves into a line of ridges when he winced. I could feel his breath on my face. His arm remained around my neck till his footing was solid.

"Get Augie out of here," he said to me. "Stay away for a couple of days, at least."

"I can help you to your car."

He shook his head. "No. But there is one thing you can do for me."

"What?"

"Load one of my guns."

I waited a minute, then said finally, "Which one?"

"The Glock. Load a few clips for me, if you can."

I went to the safe and looked for the Glock. It was resting on the top peg.

"There are a pair of gloves by the cleaning kits. Put them on."

I put on the gloves, took down the Glock, then found three clips on the shelf, beside the box of armor-piercing, police issue .40 caliber bullets. I loaded each clip and laid them together on the top shelf. The third clip I slapped into the Glock.

There was no safety. I chambered the first bullet and laid the live gun on the shelf. I took off the gloves and stepped away and looked at the Chief. He nodded once in thanks. I wondered if that hurt him more than his busted elbow.

"Give Augie and his daughter my best," he said.

I couldn't help it then, my eyes drifted to the nearest intact photograph of Tommy. I didn't know what to make of the Chief wishing well the girl his son had tried to rape. I realized then that this all started with the two of them, with Tina and Tommy, and an act of violence that begat another act of violence that left me vulnerable to the machinations of Frank Gannon. It seemed comforting to think it was all that simple, that the beginning was so easily pegged, and that this madness could be boiled down to one night seven months ago.

But of course I knew better. This had started long ago, before I was born, when Frank killed a man and buried him in his own private bone orchard.

Before I reached the door the Chief said abruptly, "MacManus." I stopped and turned. He looked me up and down, that same skeptical, unsure look on his face. Or was it disgust I saw, or contempt, or loathing? I knew what it wasn't—it wasn't forgiveness.

"You might soon learn something that's going to tear up your insides," he said. "When that happens . . . think of my boy. Do me that favor, at least."

Augie's pickup was parked in his driveway, outside the garage. I pulled George's Bug to the curb, left the keys in it, and got out in a hurry. The baggy containing the gun was in my hand. I had locked the one containing my Spyderco knife in the glove compartment. I planned on ditching it in the Shinnecock Canal right after I brought Augie the prize that, I hoped, would win back his friendship.

I entered without knocking. Tina came out of the kitchen, alarmed by the sound of the crashing door. My excitement and my condition made me clumsy. I saw that she had a glass of beer in her hand.

"Mac."

"Where's Augie?" I said. I went to the hallway that led from the living room down to the two bedrooms and Augie's study.

"He's not here," Tina said. I stopped and turned toward her. She seemed puzzled by my excitement. Tina looked down at the baggy in my hand. "What is that?"

"It's the gun that belonged to the man Augie shot."

She took two long steps toward me. "What? Where'd you get it?"

"It doesn't matter. Where is he?"

"He went out."

"Out where?"

She shrugged. "They said something about the Indian reservation."

"What?"

"They said something about the Indian reservation."

"They who?"

"Frank and the other guy."

"What other guy?"

"I don't know. I've never seen him before. Mac, what's wrong?"

"His truck is still here."

"Yeah, they went in Frank's car."

"How long ago?"

"What's going on?"

"How long ago?"

"Maybe a half hour. Mac? What's going on? Mac?"

I broke into a run down the hallway. I felt no pain. I went into Augie's office and knelt in front of his safe and dialed the combination. The safe opened and I tossed the baggy holding the gun in. There were three other guns in the safe, two Colt .45s and a Ruger .380, all but one of the Colts gunmetal blue. I took out the .45s, gave them a quick check, then grabbed five clips, all my hand could hold. The clips were all loaded. I slapped one into each Colt and put the other three in my back pocket. They stabbed my hip but I didn't care. I closed the safe door and spun the lock to the left, then the right, then the left again.

When I stood Tina was standing in the doorway.

"Mac, what are you doing?"

I checked the safeties and stuffed both .45s into the waistband of my jeans, one behind and one in front. I walked toward Tina full stride. She barely got out of my way in time. I left the study and started down the hall.

I said evenly, "You can't stay here."

"Mac, do you even know how to use a gun?"

"Call Eddie. Have him take you to Lizzie's. Don't leave her house till you hear from me. Understand?"

"Mac, what's going on?"

I took off my denim jacket, then opened the hallway closet. I dropped the jacket to the floor and grabbed one of Augie's field jackets and pulled it off a hanger. The hanger spun once, then fell to the closet floor. I began to put the jacket on as quickly as my shoulder and ribs would allow. The fact that it was too big for me was a blessing.

"Listen to me. If you don't hear from me by morning, call Gale. She was your father's nurse. Call her at the hospital. Tell her that Augie wanted me to take care of you if something happened to him, and that I wanted her to take care of you if something happened to me. Okay? Do you hear me?"

"What are you talking about? What's going to happen to you? Mac?"

"Do what I told you, okay? Lock these doors when I leave, turn off the lights, and call Eddie, have him take you to Lizzie's. And stay there. Do you understand?"

"Yes."

"Do you promise to do this for me?"

"Yes."

"It's a real promise, Tina, not a Tina Hartsell promise."

"Yes, yes, I promise. Just tell me what's going on?"

Finally the jacket was on. I was almost out of breath from the effort. I adjusted it once, quickly, then zipped it up.

I took a step toward Tina then. Her eyes were searching out mine wildly. She was on the verge of tears. She waited eagerly for whatever it was I was about to say.

"There's a check for ten thousand dollars in my apartment. If you don't hear from me I want you to take it."

"Mac, you're scaring me."

I reached into my pocket and took out what was left of the thousand dollars Curry had given me. I handed it to her, stuffing it into her palm. She hesitated at taking it.

"Please," I said. "Just take it."

"Mac."

"Just take it."

Her right hand closed over the wad.

"Just hold it for me till I get back, okay?"

"Is Augie in trouble?" Tears were beginning to slip from her narrowed eyes. As always when she cried, she

seemed more angry than sad—angry at herself for show-
ing weakness. She was her father's daughter. "Is he in
trouble?" she repeated.

"Yeah, Tina, I think maybe he is."

I transferred the three clips from my back pocket to
the right cargo pocket of the field jacket.

"Everything's going to be okay," I told her.

"Do you even know how to use a gun, Mac? I've never
even seen you touch one before."

I turned without answering and started toward the
front door. Tina followed close behind. There was a
metal dish on a table by the door with the keys to Augie's
pickup in it. I grabbed them and looked at Tina.

"Frank Gannon killed Amy," I told her. "If I don't get
a chance to, I want you to tell her father that. Do you
understand?"

She nodded. Her hands were hanging at her sides. I
took her left hand with my right. It caught her by surprise. Her eyes locked on mine.

"I'll call you at Lizzie's in a little while," I said. I let go
of her hand. She held on to mine for a while longer, then
let go. It seemed to take everything she had.

I left her then, closing the door behind me. I ran
across the lawn to the driveway and climbed up into
Augie's truck. I cranked the ignition. The engine sang. I
hit the lights and backed out into the street.

I followed Little Neck Road to its end, then turned
right and headed east down Montauk. I sped along the
blacktop without even looking at the speedometer.

I had played war here when I was a boy with kids from school, poorer kids, mostly, with whom I felt more comfortable than I did with those who lived around me on Gin Lane. I remember being happiest here, I remember those late-summer afternoons and those early nights of winter as the best parts of my unpleasant childhood. As I drove I could see in my mind's eye the place where Frank must have taken Augie—a clearing on the shore of Shinnecock Bay, surrounded on three sides by oak and ash trees and thick underbrush. It had to be the place. There was a path to it that had been there when I first started playing there and that had grown deeper when I finally left it and all boyish games behind for good.

There were, I remembered, some fallen trees, and the terrain was uneven, with crests and depressions so deep they were almost ditches. The ground was mainly earth with some grass and skunk cabbage and wild ferns growing in patches, mainly on the highest points of ground. I could understand why Frank would choose this place—the reservation was protected land, the tribe wasn't growing so fast that there would be a housing boom, and who would build there anyway when the northern and eastern edges of the reservation were on flat land with soft soil and less wilderness? The Shinnecock for the most part built their own homes, and the land by the shore wasn't the kind of land one could easily level and lay in a crawlspace foundation with shovels and picks and wheelbarrows of cement on a Saturday afternoon.

I turned off Montauk Highway and back onto the reservation and followed a dirt road as far south as it went. It came to a stop at the trunk of a fallen, rotting tree that lay across it. Beyond that was just woods, thick woods. I saw even before I reached the end of the road three cars parked side by side by the trunk. The first car I recognized was Frank Gannon's Seville. It was hard to miss. The second was a small pickup with a glossy black paint job. I didn't get a look at the third till I killed the motor and the lights and got out of Augie's truck and started toward the path that began at the end of the road. But the sight of the third car slowed me a bit. It was the dark LTD that belonged to the man with the limp, to whom I owed my life and who owed me his.

I continued toward the path. Once I reached it I stopped and listened. Above, the heavy blanket of low clouds, frayed and shredded into long strands, flew quickly past the three-quarter moon. The moon was midway up from the horizon and perfectly white and spread a pale light into the woods ahead of me. It was almost enough to see by.

Then I heard faint voices. I could tell they were shouts but they were faint to me. I couldn't hear words. I took a step onto the path and then heard a muffled pop, flat and abrupt. It was a shotgun blast. I heard more voices, more distant yelling, and then another pop. After that I heard the firecracker sound of small arms being fired, shots right on top of each other, so close they could not have come from one gun.

I ran full stride into the woods, following a path that seemed familiar only when it was directly beneath my feet. I could not predict it, but there was enough light to make out the line it cut through the dense woods, and I just aimed for that.

I reached inside the jacket and pulled the Colt from the front of my waistband. Then I reached around, under the jacket, and gripped the other one and pulled it out. That was the chrome one. I switched off each safety with my thumb.

I moved over the path, up small rises and down, around the zigzag of turns, the minor shifts in direction. I held a full-bore run for a hundred yards, then started my next hundred. My worn-out sneakers slapped the dirt with an even, rapid rhythm. I just focused on staying on the path and holding that rhythm.

I counted six shotgun bursts but could not keep track of the small-arms fire. With each pumping of my legs the sounds got louder, clearer. I could hear the voices but could not hear words over my horselike exhalations and the wind in my ears. Toward the end the path began to zigzag sharper. The terrain was rougher here, more uneven, rising and falling like a tiny roller coaster.

I hit numbness, I hit runner's high, and as the endorphins cascaded down through my brain I was struck with the euphoric belief that I could hold this pace forever.

But the euphoria didn't last. Up ahead was the end of the path. I could see into the clearing, the thick woods on both sides of me acting like blinders.

The small-arms fire was to my left. I could hear that. When the end of the path was just feet away I looked to my right and saw a man crouched behind a fallen tree that lay atop the edge of a hole in the ground. There was another man lying motionless across the trunk of the tree. The crouched man was holding a shotgun between his legs and frantically searching the pockets of the motionless man while staying covered by the tree. The small-arms fire continued, bullets cutting pockmarks in the log. The man with the empty shotgun was Augie.

He looked up just as I burst from the woods and into the clearing. I pointed my right hand to the left and just started firing. I kept my eye on Augie as I ran toward him. On his face was the look of bewildered surprise. My cover fire brought a brief end to the small-arms fire. It was surprise and the sound of the Colt firing that caused the cease-fire more than anything else. I wasn't aiming at a thing, so I knew it wasn't the threat of being shot that stopped them.

Then the shooting began again, and I knew this time it was directed at me. I was halfway to Augie and moving fast. My eyes were fixed on him and his on me. When I was maybe six yards from him I tossed the chrome-plated Colt in my left hand toward him. It was an underhand throw, and I didn't bother to see whether it was good or not. I turned my head to the left and saw three points of white light flashing in the darkness. I thought, Three shooters, close together. I aimed and kept squeezing off

rounds, but I was still running with everything I had and
had no hope of hitting anything.

I squeezed off three more rounds and then the Colt
was empty. I looked toward Augie just as he caught the
chrome-plated Colt. He gripped it with two hands and
popped up from the ditch and peeked his head up from
behind the fallen tree and laid down a covering fire
for me.

I wasn't sure if I was close enough, but being upright
and out in the open was getting tired fast. I dropped and
slid like a runner pushing for home plate. The distance
was greater than I had expected, but I had built myself a
good momentum and slid as if on ice. I dropped into a
small, freshly dug ditch Augie had adopted as his fox-
hole. I landed hard on my back against the wall of the
ditch and came to an abrupt stop.

I dropped the spent clip from the Colt, pulled out another one from my pocket, and slapped it in.

The instant I was in, Augie dropped back down into
the ditch. He lay on his back beside me, the back of his
head resting against the tree. I reached into the cargo
pocket of the field jacket and removed the remaining two
clips. I tossed both to Augie.

There was no time to waste, both Augie and I knew
that. Everything was moving fast around us, almost as if
we were suddenly aware of the earth rotating at a thousand miles an hour upon its axis. The winds gusted often
and caused the trees in the woods around us to twist and
tap branches as if crossing swords. The trees hissed, of-

fering covering noise, noise through which we could move.

I pointed to the shotgun that lay beside Augie. He looked at me and nodded. I switched on the safety and stuffed the Colt into my waistband. Augie held his in two hands and readied himself. I looked at him and nodded again. Then we rose up together and turned. Augie laid down suppressing fire and I grabbed the belt of the man lying over the tree. The sound of the .45 firing pounded my eardrums. I yanked the man down into the ditch. The body dropped to the bottom of it, and I dropped down for cover with it. Augie followed right after. He had fired five shots, expending the clip. He kicked it out and slapped in the one I had just given him. We were both even now, one clip apiece.

Very little fire had been returned. Some of the shooters were on the move. The man at the bottom of the ditch was dead, I knew that by the way he fell when I dropped him, like he was just a sack of bones. I searched through his jacket pockets for shells and found only six. I pulled them out, then rolled the body away from us, toward the other side of the ditch. All dead people looked the same, with the same stiff, surprised look, eyes half closed. I looked away from the body and loaded as fast as I could five shells into the shotgun. I pumped it once, sending one of the shells up into the chamber and making room for the sixth. I slid the sixth in and then laid the shotgun between us.

I pulled the .45 from my waistband and switched off

the safety. Augie and I lay on our backs. I peeked out around the side of the log and saw a hundred feet away an abandoned 1970 Firebird. That was most likely their cover. Before I leaned back I caught a glimpse of Augie's cane on the ground. Beside it were a shovel and pick. That would be like Frank, I thought, to make a man dig his own grave.

There was no time to wait. Maybe a minute had passed since I slid into the ditch. The longer we lay there, entrenched, the more time they had to mount an assault, if they already hadn't launched one. Augie and I had to mount one of our own, quickly. It was our only way out.

I looked at Augie and pointed to my chest, then pointed upward with my index finger and made several circling motions. I ended the round of charades by pointing south, toward the bay. Augie nodded and positioned himself, getting ready to spring up and lay down more cover. I handed him his .45. He looked at me a moment, then took it, stuffing it in the waistband of his jeans at the small of his back. I picked up the shotgun, slid the safety off with my thumb. I crouched, ready, then looked back over my shoulder at Augie. He smiled then. I smiled back. Then I nodded once, sharply, and he sprang up and began to click off rounds.

I rolled out of the ditch and down the bank toward the bay. When I was clear and had come to a stop, Augie dropped back down behind the tree. He had fired five rounds. There was only one clip after that, and only six rounds in my shotgun. He looked at me and nodded, as if to ask if I were okay. I nodded back, took one last look at him, and then crawled on my stomach till I was far enough down the bank that I was out of sight of the men behind the abandoned Firebird.

Once I was clear I got up and moved in a crouch along the edge of the bay. There was no cover here except for the bank, and I kept my eye on the ridge above and kept the shotgun ready. I waited for it, expecting at any minute to come face to face with one of Frank's killers. I waited for it to the point where I wanted it to happen just to get it over with. I wanted someone to appear suddenly on the top of that ridge and see me and take aim at me so I could send a slug into his chest and get it over with.

The way I saw it now was that I had no choice but to make my way in a hurried rush around Frank and his men, to flank them and catch them by surprise and kill them if I could. There was no choice at all, and it was this that made me feel the most like an animal.

I moved forward and kept my eye out for any movement on the top of that ridge. Maybe two minutes had passed since I had caught up with Augie in his trench. All I could hear as I moved through the darkness was my short breathing. It and the lapping of the waves against the shore of the bay were the only sounds in the night. There was no gunfire now, there were no voices, no sounds of movement, nothing. Just the waves and my breathing, each out of sync with the other.

As I moved forward the top of the bank began to sink, and gradually the Firebird came into my sight again. I could see two men crouching by the nose of the car, along the left fender. I looked to see if there was any cover that would allow me to have a clear line of everyone behind the car, but there was none. I had come as far as I could go.

I turned and lay on my back against what was left of the bank. My sweat soaked T-shirt sent a chill through my back. I laid the shotgun across my chest and waited. I closed my eyes. All I had wanted was to avoid bloodshed. Maybe two and a half minutes had passed since my arrival, and though I was lying on the bank to gather together what it would take, I could still feel the rushing of things around me, of the elements on the move over which I had no control. I knew nothing of what was going on behind that Firebird and nothing of what was going on back in Augie's ditch. I was alone out here. Alone with nothing but the thumping of my heart and a shotgun and the sound of a late November wind rushing past my ears.

I opened my eyes and started to roll onto my stomach. Something told me to look up then. I did, fast, and directly above me on the top of that short bank stood the shape of a man, his right arm raised and outstretched toward me. In his hand something glinted. I rose onto my knees and leaned back, raising the shotgun. Before I could level it at him the gun in his hand snapped and flashed blue sparks and a crack slapped my ears like a pair of cupped hands. I lost my balance and fell backward. I heard a whizzing sound, like a zipper pulled up fast, and felt a small current of heat move by me. I felt something tug at the collar of my jacket, like it was caught on something.

As I fell back I kept the shotgun level, and when my back hit the ground I ignored the jolt that rang through me and squeezed the trigger. The gun kicked hard and instantly the smell of gunpowder was in my nose. But my aim was too high. The man ducked out of reflex but was still standing, the gun still held in his outstretched arm. Before he could regain his aim I pumped the slide fast and squeezed the trigger, this time taking aim. The gun kicked hard against my ribs and the man on the top of the bank folded and fell dead.

I scurried up to him and took the gun from his hand. I sensed confusion over at the Firebird. I was about to climb back down for cover when I saw the man's face.

I stopped and my mouth dropped open. I didn't want to believe it. I looked closer to make sure but there was no mistake. It was the man with the limp I had just killed. I remembered the last thing he had said to me. His words rang in my ears.

I slid to the bottom of the bank, stood, then flung his gun with an overhand throw as far out into the bay as I could. The water swallowed it with a thump.

I pumped a new shell into the chamber, then pulled the body down to the bottom of the bank. I knelt by the body and looked up, waiting for more. None came.

I removed as fast as I could the dead man's coat. It was a navy surplus pea coat. Every few seconds I would look to the top of the bank, waiting for someone else to show. Once his jacket was off, I removed mine and made my way into his.

I heard voices then, none that I recognized, calling from the Firebird.

"Len. Len. Len. You there?"

I took the shotgun by the grip and rested it over my shoulder like it was some kind of trophy. I climbed up over the bank and limped as fast as I could toward the Firebird. My only real fear then was that Augie would shoot me. But he didn't fire a shot. I don't know if he recognized me or was under cover and hadn't seen me or what. All was quiet except for the wind and the lapping of the waves against the shore. I kept my head down to hide my face and held the trophy up for them all to see. With each step I got closer to the Firebird, closer to them.

It was when I was five feet from them that my worries came alive in my stomach. I knew these men were looking at me. One was even telling me to hurry, calling Len's name. Theirs were, I thought then, the voices of ordinary men; there was no quality of evil to them, nothing sinister or monstrous. But they were killers, just like the man with a limp was, and I was wearing his coat and walking straight into their fold.

The minute I reached the front fender I lifted my head. I saw two men and two handguns but no faces. I stepped forward and lowered the shotgun and pressed it to the chest of the nearest man. He looked more surprised at my face than he did at the barrel pushing into his chest. I held the gun with one hand and pulled the trigger. The man crumbled. The shotgun kicked upward and I caught it in my left hand and pumped the slide, then aimed it at the other man. He was raising his pistol with the same look of surprise. I pulled the trigger and the gun kicked and the deer slug crushed his chest.

I pumped a new round into the chamber and made a sweep of the area. There was no one else there.

I stood and raised my voice to call out to Augie, but another sound filled the night, the shrieking of a girl. I looked over the roof of the Firebird and saw that Augie was out of his ditch and standing by the opening to the path. That was why he hadn't fired at me, I realized. He wasn't even in the ditch when I made my walk to the Firebird. I heard male voices speaking but could not hear a word. I looked into the woods to my right, searching out a route that might bring me to the path so I could come up behind them. But before I could make out any real option I heard Augie's voice calling my name. It filled the clearing.

"Mac. Mac, come out. Come out."

I waited for a few seconds, then stepped out from behind the cover of the Firebird.

"Come here," Augie said.

I waited a moment more, then, the shotgun still in hand, started across the clearing toward him.

The air still smelled of gunpowder. I could taste it, I could feel it on my skin. A blue cloud shifted just above the clearing, moving into the bare trees.

As I got closer to Augie I could see that someone was standing in the clearing, just fifty feet from the opening to the path. Augie was facing them, ten feet away. No one said anything. As I got closer still I began to realize that there was not one person across from Augie but two, one big, one smaller. Their shapes were all I needed to know who they were. The bigger one stood behind the smaller one, holding her, it seemed, by the scruff of her neck. I saw his outstretched hand and the .45 in it.

Augie held his distance, telling Frank to let Tina go, to leave her out of this. When I was close enough to them I saw that one of Augie's .45s was on the ground between him and Frank. I looked at his back and saw the handle of the other .45 pressing against his jacket from the inside.

I looked back at Frank and Tina.

"Frank, what do you think you're doing?" I said. Frank's .45 had been aimed at Augie, but now he turned it on me.

"Not so close, MacManus. Stop right there and put the shotgun down."

I waited, then tossed the gun aside. It landed two yards away from me, on my right-hand side, near the woods. I was maybe twenty-five feet away from Frank, too far to rush him cold. Augie was to my left and ahead of me. We were maybe ten feet apart.

I looked at Tina and said, "You should have done what I told you."

She opened her mouth to speak but Frank wouldn't let her. He pulled on the hair at the back of her neck, jerking her head back. For the first time since I've known him, Frank looked frantic. His eyes were wide, his face almost white. The hand that held the .45 wasn't all that steady.

"She came here to save her boyfriend," Frank said. "You bring out such loyalty in people, MacManus. I'll never understand why." He kicked something with his foot. It slid across the ground and came to stop near Augie's .45.

It was the .380 Ruger I had seen in Augie's safe. Tina looked at me but didn't try to say anything. There was nothing to say now. She couldn't seem to make up her mind whether she was scared or angry. The gun Frank aimed in turn at her father and me frightened her, but Frank's tugging on her hair was clearly making her mad.

Frank said, smiling, "How's your shoulder doing, Mac? Healing up nice, I hope."

I didn't say anything for a moment. I looked at his eyes and could see nothing behind them but fear. His eyes were like two small storm clouds, shifting, tumbling. His smile did little to hide what was in his heart.

"You really don't want to wear such expensive cologne when you go out killing people, Frank."

Augie took a step forward. "Let Tina go, Frank," he

said. "Let Mac go, too. This is between you and me. This is all about something that went down a long time ago."

I looked at Augie for a moment. He glanced at me out of the corner of his eye, then looked back at Frank. I waited a moment more, then did the same.

"You know I can't do that, Aug. You know I can't let you go."

"You've gone too far, Frank. You've crossed the line."

"You got yourself into this, Augie."

"You sent us there to witness a murder. What did you expect me to do?"

"I didn't expect you to stick your nose in where it didn't belong. You've always been like that, since we were kids. It always gets you into trouble, and you never learn. You never fucking learn. So don't come bitching to me."

"So you're free of all blame here, Frank?"

"I've never been free of blame in my life."

I took a step forward and said, "You know, somebody must have heard all the shots and called it in by now, Frank. The cops are probably on their way now."

Frank smiled and looked at me. He waved me back with his gun. I gave back the steps I took. Frank may have been losing his nerve for the first time in his life, but he was still Frank Gannon.

"I've taken care of that," he said. "I've instructed them not to respond to any call of gunfire on the reservation. Of course, when I said that I was thinking of the two shots in the back of your head, not all this. But they won't come, not right away, at least. We've got time to do what needs to be done."

His demeanor said just the opposite. He was almost jittery, and his eyes darted back and forth between Augie and me.

"What did you give them, Frank?" I said. "How much did it take to buy the Chief's boys? How much per man?"

"Not as much as you'd think. You'd be surprised at how cheaply most men will sell out. But, of course, you don't know anything about that, do you? Just like your dear old dad."

"What do you want, Frank?" Augie said.

"I want things nice and tidy. If I'm going to get out of this alive, I can't be bothered worrying about certain loose ends."

Augie said, "Frank, I've known you my whole life. You've pulled more than your share of shit. But what did you expect us to do? She was a sixteen-year-old girl, for Christ's sake."

"It was necessary."

"She drowned in that pond," Augie said. "Alone. The last thing she knew before she died was freezing cold and fear. She was trapped in a car, underwater. She must have been crazy with terror."

"Don't expect me to feel bad, Aug. You know as well as I how the world works."

"Why was it necessary, Frank?" I said, cutting in. Augie's eyes were on Frank now. He was coiled, ready to move. I was still too far away. "Was it a warning? Was it because Concannon found out what's buried beneath our feet?"

Augie turned his head fast and looked at me then. Though I only saw him out of the corner of my eye, I could see the shock on his face.

Frank was no less surprised. He shook his head and laughed, but it died abruptly.

"Someone's been talking to you, MacManus," he said. "I can only imagine what a scene that must have been."

"It was touching, Frank, you should have been there."

"It's easy to be cool, MacManus, when you have nothing to lose."

"This isn't cool, Frank. I'm just tired. I'm so tired I just might do something desperate."

"I wouldn't, if I were you, MacManus."

I said then to Tina in Spanish, "Do what I tell you to do when I tell you to do it."

Augie looked at me. His twenty-five years in the DEA had exposed him to a good amount of Spanish. He knew what I was saying.

"What are you doing?" Frank snapped.

I continued, still in Spanish. "When I tell you to, just let yourself become dead weight and drop. Don't worry about anything else. Augie and I will do the rest."

"That's enough of your shit, MacManus," Frank demanded.

I said to her, "Do you understand?"

She nodded. I looked at Augie, then down at the .45 under his jacket, at the small of his back. He was ready, he was primed.

"I said that's enough." Frank sneered. He aimed the .45 at me, locking his elbow. He looked from me to Augie and back several times. "Now, you've got a lot of digging to do. You'd be dead right now if you didn't. I'm sure as hell not going to do it. And I haven't gone through all this just to leave your mess out in the open for everyone to find. So let's get going, huh?"

Neither Augie or I moved. Frank watched us. There was sweat on his forehead.

"Start digging," he said.

"You're going to kill us anyway. So why should we co-operate? What are you going to do if we don't?"

"I could make things unpleasant for you both before you die."

Augie said, "What's more unpleasant than digging your own grave?"

"For one, watching your little girl suffer," Frank answered. "She's not the prettiest girl I've ever seen, but her body's pretty good. Sixteen-year-old girls are so firm. I wouldn't mind having her show me just how firm she is right here. A piece of clothing at a time."

Augie and I each took a step toward him then. Frank shook his gun in warning.

"Is that unpleasant enough for you?" Frank asked.

"Leave her out of this," Augie demanded.

"It's too late for that, don't you think?" Frank nodded

toward the ditch behind us. "There's the shovel and pick, gentlemen. I suggest you get to work."

I saw something on the path then, behind Frank, some kind of motion. It moved slowly, silently, still several feet from where the path opened into the clearing, at the point in the path where it began to zigzag. I couldn't tell what it was, it was just dark motion in darkness, but I knew that whatever it was it was clearly human.

Frank caught the shift in my line of vision, the puzzled look on my face. Just then a rustling noise came from the path, the sound of someone moving through branches.

Now a puzzled look came to Frank's face. He spun around, keeping Tina in front of him, and raised his .45 and fired blindly into the dark path. He got off two fast shots.

That's when I called to Tina and told her in Spanish to move, and when Augie and I began our charge.

Tina let her knees buckle and dropped, but not before Frank spun around to face us again. He flung Tina toward Augie and raised his .45, leveling it at her. There was nothing I could do, there was too much ground to cover between me and them. As I charged I saw Augie snatch Tina with his left arm and instantly pull her into him, into a one-arm bear hug. Then faster than I thought he was capable of moving he spun on his heels, pulling Tina with him. He turned his back to Frank, putting himself directly between Frank and Tina. Augie held her close to him, bending slightly at the waist, as if he were trying to surround her with his body. The instant he had grabbed hold of Tina he began to reach back for the .45 under his jacket. He began to pull it clear of his belt and turn his head back to look at Frank. He was about to raise the gun and take aim when Frank fired one round, then another, point blank.

My heart came to a crash in my chest.

These shots slapped my ears and left the high, shrill ringing of a tuning fork in them. I was still out of reach when the first bullet caught Augie in the left kidney. I cried out but I don't remember what I said. I could see the side of Augie's face, I could see him wince. He stood there with Tina held close in front of him, still shielding her. He continued to turn his head and raise his .45 toward Frank. That was when the second round struck him in the dead center of his back.

I called out again and continued my charge forward. I wasn't covering ground fast enough. I watched, helpless, as Augie arched his back. He turned his head and we were looking at each other, me running for Frank, he holding his daughter. I saw his face and he saw mine. Augie pitched forward then, as if he were drunk, and fell, driving Tina to the ground with his mass. He landed on top of her and covered the length of her easily, like a huge blanket. Frank had no clear shot of her. Even in death Augie protected her.

My heart now turned hot in my chest. I watched as Frank took several wide strides forward and fired several times into Augie's lifeless body as he went. I came upon Frank quick and flew into him hard. But he barely moved. I grabbed his gun hand and went for a wrist lock and disarm, but he was faster and stronger than I was now. As we struggled for control of the .45, he let go with his left hand and landed two hooks into my right side. I nearly blacked out from the pain. I felt my legs wobble beneath me. While I was stunned, he grabbed hold of the collar of my jacket and spun like a discus thrower. He let go and whipped me back almost to where I had come from. I landed hard on my stomach. I rolled over onto my back. I lifted my head and looked for Frank, and that was when I saw Eddie moving out of the dark path.

He came running into the clearing on his hobbled legs, running as fast as he could, his eyes fixed on Frank. Frank was walking toward me then on long, determined strides, unaware of Eddie's approach behind him. Before I knew it Frank was standing over me and aiming his .45 point blank at my forehead. He adjusted his grip, then curled his finger around the trigger.

Frank said, "Say hello to your father for me."

Something hit Frank in the center of his back then. It hit with a thud, knocking him forward a step. He arched his back and yelled, "Fuck." He turned and aimed the .45 at Eddie, who flung another rock as he continued to rush toward him. This rock just missed Frank's head. As he continued forward Eddie looked straight into the gun but didn't blink.

I pulled myself up into a seated position then, ignoring the pain, and lunged forward and grabbed Frank around the legs. I was going for a takedown but Frank spread his legs, widening his base, breaking the hug I had around his knees. Then I felt the butt of the .45 slam into the top of my head. It hit a second time, and then once more. I fell onto my back, and then Frank was over me again. He aimed the .45 at my head again.

But he had no time to savor this hate. I watched as Frank pointed the .45 at my left eye. His finger curled around the trigger.

A gunshot ruptured the night then. I flinched sharply. But it wasn't Frank's gun that had gone off.

He dropped his gun hand to his side but held on to the piece. Then he slowly turned and faced the direction from which the gunshot had come.

I looked and saw Tina, standing in a shooter's stance, holding her father's .45 with two hands. It looked huge in her grip. She squeezed off a second shot. It hit Frank in the shoulder. The gun kicked high in her hand but she barely blinked. When Frank didn't fall she squeezed off another, this one hitting him in the collarbone. His .45 fired straight down into the ground. Tina fired again, this one hitting him dead center in the chest. Frank staggered several feet but still didn't look ready to fall.

I saw then that Eddie was still running full out on his hobbled legs toward Frank, twenty feet and closing. It was a collision course. Frank raised his right arm and pointed his .45 in Tina's direction. She fired again. This one split his gut, but Frank didn't move, his arm didn't drop. With everything he had left he took aim on Tina.

I sat up again and pulled myself to my knees and leapt forward with my right arm outstretched. I landed hard on my stomach and hooked my hand around Frank's ankle. He was wobbling but still had his .45 up, trying to put Tina in his sights. Just as I hooked Frank's ankle, Eddie closed what remained of the distance and sacked Frank from behind with a flying tackle. The instant Eddie hit I pulled on Frank's ankle, sweeping his foot out from under him. Frank flew a few feet, then landed on the ground with a thud.

Eddie crashed down into me, his momentum only slightly broken by his collision with Frank. He was a heavy rainstorm of elbows and knees. He rolled off me quick and I hacked on the pain and looked for Tina.

She was standing over Frank now, her gun hand hanging at her side. She stepped on Frank's gun hand and looked down at his face. Eddie took my arm and helped me to my feet.

Tina had no expression on her face. Even her body language seemed blank. I opened my mouth to say something to her but it was too late. She aimed her father's gun at Frank's head and pulled off three shots without flinching. Eddie and I did nothing but watch. There was nothing we could do.

When it was done I limped over to Tina. She seemed

frozen. I looked at her, but she didn't turn to look back at me. I reached down and eased the .45 from her small hand. I let it drop to the ground, then touched her shoulder.

Tina looked over at her father's body. He was face-down on the ground. She walked to him and knelt down beside him. She looked at him and touched his head with a trembling hand. I waited for her to cry but no tears came.

Eddie took a few steps forward and looked down at Augie's body. He shook his head from side to side.

"We have to get out of here, Mac," he said. "We can't be anywhere near here when it all hits the fan."

I knew he was right, but I didn't like the idea of leaving Augie there, surrounded by these kinds of men. But there is never any telling which way shit will fall in this town. I knew this.

I went to Tina and stood beside her. She didn't look up at me.

"We have to go, Tina," I said to her. "We have to leave Augie here and we have to go. This is too much trouble to explain. We have to go. We have to go now."

I looked at Eddie and nodded toward Augie's .45, the one Tina had used to kill Frank. He knew what I meant and picked it up by the trigger guard. Then he picked up the .380, the other .45, and the shotgun I had used. He gathered them all together and left us and headed down to the shore of the bay. Once there he threw them one at a time into the water. I was surprised by what a good arm he had, by how far out over the dark water he flung them.

I knelt down and put my arm around Tina.

"It's just us now," I said. "If they find us here, we won't even have that. I won't ever leave you, I promise. I will always protect you. You'll always be with me. You and I, we're all we have. Do you understand?"

She turned and looked at me. There were tears hanging in her eyes. I didn't say anything more. That was all I had to say. She looked at me for a long time, then suddenly flung both her arms around my neck and clamped on to me tight.

I laid my hands on her back. It was the first time I held her since Tommy Miller had tried to rape her, when she clung to my side as I walked her from the back of the Southampton Library to my car.

Tina and I stayed like that for a moment, and then I said, "We have to go." I got her to her feet. We took one last look at Augie, and when we turned away from him, Eddie was standing just a few feet away.

He was looking out over the clearing. There was still gun smoke churning in the cold air. The wind seemed to somehow have stopped, as if it had been chased away from this place along with so much life. The dark clearing seemed to occupy Eddie for a long time. When he finally turned and looked back at me, he was clearly awestruck.

"Jesus Christ," he said softly. "It looks like a goddamn war."

Seven

I said nothing to Tina or Eddie about Frank Gannon's private graveyard. It seemed to me for the best that they didn't know. The events of that night in the clearing were enough to bear as it was, and anyway it had nothing to do with them. Three days after Augie's military funeral in a veteran's cemetery in Riverhead, the yellow police tape surrounding the clearing was taken down, and the investigation, or what passed for an investigation, was over. A detective came to the Hansom House one afternoon to interview Tina, but his questions were mostly formalities and he left after ten minutes. I stood by the door and watched him closely as he sat and spoke with her and got the impression they thought her father and Frank were killed by drug dealers, that they were working together. I didn't know if they knew the truth and that was just their cover story, something Frank's men came up with for the press, or if they actually believed it themselves. As the cop left his eyes met mine, and he nodded without a word.

Tina stayed with me for a week after the funeral. We spent every moment together but barely spoke. At night she slept in my bed while I slept on the couch. Once she woke up an hour before dawn crying and we sat up at my kitchen table and drank cold tea and said nothing. I gradually came to see that the nonsense between us was over. Augie's absence had done something to us, made somehow our presence in each other's lives much more important, much more vital.

Not long after that night in the clearing, while Tina was at Lizzie's house, James Curry paid me an unannounced visit at the Hansom House. He arrived at my door one stark evening, and after a moment of staring at him I stepped aside to let him in. He was carrying a briefcase and was dressed in jeans, a shirt, and a black leather coat lined with dark fur. After he entered I took a look down the dim hallway to be certain that no one else was with him. Then I closed my door and folded my arms across my chest and leaned against the door frame and waited.

Curry went to my couch and laid the briefcase on its arm. Outside was a silent and motionless dark. It was more frozen void of space than night. I looked at the side of Curry's face as he opened his briefcase.

"I didn't come at a bad time, did I?" he said.

I waited a while, hearing what he said, dealing with the feelings his choice of words brought up in me, the sense of having come somehow full circle. "What do you want, Curry?"

He withdrew a folder from his briefcase and stood up straight and turned to face me. There was bulk to the folder. My eyes lingered on it, then back to his face.

"I don't have much time," he began. "So excuse me if I seem in a hurry." His attitude was somehow both denim casual and all business. "What I like about working with you the most, Mac, is you don't care. You don't want to get involved. You're no hero, no crusader. You don't care who gets rich or goes broke. You couldn't be bothered. So I know that you'll keep to yourself things that you may have heard or may have learned along the way. None of this has anything to do with you, and you have the smarts to stay out of things that don't have anything to do with you. Do you understand me so far?"

I said nothing, just looked at him.

"Thanks to you, Mac, I'm about to become a very rich man."

"I thought you were already rich."

"You can always be richer. Anyway, the deal is close to going through."

"What deal?"

He looked at me. "The Shinnecock Indian Reservation. It's my deal. I'm buying it."

"What?"

"It's a deal that benefits everyone. It will release the

Shinnecock from four hundred years of poverty and significantly increase land values around here, once I've put
my finishing touches on it."

I said nothing.

"Why'd I think you would have figured all this out by
now?"

"You hired me to find Amy's killer."

"I already knew who that was. I hired you to stop
Frank."

"What are you talking about?"

"Your relationship with Frank isn't exactly a big secret
around town. He was close to fucking up the whole deal.
I knew if anyone could bring him down, you could. I
thought maybe if you got in his way that's exactly what
would happen. You have nothing to lose, Mac, that's the
beautiful thing about you. That's what makes you so
dangerous. That's why, in a dogfight between Frank Gannon and you, I'd put my money on you. And, in effect,
that's just what I did."

"Why did Frank kill Amy?"

"The town hired Concannon to assess the ecological
impact of my plans for the land. Environmentalists
wanted the deal killed. They're worried about erosion
and coastline construction and bullshit like that. So I put
Concannon on my payroll. He was more than eager.
When he found the bones, he called me. The next day
Frank Gannon appeared at my house. He knew all about
my conversation with Concannon. He had put a tap on
Concannon's phone the day the town hired him. He

wanted to know what I planned on doing with the information. I told him I had no interest in going to the cops or FBI. Do you think people would be lining up to buy luxury condos on land that had once been full of shallow graves?"

"So you struck a deal?"

"We couldn't do anything till I owned the land. Then we could move the bodies and no one would know. We'd hire a crew to work by hand at night, in secret."

"So why did Frank go nuts?"

"Frank gave a map to Concannon, so we could mark all the graves and waste little time once the deal went through. Amy stole the map from Concannon and hid it."

"Why?"

"Concannon told her what we were up to, the idiot. Amy wanted to kill the deal. She liked to call herself an environmentalist, but really she just liked to do anything she could to hurt me. She'd join any group opposed to my land deals and fund them with money she stole from me. She started up with Concannon just to hurt me. She did everything a woman could to influence him and sway him against me."

"She must have been very angry with you to go that far."

"She hated my guts."

"So Frank killed her to shut her up and ransacked her room to get back the map," I said.

"He panicked. He wanted everyone who knew anything about the bones dead."

"Including you?"

"I don't think he'd dare try to kill me."

"Because you're rich?"

"Because I'd squash him like a bug."

Curry took a step toward me. "I want the Shinnecock land deal to go through and you want to live your life and not give a shit about what goes on around you. I'm prepared to give you what you want, which is to be left alone, and all you have to do is do what you do best. Mind your own business and keep your mouth shut. We're the only two people alive who know about Frank Gannon's private little graveyard. I wake up one morning and find that clearing crawling with FBI agents, well, then neither of us gets what we want, if you know what I mean. I make one phone call, and before the end of the day you're dead and buried where no one will ever find you. Do you understand?"

I said nothing, just looked at him.

"All I'm asking is for you to be yourself. That's all. It has nothing to do with you. All I'm asking you to do is remember this."

The dim lights in my living room created a pale pocket of yellow light. Curry and I were the only ones standing in it. I wondered then how a half-dozen or so people could be killed and nothing really change all that much. The world was still the world.

"You see," Curry began, "the trick, Mac, is finding a man's price." He held up the folder and then tossed it onto my couch.

I looked at it and waited for a while before I said, "I don't want your money."

"It's not for your silence. We had a deal, remember. I honor my deals."

"You hired me to find your daughter's killer."

"I hired you to bring Frank Gannon down, and you did. Take the money. I insist." He gestured toward the folder with his head. "It's a check for the other ten grand I promised, plus a stocks fund. It's ten grand and it's in a Thornburg fund. Leave it be, and in twenty years it could be a million dollars. A little something for your future."

I didn't make a move toward the folder. After a moment Curry picked up his briefcase and snapped it closed and stood before me, ready to go.

"I know all about you, Mac. I know about what that asshole Van Deusen put you through. I know that he thought he owned you and that you thought he wouldn't ever let you go. You were right, he wouldn't. He'd invested quite a bit in you, seeing to it you learned all those languages you know, arranging all that hand-to-hand combat training, making you his little bodyguard. He'd never walk away from that kind of investment. Plus, you were plenty scared of him, too, weren't you? That meant a lot to him. It's okay, we were all scared of him. But it was a good thing for you that that boating accident just happened to come along when it did, though, don't you think? Damn good thing. I don't know, maybe it was an accident, maybe it wasn't. Maybe it was a little of both.

"Maybe I'm right in thinking what I think about what happened that day, and that's why you live the way you do. Maybe you think this shitty little life you live is all you deserve. And maybe it eats away at you. Maybe you're trying to pay your debt in your own way. But let me tell you one thing I do know for certain. You're no different from me, or from Frank Gannon, for that matter, Mac. So don't fool yourself.

"You did whatever it was you did that day to get out alive. And because of that you now know, deep down in your heart, that you're capable of anything, just like the rest of us motherfuckers you hate. That's why Frank Gannon wanted you around, that's why he wanted you on his payroll. You were just like him. And that's why I want you around. Because you're just like me."

I looked at him and said nothing. My heart pounded as hard as it pounded that long-ago day out of Sag Harbor, the day the sailboat went down and I made my choice.

"Maybe we'll work again sometime," Curry said.

He moved past me then. I didn't look at him. I heard him close the door behind him and walk down the hall. I listened till he was down both flights of stairs, then picked up the folder and held it for a moment before tossing it onto my coffee table. I left it there and went into my bedroom and sat on the edge of my bed in the dark and looked out the window.

The folder lay unopened on my coffee table for three days. I tried to forget that it existed but I could see it from almost every point in my apartment. I knew it was just numbers on paper, but it connected me to some-

thing that I wanted to be over and done with and far behind me.

On the fourth morning after my visit from Curry I
got up, opened the folder, and pulled out the cover sheet.
On the letterhead was the broker's contact information.
I took it and went to my phone and dialed. A woman answered, and I told her my name and who I wanted. Almost immediately a deep and cheerful male voice came
on the line.

"Mr. MacManus, good morning. This is Gordon
Banks. How can I help you?"

"I have a question about the Thornburg stock fund
James Curry set up for me," I said. "Could I have it put
in someone else's name?"

"Of course."

"I would like to do this anonymously, if possible."

"I can take care of everything for you."

"I also have two checks for ten thousand dollars. I'd
like it all to go to the same person."

"Very well. To whom would you want this to be transferred?"

I went to my window and looked down on the train
station. A woman waited for the 9:33 eastbound. There
was no one else on the platform. She was wearing jeans
and a man's overcoat and running shoes. Sitting at her
feet, like a pet, was a large suitcase. Her hair was dark
brown and thick and shoulder length, like Catherine's
had been the day she left for New York.

"Mr. MacManus?"

"Yes."

"I asked to whom did you want these funds to be transferred."

"His name is Tommy Miller," I said. "Tommy Miller."

"A relative of yours?"

I waited a moment, watching the woman waiting on the platform. She had a fifteen-minute wait for her train. I knew I would stand there and watch her till she got aboard.

"What?"

"I said, is he a relative of yours?"

Somewhere on Elm Street someone sounded a car horn. I heard silence from the other end of the phone.

"Yeah," I said. "In a way, yeah."

Winter was coming, and days passed faster than I could keep track of, or even cared to. During the first week of December I found a bank to lend me the money to buy a secondhand taxi from a cab company in the city and went into business with Eddie. We formed a cab and car service, and I drove six days a week, twelve hours a day, and in my first week I took home fifteen hundred dollars. I made four runs to JFK in three days at a hundred and fifty dollars a pop. Tina put the house on Little Neck Road up for sale and left my apartment over the Hansom House and moved into Lizzie's parents' house across town. I got her to see that she needed a family and that I couldn't be enough for her. I would, as Augie's will specified, be her legal guardian, as well as the trustee of the nearly quarter of a million dollars his life insurance paid to her, until she reached the age of eighteen. As close as we were, and as much as we understood each other now, she could not live with me under the same roof. Our town was just too small for that kind of thing, and anyway what kind of life was this for a girl like her?

Less than a week before Christmas I ran into Gale in the grocery store in town. She was wearing a dark wool coat over her nurse's scrubs. Her cheeks were red from the cold and by her eyes I could tell she was tired. She seemed tense and had very little makeup on.

We left the store and went to a café on the corner of Nugent and Main for coffee. We got service from the woman behind the counter and then picked a table by the window. The first thing Gale asked me when we sat down was how my shoulder was.

I shrugged. "It's fine. I took the stitches out myself. Thank my doctor for me."

She said nothing to that. She held her cup of coffee in both hands for the warmth. She looked out the window for a while, at nothing in particular, I guessed, before she finally spoke.

"I was kind of hoping I would never see you again."

"I'm sorry I put you on the spot like that."

"No, it was okay. I thought of calling you a hundred times, to see if you were okay. But I figured if something happened I would have read about it in the paper, that or Eddie would have told me. I figure I would have heard somehow." She looked at me. "I'm sorry about Augie. I wanted to go to the funeral."

"Why didn't you?"

She looked down. "I just didn't think it was a good idea." She wouldn't look at me. "How's Eddie?"

"Eddie's fine."

"I hear the Chief is in a real fight for his life, career-wise. He's firing cops left and right, trying to look good for the FBI. I guess if anybody can squirm his way out of this kind of trouble it's him, right?"

I looked at her for a moment, then said, "What's wrong, Gale?"

She shrugged. It took her a while before she spoke. "There's nothing really wrong, Mac. Who you are and what you do, they're the same thing. With you, what you see is what you get, and for some reason I just can't stop thinking of that."

She glanced out the window at the people passing on the sidewalk and said, "So I seem to have a problem. And I don't know exactly what to do about it."

I wasn't sure what to say to her, so I said nothing. I looked at her for a long time. I thought of those long-ago nights in the hospital, when she was all I knew, when her presence was all I hoped for. Then I thought of her in her blue turtleneck and lavender panties, of her lying beside me.

I wanted to reach out and touch her hand but didn't. Finally I nodded my head once and said, "I'm not going anywhere, Gale. I'm not going anywhere."

She smiled at that. We sat there and drank our coffee and said nothing. She reached across the table and took my hand for a minute.

The next afternoon I went to the house on Little Neck Road to help Tina move what was left into storage. I found her in the basement, surrounded by boxes and boxes of her father's things. She was sitting cross-legged on a fragment of rug on the cement floor, going through papers. Around her lay envelope after envelope of surveillance photographs and her father's notebooks. Beside her right knee was an old photograph album. It seemed older than I.

Tina hadn't heard me come down the stairs and looked when I said her name.

"Mac," she said.

"What are you doing?"

"I've been looking through Augie's notebooks and junk. He kept a record of everything."

"He was a thorough man."

"Yeah, that's putting it mildly."

"I was trying to figure out what to make for din—"

"Did you know that he'd been spying on Frank since we moved out here? Over something that happened a long time ago, as far as I can tell. It almost seems that's why we moved out here. He has notes from conversations between him and the Chief about it. I'm beginning to think that Augie went to work for Frank just to get closer to him, to find something out."

"What?"

"I don't know."

"There isn't anything in there by any chance about why he didn't tell me that he knew my father?"

"No. I'm sorry. You know, I've been meaning to tell you, he didn't stay mad at you long, Mac. Last Thanksgiving, I mean. And I don't think he was really mad. I think he was more scared than anything else."

I paused, then nodded. "We should get started," I said. "There's a lot to do." I turned toward the stairs. When she spoke I turned back to her.

"Wait. C'mere. I want you to see something."

"What?"

"Something I found mixed in with some surveillance photos."

I walked over and stood behind her, looking over her shoulder. She held up a faded black-and-white photograph of four men. A crease ran down the middle of it. Tina pointed to one of the two men in the center.

"That's Augie," she said. She sounded happy, almost proud.

My interest piqued, I knelt, leaning in close for a better look. I smiled at the sight of his young, still-forming face. He looked like an early model of himself. "You're right, it is," I said.

All the men in that photo were young, not yet in their twenties. They wore chinos and cloth jackets and stupid grins. They could have been Jack Kerouac and his boys. Tina pointed to one with longish hair on the right flank of their line.

"Any idea who that is?"

I leaned in even closer. I laughed once. "Jesus, that's the Chief," I said.

"No."

"Yeah. Look."

She brought the photograph closer to her face. "Oh my God. The hair." She pointed to the man at the left flank. "So could this be Frank?"

I looked closer still. "Yeah, I think it is."

Then she pointed to the man between Augie and Frank. "So then who's this?"

I looked at the face and my smile faded.

"That's my father."

Tina turned to look at me. "You're kidding."

I shook my head as casually as I could. "No."

She looked back at the photograph. "My God, Mac. When was this taken, I wonder?"

"Nineteen sixty-five, maybe sixty-six."

"How can you tell?"

"Augie joined the marines in sixty-seven. He doesn't exactly look like a marine yet, does he?"

"No." She ran her fingers over the surface of the photograph. "They were so young."

"They're all so thin. They're all as much boys as they are men."

"Do you have a photo of your father?"

"No."

She looked over her shoulder again and held it out for me. "Take it," she said.

"It's yours, Tina. It belonged to Augie."

"I've got other pictures of him. Tons. Take it. I want you to have it, if you want it."

I hesitated, as if taking it would commit me to something. Then I took it from her hand and looked at it closely.

I hadn't seen my father's face since I was seven. He was smiling widely in the photo, laughing wildly. They all were, their eyes focused on something behind the camera. They were standing shoulder to shoulder, holding short-necked bottles of Schaffer beer, arms around each other, making a kind of chain of men. They were standing on a dirt road, and behind them were spring trees.

When I got back to the Hansom House I placed the photograph in the top drawer of the bureau in my living room, where I used to keep my Spyderco knife. I laid the photo next to the one of Catherine. These were the only two photographs I owned. As the night went on I became more and more aware of the bar buzzing two floors below me. It felt at times like the engine of a ship humming up through the decks.

That night I couldn't sleep. Sounds for the first time in my life kept me awake. I could hear everything from every corner of the Hansom House, from basement to attic.

I got out of bed and sat in my chair and looked out my window. I watched the night bleed pale. In my mind I kept seeing that photograph of the four of them. Eventually I got up and took the photo out of the bureau drawer and held it again. I kept looking at Augie's face, nothing else, just his face, and it wasn't long before I knew what I had to do.

I went down the two flights of stairs to the bar and closed the door of the old-fashioned phone booth behind me and opened the phone book. I didn't care about James Curry anymore, about our deal, about the reservation, about who killed his girl and why. I didn't care what he thought he knew about me, about the secret I keep. I didn't care about anything except this truth: Men like Augie Hartsell don't die so rich men can get richer. There was no way I was going to let that happen.

I looked up the number of the local branch of the FBI and dropped two quarters and dialed. It was early but I was connected to an agent and told her just what to look for and where to look for it. Then hung up and went back upstairs to my apartment. My heart was pounding. I didn't give a damn about Curry now, or his land deal. I didn't care about anything, just like he wanted me to.

A few days before Christmas I was coming back from JFK when Angel called me on the dispatch and told me that Eddie wanted to see me. I told her I was a half hour away. I heard nothing more for a minute, and then her voice came over the speaker again. "He'll meet you at Road D in a half hour," she said.

That didn't seem right to me for some reason. I had a half hour to think about it. I did nothing else. I felt curious and guarded when I made the turn off Dune Road onto the short dead end called Road D. Eddie's old repainted Checker was the only other car in the lot. I parked beside it. He wasn't behind the wheel. I got out, looked around, then headed between the dunes to the beach. It was the only place he could be.

When I spotted him, he was a hundred yards away, at the shoreline, facing the ocean. When I finally reached him I said, "Eddie, what's up?"

He turned his head to look at me but kept his body facing the ocean. The ocean looked like melted steel just before it hardened.

Eddie looked at my denim jacket. I had sewn the slice in the left sleeve closed and had scrubbed out most of the blood. It was by my standards presentable, no worse off looking than I was.

"You need a winter coat," he observed.

"I think Tina got me one for Christmas."

He was looking out over the ocean again. I studied the side of his wrinkled, black face. He chewed on his unlit cigar pensively.

"What's going on, Eddie?" I said.

"I need to talk to you, Mac."

"What about?"

"There's something you should know."

"What?"

"I just heard it myself an hour ago. I don't think too many people know yet."

"Know what?"

"It's about Frank and—"

"And what?"

Eddie said nothing. He couldn't look at me. He stared at the waves rolling in. The tide was moving out, somewhere between high and low.

"Frank and what, Eddie?"

He still didn't say anything.

"Eddie."

He turned his head and looked at me then. He had tears in his already glassy eyes.

"You heard about the FBI finding bodies in that clearing on the reservation?"

"Yeah."

"In the last three days they've found eight, and they're still looking."

I shrugged, as if to assert that it had nothing to do with me now. "Okay."

"They've been running checks, trying to identify them, trying to find out who they were back when they were alive. They had four of the eight identified, but just a little while ago they figured out who the fifth was. According to the FBI this body had been buried there longer than any of the others they've found so far. They're thinking that it might be the first body that had been buried there, the first victim. That's their word, 'victim.' They think that body has been in the ground for twenty-five years."

The wind moved past my ears. I waited for more from Eddie, uncertain still what this had to do with me.

"I'm sorry, Mac, I don't know how to tell you this."

"Tell me what, Eddie?"

"Everything's going so good for you now. But that's when it hits us, right?"

"Eddie. Eddie. Jesus. What is it you can't tell me?"

Tears sprang from his eyes and wormed their way down the creases in his skin.

"The body they just identified was—"

"It was what, Eddie?"

He looked at me square then.

"It was what, Eddie?"

He said something then that at first sounded to me like some kind of foreign language. It had no effect on me that I was aware of. But then the words arranged themselves into English in my brain and I took all of it, all it meant and all it was, right between the eyes.

A wave crashed and hissed. I heard birds, seagulls or egrets. It hit me hard, and I never saw it coming.

"It was your father, Mac," Eddie had said. "It was your father."

Tomorrow is Christmas. It is clearly winter now. The trees are all bare and the ground and everything in it is frozen hard. I do little. Tina comes by with things and is sweet. There is suddenly so much silence in my life. There is so much time to think about all the cripples: Augie, Tommy Miller, Eddie, the man with the limp, the Chief, me, even Tina. So many pieces lost. It seems now finally done, all of it, though I'm not sure what to make of that. But I do know now that this didn't start with Amy Curry dying in a freezing pond. It didn't start when Tommy Miller and his friends tried to rape Tina. This all started some thirty years ago, when Frank caved in my father's skull with a crowbar and buried him and the murder weapon in that clearing by the bay on the Shinnecock Indian Reservation.

I hear they know all kinds of things, all kinds of remarkable details, that forensics is an amazing science. But I don't really care about that. I know all I need to know. My father is dead, and has been most of my life. He is no longer just missing, and there is no need to wonder any longer just why it was he left and why he couldn't take me with him. I realize that he has been out here all along, always nearby—under my feet as I played in that clearing as a boy, a mile from Augie's home, a mile from the college where I met Catherine, waiting in a shallow grave just south of Montauk Highway, just waiting for the day he would be found.

Soon Tina will arrive and ask if I want anything. I seldom eat or drink. I just sit here in this chair by this window and look at the photograph Tina has given me of four smiling friends, of my four fathers, and know that I am what I am because of them and that is all there is to it. They each, Frank, the Chief, Augie, and my father, have in one way or another made me, shaped me into what I am. I cannot fight it any longer. I know my place in this town for the first time in my life. I needn't hide from it anymore. I sit now in my rooms and wait, wait for my next chance meeting with Gale, wait for some kind of move from the Chief, wait for Curry to take his revenge against me, and I know now for once just what I am.

I am Declan MacManus, and tomorrow is Christmas, and what I hope for is a good winter coat all my own.

If you enjoyed *The Bone Orchard*,
turn the page for an exciting
preview of D. Daniel Judson's
new Declan MacManus novel,
coming soon from Bantam

It wasn't long before the door to the bar opened. We both sat up and watched as a man stepped out onto the sidewalk and stood under the small awning over the door. He was immediately followed by another.

Even across this distance and through the rain I could tell that the one who had exited the bar first was Vogler. The second man out had black hair that hung halfway down his back. Neither of them was a terribly big man. They stood face-to-face and talked.

"That's him," Augie said. He reached down and turned the ignition. The starter motor cranked twice, then the engine caught with a burst of vapor tumbling down the dual exhaust below the rusted-out floorboards.

Augie gripped the steering wheel with his left hand and rested his right hand over the knob of the gear shift.

I could see it shake from the vibrations of the motor. He sat completely still and waited, watching through the driver's door window the scene at the end of the block.

"Someone's not happy."

The kid, Vogler, and the guy with the long black hair were going at it, arguing and yelling at each other, their faces just inches apart. Vogler pointed his finger in the second guy's face, but the second guy swatted it away and pointed back, only at Vogler's chest. He jabbed Vogler hard, and Vogler just took it. He stopped yelling and listened to whatever it was the second guy was telling him. After a while Vogler turned and stepped out into the street. The second guy yelled at him as he went, but Vogler just kept going without looking back. He crossed the rain-swept street and got into an old Dodge Rambler. The lights came on and I heard the sound of its motor start. It barely stood out against the rain. The reverse lights came on, and then the Rambler backed out onto Main Street.

Augie flipped on his headlights and shifted into reverse. He waited till the Rambler was moving forward, then let out the clutch and backed us away from the curb. He shifted into first and we moved slowly forward. I listened to the transmission whine.

But before Augie could shift into second gear an old black Caddy whipped around the corner, turning from Bay Street onto Main, skidding to a sudden stop in front of the Rambler, cutting it off. It and the Caddy formed a perfect T shape, the driver's door of the Caddy facing the windshield of the Rambler. The instant the Rambler stopped, Augie pushed in the clutch and down on the brake pedal. His truck slowed, twenty-five feet from the other two vehicles at the end of Main.

The brake lights of the Rambler reflecting off the rainy street looked to me like an illustration of fire. I sensed something and my stomach tightened. Just seconds after the near collision the driver's door window of the Caddy rolled down far enough for a hand to extend out. Augie and I instantly saw the gun it held, but there was nothing we could do.

Six shots, one right after the other, punched holes in the Rambler's windshield. The first shot sent a jolt through me. My muscles flexed hard. The same jolt tore through me with each successive shot. When it was done, when the revolver was empty and the Caddy began to back away, its tires slipping on the wet pavement, I said, "Jesus," reached for the door handle and stepped down to the street, into a good inch of water. I heard Augie call my name, but I ignored him and started toward the Rambler in an all-out run.

The Caddy backed onto Bay Street, the driver cutting the wheel sharply. It spun around, then paused long enough for the driver to shift into drive before it sped forward, heading toward the bridge to North Haven.

I looked for a license plate but the Caddy was moving too fast. The scratches on my face stung in the rain and I felt my legs hollow a little from fear.

By the time I reached the Rambler the driver's door had swung open and Vogler had slumped out from behind the wheel and was lying on the street. The water around his head was dark with blood. The darkness was spreading out fast.

I came to a stop and crouched to see his face. I had to lean around him to do so, and my chest touched his shoulder. His body was motionless, his limbs fallen to rest at odd angles. One bullet had creased his temple, the other had shattered his cheekbone. Part of his right ear was missing. There was another bullet wound in his chest, and I could hear air being sucked through it. I saw then that his eyes were open, searching. His eyes met mine and there was cognition. There were bits of shattered windshield glass in his wounds. He tried to move his mouth but the nerve damage to his face was so severe, his jaw wouldn't work.

I took off my denim jacket and laid it over his torso. He was on his side. I could see that the bullet had entered his chest and exited through his back, just below his left shoulder blade. I knew enough to guess that he would probably be dead before an ambulance could get to him. The nearest hospital was in Southampton, twenty miles away. The nearest ambulance station was only a little over a mile from here, but in his condition it might as well have been a hundred.

Still, I lifted my head and looked toward the entrance to The Dead Horse, where a handful of people had collected, among them the kid with the long black hair, the one Vogler had been arguing with.

"Call an ambulance," I yelled. The rain was a steady

peal in my ears, as heavy as a waterfall. My voice barely cut through it.

Nobody moved at first; they all just stood there and stared at me. I glanced through the storefront window and saw that the bartender was on the phone, her eyes fixed on Vogler and me. Gurgling sounds added to the sucking sound coming from his chest wound. I looked down at him. His eyes were fixed on me, but they were becoming glassy and dimming. Any minute they would roll back in their sockets and his lids would half close and the look of dulled surprise worn by every corpse I have ever seen will show itself on his face.

I said, "Hang on," but I knew he couldn't hear me. He was bleeding out of this world, and quickly. I felt his neck for a pulse, but what I found was more of a flicker interrupted by long stretches of nothing.

I looked back up at the people gathered outside The Dead Horse. They continued to stand there dumbfounded, watching me. After a moment, the guy with the long black hair turned away and returned inside the bar. He casually removed a cell phone from his belt, opened it, pressed two buttons, then brought the phone to his face.

I looked back at the people outside the bar and called, "Somebody get a blanket." But before anyone could move, Augie's ancient pickup truck skidded to a stop behind me. I turned and saw that the passenger door was open and that Augie was leaning across the seat, holding the door so it wouldn't kick back and shut. He waved me in.

"C'mon, let's go."

I looked back down at the kid. His eyes were vacant. There was no one behind them now.

I heard from behind me, "C'mon, Mac, let's go."

I stood and looked once more at the crowd, then looked down at Vogler's body again before turning and climbing up into the passenger seat of Augie Hartsell's pickup.

We were in motion before I could close the door. I fastened my seat belt as we steered through the stop sign and around the corner. Augie gunned it through to fourth gear as we crossed the bridge and went after the black Caddy.

I sensed him glance at me once we hit the straightaway of Long Beach Road. I felt his stare for a moment but didn't look at him. I kept my eyes fixed straight ahead, looking for the Caddy's taillights on the dark and rainy road.

To our right was Great Peconic Bay, though it was hard to make out in all this rain and dark. It seemed to me like a void in the night, more an absence than a presence. If I wasn't a local I might not have even known it was there. It was hard right then to see things for what they were.

A few hundred feet ahead on the narrow beach road the distinctive rear lights of the Caddy suddenly appeared. Augie flattened the accelerator, and together we raced toward violence.

We pulled in tight behind the speeding Caddy on Noyac Road and followed it closely along the rim of the bay. As far as I could see there was only the driver. Augie had the truck in fourth gear, the engine whining. I looked at the rear license plate but it was blacked out with tape. Several times during that first minute Augie nearly lost control in one of the many sharp and sudden corners in the road. But he always caught it and pulled us out right away. He looked intense, wedged in behind the wheel, and it wasn't long into this confusion before he reached back and removed his .45 from the holster on his belt and laid it on the seat between us. I looked at it but didn't touch it. He returned his hand to the steering wheel, his eyes fixed on the road ahead. His left foot hovered over the clutch, his right holding the gas pedal to the floor. All I could do was hang on to the frayed door strap with my right hand and grip the dashboard with my left and trust in Augie's skills.

He kept the nose of his truck right there on the tail of the Caddy for several miles, till Noyac Road veered away from the bay and followed a wavering line through the woods. We passed through middle-class neighborhoods, during which I kept an eye out for cars pulling out of driveways and late-night joggers. Then the neighborhoods gave way and we entered a long stretch of barren woods. Here the streets were unlit and sharp corners came up unannounced. The driver of the Caddy was having as difficult a time as Augie keeping his vehicle on the road. At one point it fishtailed sharply and looked about to spin out of control. Augie hit the brakes and backed off so the truck didn't clip the swerving Caddy. But it regained control soon enough and continued on, and once it did Augie pushed the accelerator down to the floorboard again and we surged forward and right back on the Caddy's tail.

The speed limit was thirty-five and we were easily doing eighty, sometimes more in brief stretches of straight road. Several times Augie tried to get around the Caddy, but the driver always cut him off. We were only a few miles from the village of North Sea. Beyond that was the town of Southampton. All we needed was to drive the Caddy into either village, where it wouldn't go unnoticed by the local boys who sat in patrol cars on North Sea Road waiting for teenagers or drunk drivers.

But Augie didn't seem content to just push the Caddy toward the authorities. He was determined to run it off the road or get around it and cut it off. I could see his knuckles were white from the force of his grip on the steering wheel.

About a mile from North Sea we hit a good straight patch of back road, and that was when Augie made his move. He dropped down a gear and pulled into the other lane to cut around the Caddy. His nose was even with the rear door when the driver veered toward the truck to scare Augie away. But it didn't work that way. Augie veered into the Caddy instead, his front bumper denting the rear driver's side door of the Caddy. But the Caddy wouldn't give.

We rode side by side, metal smashing metal. Each jolt rocked the cab of the truck, and Augie and me with it. But he hung on to the wheel and wouldn't budge. He began to move the Caddy toward the shoulder of the road. Then he dropped it down another gear and gunned the gas. I saw the tachometer arc up to the red line. The engine screamed and the truck lurched forward till my window was almost even with the driver's door. I could see the back left side of the driver's head but nothing more. His window was streaked with rain. The inside of the Caddy was dimly lit by the dashboard lights. Augie jerked the wheel hard, hitting the Caddy with the full length of his pickup. The Caddy swerved away, then swerved back again. Its right-hand tires were off the road and onto the shoulder now, kicking up clumps of grass and mud. The traction slowed it enough to allow Augie to pull up and then slightly ahead of the Caddy. He was about to cut the wheel one last time and drive the Caddy off the road. But before he could, something rammed us hard from behind. It rammed us again before I could turn to look back.

The distraction had allowed the Caddy to cut back onto the road. It hit the pickup broadside. Augie did what he could to keep control of the wheel, but we took another hit from behind and the truck turned into a fishtail and began a sideways slide. I felt myself pulled into the seat, and I knew by this that my side of the truck was lifting off the road. The nose of the truck hit the Caddy one last time, in the front fender. It was like a chain reaction. The Caddy lost control then and began to spin. It rode back up onto the shoulder, kicking up earth and grass. The feeling of being lifted increased and I braced myself for a roll. But instead of rolling we slid sideways down a short ditch and stopped dead against the trunk of a tree. We slammed with such force I felt my kidneys shift in their sockets.

Augie's side of the truck had impacted with the tree. The driver's door window had been shattered by the side of his head. The force of the sudden stop had flung me so hard against my seat belt that I thought I might have popped a rib.

Augie was dazed. His eyes looked glassy and his lids blinked a lot. He looked surprised and there was blood in the creases in his forehead. I heard a car skid to a stop on the rainy road above, but I couldn't see anything. The windshield had shattered and popped out and there was rain in my eyes.

I looked over at Augie. Both his arms were up and out in front of him, like he was trying to find his way in the dark. We didn't have much time.

"Augie," I said. "Augie."

He looked at me but I don't think he saw me.

"Can you move?" I reached down for my belt and undid the buckle. It came free easily. "We have to move."

From the street above I heard a car door open and close. With the windows gone the rain sounded louder. Fine drops bounced up from the dashboard into my face.

I reached over and fumbled for Augie's seat belt.

"Can you move?" I said.

He looked at me. It took a moment for his eyes to focus. He nodded once. I undid the belt and heard voices coming from the street above.

"Are you hurt?" I whispered.

He said nothing. I reached up and took hold of his large head with both hands and looked at the cut on his forehead. It looked superficial to me. I aimed his face at mine and checked his eyes. He looked at me, and there was a degree of cognition.

"We have to move. We have to move now."

My words seemed to reach him then. I could see it in his eyes. He nodded again. This time there was more certainty in it.

"My .45."

"What?"

"My .45. Where is it?"

"I don't know."

"It must have fallen off the seat."

"We don't have time to look for it."

I grabbed the passenger door handle and jerked it up. The door swung open on a creaking hinge. I slid out and grabbed Augie by his jacket and pulled him across the seat. Once he made it through the door it became clear fast that I wasn't going to be able to hold him. But before either of us could do anything he fell. I went down to the mud with him. He was as heavy as a refrigerator when he landed on top of me. Most of his weight was on my legs. I was pinned and couldn't move.

We heard two voices up on the street then and waited where we were, listening. I could hear only some of their words clearly through the rain.

"It went down this ditch . . . over here. . . . They saw the whole fucking thing. . . . No . . . over here . . ."

I scrambled out from under Augie and got up. I tried to pull him to his feet. He did what he could to help. We fumbled but he finally got up. I got in next to him and wrapped his left arm around the back of my neck. Side by side we stumbled through the mud and around the truck. Augie was still too dazed to walk well, and he was too heavy for me to shoulder and carry. After a few feet we dropped to the ground again behind the tree the pickup had crashed into. I landed on a root and felt it dig hard into my side. I was out of breath already, my chest heaving. Augie seemed to be struggling toward consciousness. There was nothing we could do but lie there together in the mud by the base of that tree and wait.

I looked around the tree and spotted the first man as he appeared at the top of the bank. He was just a silhouette in the rain. He looked down at the truck, then glanced over his shoulder and waved someone behind him to follow.

"Hurry," he called.

A second man appeared then. He held a flashlight in his hand. The first man took it, switched it on, and shone it down at the wrecked truck.

The drops of rain looked like tiny blurs in the beam of light. The first man shone it on the opened passenger door and into the cab. The inside of the truck seemed evenly divided between bright light and sharp shadows, both of which moved with each motion of the man's hand. He led the second man down the mud bank. They looked inside the cab, then under it. It only took them a minute to spot the footprints. I saw then that the second man had a gun in his hand. I saw small drops of rain bouncing off it. But I couldn't see either of their faces, only the shapes of them in the night, the flashlight, and the gun.

About the Author

D. DANIEL JUDSON was born and raised in Connecticut. He writes full time from his home and is currently at work on another novel.